"EXPECT TO BE SPELLBOUND"*
by the worlds of Patricia Briggs

Praise for the Alpha and Omega novels

CRY WOLF

"Anna and Charles are intriguing new characters to add to the world Briggs created." —*The Parkersburg News and Sentinel*

"A brisk pace and strong character development, coupled with the unusual abilities of an Omega and what she is capable of, will keep the pages turning well into the night."
—*Monsters and Critics*

"The ancient Moorish werewolf is a fascinating character."
—*Midwest Book Review*

"Solid writing, solid world building, and solid characterization made this urban fantasy hard to put down."
—avidbookreader.com

"This utterly gripping novel races to its climax. Briggs is truly a master storyteller." —*Romantic Times*

"Once in a while there comes a book that sweeps you off your feet, a book you fall in love with so completely that it is hard to do justice to that love in a review. *Cry Wolf* made me feel that way." —*Dear Author*

"A great start to [a] new werewolf series. Ms. Briggs is a fantastic storyteller . . . The action is filled with dangerous surprises, and the romance will find a way into your heart." —*Darque Reviews*

"Patricia Briggs is one of my favorite urban fantasists as she makes her alternative world filled with werewolves, witches, and spirits (oh my) seem genuine." —*Genre Go Round Reviews*

*Lynn Viehl, *New York Times* bestselling author

continued . . .

Blood Bound

"Be prepared to read [it] in one sitting."   —*SFRevu*

"In the increasingly crowded field of kick-ass supernatural heroines, Mercy stands out as one of the best."   —*Locus*

"The plot keeps the pages flapping."   —*Booklist*

"Briggs has created a believable alternative world populated with strong, dynamite characters, deadly adversaries, and cunningly laid plots that leave the reader looking for more."
                    —*Monsters and Critics*

"A compelling and fascinating supernatural tale."
                    —*The Best Reviews*

"Fans of Kim Harrison and Laurell K. Hamilton will enjoy this tightly plotted and fast-paced tale set in a world of vampires, werewolves, fae, and one shapeshifter named Mercy."
                    —*Romantic Times*

Moon Called

"Plenty of twists and turns . . . It left me wanting more."
                    —Kim Harrison, #1 *New York Times* bestselling author of
                    The Witch with No Name

"Patricia Briggs weaves her magic on every page."
                    —Lynn Viehl, *New York Times* bestselling author of
                    the Darkyn series

"Will have you on the edge of your seat."   —*Romance Junkies*

"Inventive and fast paced . . . entertaining from start to end."
                    —*Fantasy & Science Fiction*

"A thoroughly entertaining read."   —*Monsters and Critics*

"Mercy's a compelling protagonist."   —*Romantic Times*

"An exciting new entry in the field of dark urban fantasy."
                    —*Rambles.net*

HUNTING GROUND

PATRICIA BRIGGS

ACE BOOKS, NEW YORK

ACE

**An imprint of Penguin Random House LLC
375 Hudson Street, New York, New York 10014**

HUNTING GROUND

An Ace Book / published by arrangement with Hurog, Inc.

ISBN: 978-0-441-01738-6

PUBLISHING HISTORY
Ace mass-market edition / September 2009

PRINTED IN THE UNITED STATES OF AMERICA

18 17 16 15 14 13 12 11 10 9

Cover art by Daniel Dos Santos.
Cover design by Annette Fiore DeFex.
Interior text design by Kristin del Rosario.
Map illustration by Michael Enzweiler.

Penguin
Random
House

Boo. To my home team,
who puts up with "get your own meals,"
frozen pizza, and glop so I can get the book done.

Love you all:
Michael, Collin, Amanda, and Jordan.

ACKNOWLEDGMENTS

Thanks to the daring young men and their flying machines, for letting us pick their brains: Clif Dyer of Sundance Aviation, and John Haakenson, director of airports and operations at the Port of Benton.

And to the usual suspects who read it when it's bad so you don't have to: Collin Briggs, Michael Briggs, Dave and Katharine Carson, Michael Enzweiler (who also does a terrific job on the maps), Debbie Hill, Jean Matteucci, Ann Peters, Kaye and Kyle Roberson, and Anne Sowards.

And a very big thank-you to Cthulhu Bob Lovely for "Running Eagle." I'm sure Charles will forgive us eventually.

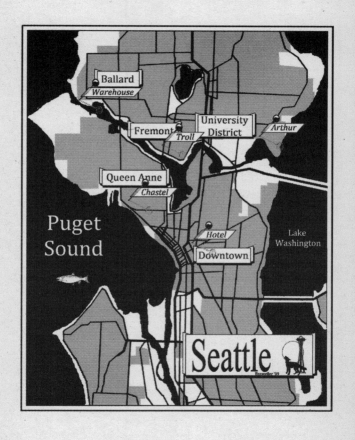

ONE

SHE observed him from her chosen cover, as she'd done twice before. The first two times he'd been chopping wood, but today, after a heavy snowfall appropriate for the middle of December, he was shoveling the sidewalk. Today was the day she'd take him.

Heart in her mouth, she watched as he cleared the snow with carefully controlled violence. Every movement was exactly the same as the one before. Each slide of the shovel was strictly parallel to previous marks. And in his fierce control, she saw his rage, tamped and contained by will alone—like a pipe bomb.

Flattening herself and breathing lightly so he wouldn't see her, she considered how she would do it. From behind, she thought, as fast as possible, to give him no time to react. One quick movement and it would all be over—if she didn't lose her courage, as she had the first two times.

Something told her it had to be today, that she wouldn't get a fourth opportunity. He was wary and disciplined—and if he hadn't been so angry, surely his senses, werewolf sharp, would have discovered her hiding place in the snow beneath the fir trees lining his front yard.

She shook with the stress of what she planned. Ambush. Weak and cowardly, but it was the only way she could take him. And it needed to be done, because it was only a matter of time before he lost the control that kept him shoveling to a steady beat while the wolf raged inside him. And when his control failed, people would die.

Dangerous. He could be so fast. If she screwed this up, he could kill her. She had to trust that her own werewolf reflexes were up to this. It needed to be done.

Resolution gave her strength. It would be today.

CHARLES heard the SUV, but he didn't look up.

He'd turned off his cell and continued to ignore the cool voice of his father in his head until it went away. There was no one who lived near him on the snow-packed mountain road—so the SUV was just the next step in his father's determination to make him toe the line.

"Hey, Chief."

It was a new wolf, Robert, sent here to the Aspen Creek Pack by his own Alpha because of his lack of control. Sometimes the Marrok could help; other times he just had to clean up the mess. If Robert couldn't learn discipline, it would probably be Charles's job to dispose of him. If Robert didn't learn *manners*, the disposal job wouldn't bother Charles as much as it should.

That Bran had sent Robert to deliver his message told Charles just how furious his da was.

"Chief!" The man didn't even bother getting out of the car. There weren't many people Charles extended the privilege of calling him anything but his given name, and this pup wasn't one of them.

Charles stopped shoveling and looked at the other wolf, let him see just what he was messing with. The man lost his grin, paled, and dropped his eyes instantly, his heartbeat making the big blood vessel in his neck throb with sudden fear.

Charles felt petty. And he resented it, resented his pettiness and the roiling anger that caused it. Inside him Brother Wolf smelled Robert's weakness and liked it. The stress of defying the Marrok, his Alpha, had left Brother Wolf wanting blood. Robert's would do.

"I . . . ah."

Charles didn't say anything. Let the fool work for it. He lowered his eyelids and watched the man squirm some more. The scent of his fear pleased Brother Wolf—and made Charles feel a little sick at the same time. Usually, he and Brother Wolf were in better harmony—or maybe the real problem was that he wanted to kill someone, too.

"The Marrok wants to see you."

Charles waited a full minute, knowing how long that time would seem to his father's message boy. "That's it?"

"Yes, sir."

That "sir" was a far cry from "Hey, Chief."

"Tell him I'll come after my walk is cleared." And he went back to work.

After a few scrapes of his shovel, he heard the SUV turn around in the narrow road. The vehicle spun out, then grabbed traction and headed back to the Marrok's, fish-tailing with Robert's urgent desire to get away. Brother Wolf was smugly satisfied; Charles tried not to be. Charles knew he shouldn't bait his father by defying his orders—especially not in front of a wolf who needed guidance, as Robert did. But Charles needed the time.

He had to be in better control of himself before he faced the Marrok again. He needed *real* control that would allow him to lay out his argument logically and explain why the Marrok was wrongheaded—instead of simply bashing heads with him the way they had the last four times Charles had spoken to him. Not for the first time, he wished for a more facile tongue. His brother could sometimes change the Marrok's mind—but he never had. This time, Charles *knew* his father was wrong.

And now he'd worked himself up into a fine mood.

He focused on the snow and took a deep breath of cold air—and something heavy landed on his shoulders, dropping him facedown in the snow. Sharp teeth and a warm mouth touched his neck and were gone as quickly as the weight that had dropped him.

Without moving, he opened his eyes to slits, and from the corner of his eye, he glanced at the sky-eyed black wolf facing him warily . . . with a tail that waved tentatively and paws that danced in the snow, claws extending and retracting like a cat's with nervous excitement.

And it was as though something clicked inside Brother Wolf, turning off the fierce anger that had been churning in Charles's gut for the past couple of weeks. The relief of that was enough to drop his head back into the snow. Only with her, only ever with her, did Brother Wolf settle down wholly. And a few weeks were not enough time to get used to the miracle of it—or to keep him from being too stupid to ask for her help.

Which was why she'd planned this ambush, of course.

When he was up to it, he'd explain to her how dangerous it was for her to attack him without warning. Though Brother Wolf had apparently known exactly who it was who'd attacked: he'd let them be taken down in the snow.

The cold felt good against his face.

The frozen stuff squeaked under her paws, and she made an anxious sound, proof that she hadn't noticed when he'd looked at her. Her nose was cold as it touched his ear and he steeled himself not to react. Playing dead with his face buried in the snow, his smile was free to grow.

The cold nose retreated, and he waited for it to come back within reach, his body limp and lifeless. She pawed at him, and he let his body rock—but when she nipped his backside, he couldn't help but jerk away with a sharp sound.

Faking dead was useless after that, so he rolled over and rose to a crouch.

She got out of reach quickly and turned back to look at him. He knew that she couldn't read anything in his face. He *knew* it. He had too much practice controlling all of his expressions.

But she saw something that had her dropping her front half down to a crouch and loosening her lower jaw in a wolfish grin—a universal invitation to play. He rolled forward, and she took off with a yip of excitement.

They wrestled all over the front yard—making a mess of his carefully tended walk and turning the pristine snow into a battleground of foot-and-body prints. He stayed human to even the odds, because Brother Wolf outweighed her by sixty or eighty pounds and his human form was almost her weight. She didn't use her claws or teeth against his vulnerable skin.

He laughed at her mock growls when she got him down and went for his stomach—then laughed again at the icy nose she shoved under his coat and shirt, more ticklish than any fingers in the sensitive spots on the sides of his belly.

He was careful never to pin her down, never to hurt her, even by accident. That she'd risk this was a statement of trust that warmed him immensely—but he never let Brother Wolf forget that she didn't know them well and had more reason than most to fear him and what he was: male and dominant and wolf.

He heard the car drive up. He could have stopped their play, but Brother Wolf had no desire to take up a real battle yet. So he grabbed her hind foot and tugged it as he rolled out of reach of gleaming fangs.

And he ignored the rich scent of his father's anger—a scent that faded abruptly.

Anna was oblivious to his father's presence. Bran could do that, fade into the shadows as if he were just another man and not the Marrok. All of *her* attention was on Charles—and it made Brother Wolf preen that even the Marrok was second to them in her attentions. It worried the man because, untrained to use her wolf senses, someday she might not notice some danger that would get her killed. Brother Wolf was sure that they could protect her and shook off Charles's worry, dragging him back into the joy of play.

He heard his father sigh and strip out of his clothing as Anna made a run for it and Charles chased her all the way around the house. She used the trees in the back as barriers to keep him at bay when he got too close. Her four clawed feet gave her more traction than his boots did, and she could get around the trees faster.

At last he chased her out of the trees, and she bolted back around the house with him hot on her trail. She rounded the corner to the front yard and froze at the sight of his father in wolf shape, waiting for them.

It was all Charles could do to not keep going through her like a running back. As it was, he took her legs right out from under her as he changed his run into a slide.

Before he could check to see if she was okay, a silver missile was on him and the whole fight changed abruptly. Charles had been mostly in control of the action when it was just he and Anna, but with the addition of his father, he was forced to an earnest application of muscle, speed, and brain to keep the two wolves, black and silver, from making him eat snow.

At last he lay flat on his back, with Anna on his legs and his father's fangs touching the sides of his throat in mock threat.

"Okay," he said, relaxing his body in surrender. "Okay. I give up."

The words were more than just an end to play. He'd tried. But in the end, the Alpha's word was law. Whatever followed would follow. So he submitted as easily as any pup in the pack to his father's dominance.

The Marrok lifted his head and removed himself from Charles's chest. He sneezed and shook off snow as Charles sat up and pulled his legs out from under Anna.

"Thanks," he told her, and she gave him a happy grin. He gathered up the clothes from the hood of his father's car and opened the door to the house. Anna bounced into the living room and trotted down the hall to the bedroom. He tossed his father's clothes into the bathroom, and when his father followed them, shut the door behind the white-tipped tail.

He had hot chocolate and soup ready when his father emerged, his face flushed with the effort of the change, his eyes hazel and human once more.

He and his da didn't look much alike. Charles took after his Salish mother and Bran was Welsh through and through, with sandy hair and prominent features that usually wore a deceptively earnest expression, which was currently nowhere in evidence. Despite the play, Bran didn't look particularly happy.

Charles didn't bother trying to talk. He had nothing to say anyway. His grandfather had often told him that he tried too hard to move trees when a wiser man would walk around them. His grandfather had been a medicine man and liked to speak in metaphors. He had usually been right.

He handed his da a cup of hot chocolate.

"Your wife called me last night." Bran's voice was gruff.

"Ah." He hadn't known that. Anna must have done it while he'd been out trying to outrun his frustrations.

"She told me I wasn't hearing what you were saying," his da said. "I told her that I heard you tell me quite clearly that I was an idiot for going to Seattle to meet with the European delegation—as did most of the rest of the pack."

Tactful, that's me, thought Charles, who decided sipping his cocoa was better than opening his mouth.

"And I asked him if you were in the habit of arguing with him without a good reason," said Anna breezily as she slipped by his father and brushed against Charles. She was wearing his favorite brown sweater. On her it hung halfway down her thighs and buried her shape in cocoa-colored wool. Brother Wolf liked it when she wore his clothes.

She should have looked like a refugee, but somehow she didn't. The color turned her skin to porcelain and brought out rich highlights in her light brown hair. It also emphasized her freckles—which he adored.

She hopped up on the counter and purred happily as she snagged the cocoa he'd made for her.

"And then she hung up," said his father in disgruntled tones.

"Mmm," said Anna. Charles couldn't tell if she was responding to the hot chocolate or his father.

"And she refused to pick up the phone when I called back." His father wasn't pleased.

Not so comfortable having someone around who doesn't instantly obey you, old man? Charles thought—just as his father met his eye.

Bran's sudden laugh told Charles that his da wasn't really upset.

"Frustrating," Charles ventured.

"He yelled at me," Anna said serenely, tapping her forehead. The Marrok could speak to any of his wolves mind to mind, though he couldn't read their thoughts no matter how much it felt like that was what he was doing. He was just damnably good at reading people. "I ignored him, and he went away eventually."

"No fun fighting someone who doesn't fight back," Charles said.

"Without someone to argue with, I knew he'd have to think about what I said," Anna told them smugly. "If only to come up with the right words to squelch me the next time he talked to me."

She hadn't reached even a quarter of a century yet, they hadn't been mated a full month—and she was already arranging them all to suit herself. Brother Wolf was pleased with the mate he'd found for them.

Charles set down his cup and folded his arms over his chest. He knew he looked intimidating; that was his intention. But when Anna leaned away from him, just a little, he dropped his arms and hooked his thumbs in his jeans and made his shoulders relax.

And his voice was gentler than he'd meant it to be. "Manipulating Bran has a tendency to backfire," he told her. "I'd recommend against it."

But his father rubbed his mouth and sighed loudly. "So," said his father. "Why is it that you think it would be disastrous for me to go to Seattle?"

Charles rounded on his father, his resolve to quit fighting Bran on his decision to go to Seattle all but forgotten. "The Beast is coming, and you ask me that?"

"Who?" Anna asked.

"Jean Chastel, the Beast of Gévaudan," Charles told her. "He likes to eat his prey—and his prey is mostly human."

"He stopped that," Bran said coolly.

"Please," Charles snapped, "*don't* mouth something *you* don't believe to me—it smells perilously close to a lie. The Beast was forced to stop killing openly, but a tiger doesn't change his stripes. He's still doing it. You know it as well as I do." He could have pointed out other things—Jean had a taste for human flesh, the younger the better. But Anna had already experienced what happened when a wolf turned monstrous. He didn't want to be the one to tell her that there were worse beasts out there than her former Alpha and his mate. His father knew what Jean Chastel was.

Bran conceded the point. "Yes. Almost certainly he is. But I'm not a helpless human, he won't kill *me*." He looked at Charles narrowly. "Which you know. So why do you think it will be dangerous?"

He was right. Take the Beast out of the picture, and it still made him ill to think of his father going. The Beast was the most obvious, provable danger.

"I just know," Charles said, finally. "But it is your decision to make." His gut clenched in anticipation of just how bad it was going to be.

"You still don't have a logical reason."

"No." Charles forced his body to accept his defeat and kept his eyes on the floor.

His da looked out the little window where the mountains lay draped in winter white. "Your mother did that," he said. "She'd make a statement without any real support at all, and I was supposed to just take her word for it."

Anna was looking at his da with bright expectancy.

Bran smiled at her, then raised his cup toward the mountains. "I learned the hard way that she was usually right. *Frustrating* doesn't come close to covering it."

"So," he said, turning his attention back to Charles. "They are on their way already, I can't cancel it now—and it needs to be done. Announcing to the real world that there are werewolves among them will affect the European wolves as much, if not more, than it does us. They deserve their chance to be heard and told why we are doing it. It should come from me, but you would be an acceptable substitute. It will cause some offense, though, and you will have to deal with that."

Relief flooded Charles with an abruptness that had him leaning against the countertop in sudden weakness, as the all-consuming sense of absolute and utter disaster slid away and left him whole. Charles looked at his mate.

"My grandfather would have loved to have met you," he told her huskily. "He would have called you 'She Moves Trees Out of His Path.'"

She looked lost, but his da laughed. He'd known the old man, too.

"He called me 'He Who Must Run into Trees,'" Charles explained, and in a spirit of honesty, a need for his mate to know who he was, he continued, "or sometimes 'Running Eagle.'"

"'Running Eagle'?" Anna puzzled it over, frowning at him. "What's wrong with that?"

"Too stupid to fly," murmured his father with a little smile. "That old man had a wicked tongue—wicked and clever, so it stuck until he dinged you with your next offense." He tilted his head at Charles. "But you were a lot younger then—and I am not so solid an object as a tree. You'd feel better if you—"

Anna cleared her throat pointedly.

His da smiled at her. "If you *and Anna* go instead?"

"Yes." Charles paused because there was something more, but the house was too busy with modern things for the

Two

"I love Seattle." Krissy folded her arms around herself and spun in a circle. She looked up with a practiced little-girl grin, and her lover smiled down at her.

He reached out and tucked a gold curl behind her ear. "Shall we move here, princess? I could get you a condo that looks over the water."

She thought about it and finally shook her head. "I'd miss New York, you know I would. No place has shopping like New York."

"All right," he said, his voice an indulgent purr. "But we can come here to play now and again if you like it."

Krissy tilted her head and caught the rain in her mouth, a quick snap like a bat taking a bug out of the sky. "Can we play now?"

"Work before play," said Hannah, the spoilsport. She'd been Ivan's playmate before Krissy. Krissy had taken her place in his bed and in his heart, and it made Hannah pissy.

"Ivan," Krissy coaxed, putting a hand on either side of

his shirt and tugging him down so she could lick his lips. "Can't we go play? We don't have to work tonight, do we?"

He let her take his mouth, and when he raised his head, his eyes were hot. "Hannah, take the others to our hotel and contact our employer. Krissy and I will be there in a few hours."

It was raining again, but Jody had been raised in Eugene, where it only rained once a year—from January to December. Besides, he was a Pisces; water was his element.

He raised his face and let the rain wash down it. Practice had run a little late and the sun had set before he'd gotten out. The music had been good tonight; they'd all felt it. He pulled the sticks out of his back pocket and beat the air in a rhythm only he could hear. There was something he should change in that last measure . . .

He took the shortcut to his apartment—a dim little street barely wide enough for a car and a half. It wasn't late, but there was no one around except for an older man and a girl who looked about sixteen. They were both drenched and hurried toward him.

"Excuse me," said the man, "We're visiting and seem to have gotten turned around. Do you know where the nearest restaurant is?" The coat he wore was expensive— wool, Jody thought—and he had a bright gold watch on his wrist that looked like it cost a bundle. The girl—as they got closer he was pretty sure that there was more than a generation between the old gent and the girl; maybe she was his granddaughter—was wearing four-inch heels that made her feet look tiny.

She caught him looking and enjoyed his admiration. He couldn't help but smile back. She put her hand on his wrist, and said, "We need to find some food." And her smile widened a little more, and he saw fangs.

Strange, he thought, she didn't look like she belonged in the groups his ex-girlfriend had hung out with, where they all wore fangs and played that stupid game . . . not D&D, which was cool . . . something with vampires.

This girl wore a ponytail and looked more like Britney Spears than Vampirella. Her shoes were hot pink, and there wasn't a piece of her clothing that was black.

He didn't like it that his throat tightened in fear because she was wearing acrylic fangs.

"There's a place a few blocks away," he told her, twisting his wrist gently to get her to let go. "Serves Italian food. They have a great red sauce."

She licked her lips and didn't let go of his wrist. "I love red sauce."

"Look," he said, jerking his wrist free, "cut it out. That's not funny."

"No," breathed the man, who had somehow gotten behind him while Jody had been talking to the girl. "Not funny at all." And there was a sharp pain in his neck.

"Where is someplace private?" the old man asked after a little while. "Someplace we might play together for a while without anyone seeing us?"

And Jody led his new friends a few miles away to a place on the Sound where he knew no one would come.

"Good," said the man. "Very good."

The girl closed her eyes and smiled. "The traffic will drown out the screams."

The man leaned over and put his mouth to Jody's ear. "You can be scared now."

Jody was scared for a very, very long time before they threw him into the water for the fish.

*   *   *

"THE rocks will keep him underwater until they won't be able to tell how he died," said Ivan.

"I still think we should have left him naked hanging from a tree like that girl in Syracuse."

Ivan rubbed the top of her head. "Dear child," he said, and sighed. "That was a special case; she was a message to her father. This one was just play, and if we let the silly humans know we killed him, it would interfere with business."

She looked at the bloody drumsticks and sighed, tossing them in after the body. "And nothing interferes with business."

"Business keeps a roof over our heads and lets us travel when we want to," Ivan told her. "You need to wash your face, princess, and put your clothes back on."

A great mountain peak broke through the white mist and ruled in awesome splendor over the soft sky and Anna held her breath. Mount Rainier, she thought, though her geography of the Cascades was shaky. There were mountains spread out below them, but this one was orders of magnitude larger than the lowly ripples in the land below it. Gradually, other great peaks revealed themselves in the distance, drowning in clouds.

"Hey, Charles?"

The mountains were on Charles's side of the plane. Anna leaned as far toward him as she could without touching him—he was flying the plane, and she didn't want to distract him.

"Yes?"

They were wearing headsets that protected their sensitive ears from the noise of the engine and miked their voices to each other. In her headphone, his voice was low enough to make the speaker in her ear buzz even though it was turned to the lowest setting.

"Just how many planes does the pack have?"

This was the second she'd been in.

"Just the Learjet," he told her. "If you lean any farther, you're going to strangle yourself. This Cessna is mine."

He owned a plane? Just when she was starting to think she knew him, something else would come up. She knew that he handled the pack finances—and that their pack was not in any danger of being penniless anytime soon. She knew that he himself was financially stable, though they hadn't really talked about it much. Owning a plane was a whole different category of financially stable, like Mount Rainier was a whole different category of mountain from the hills she'd known in Illinois.

"Aren't we on pack business?" she asked. "Why did we take this one?"

"The jet needs five thousand feet to land," he said. "That means Boeing Field or Sea-Tac, and I don't want the government to be following us around all week."

"The government follows you?" She had a sudden picture of Charles strolling along with dark-suited men creeping behind him, trying to stay out of sight and failing, with cartoonish exaggeration.

He nodded. "We may be a secret from the rest of the world—but the wrong people know who we are."

And that was why the Marrok had decided it was time to bring the werewolves out to the public. "So the wrong people are following you?"

He smiled wolfishly. "Only when I want them to."

She considered that smile and decided she liked it on him. "So where *are* we landing?"

"At an airstrip maintained by the Emerald City Pack. It's about thirty miles from Seattle."

The plane bounced, dropping fast and tickling her stomach. She gripped her armrests and laughed as Charles brought the plane back to level. "I really like flying."

He dipped his head and looked at her over the top of his dark lenses for a moment. Then his mouth quirked up, and he turned his attention back to his instrument panel. The plane tilted to the left.

Anna waited for him to right it, but they just kept tilting all the way upside down and continued smoothly over until they were back upright again.

Over her laughter, he said, "This plane isn't rated for aerobatics, but a roll is only a one-gee maneuver." He tilted the plane over the other way, and said, "Properly done." And then he danced the plane through the sky.

She was breathless, and her diaphragm ached from laughing by the time the plane settled back on level flight. She glanced at Charles, who wasn't even smiling. He might have just as well been flying patterns over a grain field.

He hated planes just as he hated most modern technology. He'd told her so. But he owned one—and by golly he knew how to fly it. When he drove his truck, he was cautious and controlled. So why had he decided to play barnstormer in the Cessna? Was he just entertaining her, or was he enjoying himself?

A woman should know more about her mate. When the mate bond had first settled in, she'd believed she would. But her initial ability to feel him had faded, buried under his self-control and her defenses. She could feel the bond between them, strong and shining and impenetrable. She wondered if it felt the same to him, or if he could read her through it whenever he chose.

"This is Station Air November one eight eight three Victor requesting permission to land," he said, and it took her a moment to realize he was talking to someone other than her.

"Go ahead, sir. I mean, go ahead, eight three Victor," said a stranger's voice. "Welcome to Emerald City Pack territory, sir."

Charles dropped them abruptly through the scattered clouds, past white-coated mountains, to the soft green valley below. Before she realized there was a landing strip, the wheels touched down with a gentle bump.

The place where they landed looked nearly as remote as Aspen Creek. Though there was snow a hundred feet or so up the foothills, down where they had landed it was as green as if it were summer. Greener. Except for the landing field and a hangar, the land was awash in trees and bushes.

People jogged up to the plane from the hangar as Charles pulled his headset off and unbuckled.

He withdrew from her, thinning the bond between them painfully. If he'd warned her beforehand, she would have kept quiet: three years in her first pack had given her power over her pain. It was surprise that forced the whine out of her throat.

Charles pulled his sunglasses off his face and looked at her with a frown. Sudden comprehension widened his eyes—"I never thought . . ." He turned his head and said, not to her, "All right. All right." And the painful collapse of their bond ceased.

Wolf-eyed, he leaned toward her and touched her face.

"I'm sorry," he told her. "I didn't mean to shut you out. I just . . ."

He stopped, apparently at a loss for words.

"Donning your armor?" she suggested. "It's okay, I just wasn't expecting it. Do what you have to."

But he didn't. Instead, he said, looking out at the approaching men, "These are not the enemy. Not this time, anyway."

He was out of his seat before she could say anything. *And what would I have said?* He closed himself up so that he could kill if he had to, so that he wouldn't like any of them too much. So he wouldn't hesitate in carrying out whatever had to be done.

She did know something about her mate after all. She climbed out behind him, following him out of the plane and into the presence of strange wolves, still trying to decide if it should reassure her or worry her.

"Glad you made it in, sir," said the one who was in charge. It still freaked her out sometimes how she could tell who was in charge by the subtle cues of body motion and position. Real people—normal *humans*—didn't need to know who was first and who was last.

"We were following you on our radar, and Jim here was worried you might have had some trouble because your speed seemed a little erratic."

Charles gave them a neutral face, and Anna wondered what his aerobatics had looked like on radar.

"No trouble," he said.

The other wolf cleared his throat and dropped his gaze. "Good. I'm Ian Garner of the Emerald City Pack, and I'm to help you in any way that I can."

As Charles and the other wolves unloaded the luggage and discussed how the plane was to be cared for and stored, Anna stood a little apart. She wasn't as nervous with the strangers as she expected to be—and it took her a minute to pinpoint why.

Ian was middle of the pack and leader here. So this group was not the Alpha's top tier of wolves, nowhere near the most dominant; they were wolves who wouldn't spark a dominant male's instinct to put them in their places. Angus Hopper, the Emerald City Pack Alpha, was a smart man. Not that he had to worry about Charles's control, but playing it safe was always a smart move.

Angus wouldn't have done it because strange dominant males still scared Anna, but a part of her was grateful nonetheless.

There would be enough dominant males to drown in later, when the meetings took place. The wolves coming from Europe each ruled their own territories; some of them had been in power for centuries. No one would hurt her, not while she was with Charles. She knew it, but her fear of male wolves had taken a few years to beat into her and would take more than a month or two to free herself from.

"They'll take care of the airplane," said Ian. He picked up the nearest piece of luggage and, with a dropped shoulder and a deferential swing of his head instead of words, invited them to follow him up a stone pathway through the trees. Charles took his own suitcase and waited for Anna to precede him.

Once he had them moving, the Emerald City wolf started talking in a rapid all-business voice that might have masked his anxiety from someone who was purely human. Charles did that to people, even in his own pack, and she didn't think even his father knew how much it bothered him.

"Angus is at work," the wolf said. "He says you're to have free access to the house." Anna remembered getting a glimpse of a house as they landed, but from the ground, it was well hidden by the trees. That must be where they were headed toward. "You're welcome to anything any of us have, but the pack itself has a newish Land Cruiser and a Corolla that has seen better days. Angus says you can use his BMW if you'd rather."

"We'll take the Corolla," Charles told him. "And we're

staying in a hotel downtown. This is too far for an easy commute to the meeting place."

"He thought you would feel that way. Angus invites you to stay with him at his condo in the city."

"Not necessary," said Charles. Anna wasn't sure he noticed the other man's mouth flatten. More probably he just didn't care.

The Emerald City Pack was hosting the meeting, and for Charles to refuse housing might look like he was not acknowledging them as allies. Charles preferred to be independent—separate from the people he might be called upon to kill. Charles was his father's assassin and justice dealer, and that grim responsibility affected everything he did. He didn't go out of his way to make friends among the werewolves, not even in his own pack. He would feel more comfortable on his own.

That didn't mean that Anna couldn't smooth things over.

"We appreciate the offer," Anna told Ian. "But we're newly mated and . . ." It didn't require any effort on her part to blush as her voice trailed off. And whatever offense he'd felt was overshadowed by interest.

"So it's true?" Ian glanced at Charles, then quickly away. "I had heard that."

"Shocking, I know," murmured Charles.

The other wolf stiffened and gave Charles a worried look, too wary of Charles to hear the humor.

"He's a terrible tease," she told Ian, trying to help.

The Emerald City wolf's face loosened in utter disbelief.

Charles saw it and grinned at her. It was too bad Ian didn't see her mate's expression, but Charles's usual-in-public granite facade was back before the other wolf glanced his way.

"Right," Ian said. He cleared his throat and changed the subject. "Well . . . Angus asked me to tell you that the only people we're waiting for are the Russians and the French. He thought you might also be interested to know that the British Alpha came alone with his mate. We'll know when the Russians get here—they're staying in the apartment Angus's company owns."

"Angus's company?" asked Anna—they'd packed in a hurry, and she hadn't asked him much about what they'd actually be doing here.

"Angus runs a high-tech company," Charles explained. "They put together programs to keep other companies running. We'll be using his facilities this week—he's given his staff an early vacation for Christmas." He looked at Ian. "I'd wager the French wolves have arrived already. Chastel will want to check out his hunting grounds before the prey arrives."

"They haven't checked into the hotel they booked."

Charles shook his head. "Tell Angus that Chastel would never stay in a hotel. Too public. He'll have rented a house, something nice. He's here, probably has been here for a week or two."

Charles claimed not to be good with people, not to understand them . . . and maybe that was true. But he understood predators just fine.

The trees thinned, and a house emerged from the forest. Like Bran's house, it had been built to take advantage of the natural topography, and the surrounding trees effectively hid a good deal of its bulk. Angus's company must be pretty lucrative.

"Angus says it is the Frenchman who will cause the most trouble," said Ian.

"Don't underestimate the Russians," Charles said. "But Angus is probably right. Jean is powerful, scary, and mad as a hatter. He likes killing, especially if his prey is weak and frightened—his life wouldn't hold up to the kind of scrutiny we're inviting by introducing ourselves to the world."

"Angus says that Jean Chastel will carry the vote because everyone else is scared of him."

Charles smiled wolfishly, his eyes cold and clear. "This is not a democracy: there is no vote. Not on this. The Europeans have no say in whether or not we tell the world about ourselves. I'm here to listen to their concerns and decide what we can do to help them mitigate the impact of becoming public."

"That doesn't sound like what I've picked up from the European delegations who've arrived." Ian was careful not to sound as if he were disagreeing with Charles.

"What about the Asian werewolves?" Anna asked. "Or African and Australian? And South American?"

"They don't matter." Ian dismissed her question.

"They matter," said Charles softly. "They have been dealt with differently."

The sharp scent of fear coiled around Anna's nose; there had been a threat in Charles's voice when he thought the other wolf had overstepped himself—and Ian had clearly caught it. She gave Charles a frown. "Stop terrorizing him. These are things I ought to have known. Tell me about the non-European werewolves."

Charles raised an eyebrow at her but answered her readily enough. "Werewolves are a European monster, and we've done pretty well here in this part of the New World, too. There are a few of us in Africa and even fewer in Asia, where there are other monsters who don't like us very well. There are two packs in Australia, about forty wolves. Both of their Alphas have been informed of our plans, and neither voiced objections. Bran has also discussed his intentions with the South American wolves. They were less happy—but, like the Europeans, they have no say in what my father does or does not do. Unlike the Europeans, they know it. We've offered them the same sorts of aid we're offering the Europeans, and they are happy with that. They were invited but chose not to come."

THE battered and abused Corolla was a four-speed stick shift with a touchy clutch, and it kept Anna's attention firmly on driving until they were on the interstate headed for the city.

"Okay," she said. "I need to understand more. I should have asked more questions, but this came up awfully fast. The British Alpha, by not bringing more wolves, is telling everyone he can handle anything anyone can send after him?"

Charles nodded. "There's some bad blood between Arthur Madden, the British Alpha, and Angus." He paused. "Actually, I think there's some bad blood between Arthur and my father, too. If it looks like an issue, I'll call Da and see what it was about. Da says that Arthur's the only Alpha who will stand up to Chastel—and that's a good thing to have. We'll need every advantage we can get."

He sounded . . . not worried. Intrigued. It was, Anna thought, going to be a different manner of fighting this week; not fangs and blood but a battle of wits. All those dominant wolves . . . most of the Alphas in the same room. Arguing. Maybe it wasn't going to be a different way of fighting. But for now, she was driving and had absolutely no idea where they were headed.

"Are we going to the hotel?"

"Yes." And he gave her directions. But as they turned off the highway and onto the streets of downtown Seattle, he said, "Let's do something first. Why don't we go see Dana, the fae who's agreed to moderate this mess." And maybe, like his father, he'd been doing some mind reading. "She's not just . . . a stand-in for a UN ambassador, a graceful host to help Angus. She's the one who's going to keep this civilized and keep us from paying to have Angus's carpets cleaned of bloodstains. I have a gift to give her from my father, to thank her for the help we are paying her a small fortune for."

"I didn't hear about the fae." Anna had never seen a fae before, not one she knew was a fae anyway. She felt a frisson of excitement and tightened her hands on the steering wheel. "Bran brought a fae into werewolf business?"

"It's necessary to have a neutral party to make sure the violence doesn't get out of hand."

Anna thought about the wolves she had known: the violence that had *always* gotten out of hand. She tried to imagine someone who could put a stop to it. Bran, Charles—but they would have to do it with more violence. "She can do that?"

"Yes. And more importantly, everyone knows it."

"What kind of fae is she? Isn't Dana a German name? I thought most of the fae were British—you know, Welsh, Irish, and Scots."

"Most of the fae we see in the US are Northern European: Celtic, German, French, Cornish, English. Dana isn't her real name. This decade or so she's been using the name 'Dana Shea,' a variant of *daoine sidhe.* A lot of the older fae and some of the witches won't use their own names— anything that belongs to them for such a long time develops power over them and can be used against them, the same way scraps of hair or fingernails can."

"Do you know what her real name is? Or what kind of fae she is?"

"I don't know it—I don't think even Da knows it. Though

she is a Gray Lord, one of the most powerful fae. They rule the fae sort of like Da does the wolves." He glanced at her. "If Da was a psychotic serial killer, maybe. I do know what kind of fae she is, though. You meet her and talk to her a bit. Then tell me what you think."

Anna gave a half-amused huff. "What do I get if I'm right?"

His eyes lightened with the wolf who lurked inside him, and the hunger in his gaze told her exactly what he meant when he said, "The same thing you get if you're wrong."

She waited for the fear or even trepidation that thoughts of sex had usually brought to her—but it never came. Just a welcome tickly feeling in her stomach. In less than a month's time, he'd made serious inroads on her problems in that area. "Good," she told him.

He smiled at her and relaxed against his seat.

SEATTLE highways had a lot more vertical variation than those in Chicago. The roads rose above water, tangled and burrowed under hills where houses sat unmoved by the thousands of cars that traveled beneath them. Over the smell of the cars was the scent of water and salt from the Puget Sound and various other saltwater lakes and ponds. The gray skies leaked here and there, not enough to turn the wipers on full but too much to let the rain accumulate long.

Following Charles's directions, she exited the highway and found herself tootling along a slower road in what could just as well have been a small town in Britain as a part of Seattle. It looked old, quaint, and beautiful, if a little self-conscious. On the water to her right was a series of docks with boats and houseboats, while on her left, narrow buildings covered the side of a hill that got progressively steeper as she drove.

A huge silver bridge arched over the water and the road she was driving, soaring up to land on the top of a steep hill above. The name of the cross street that ran directly under the bridge had Anna pulling her foot off the gas so she could be sure that she was reading the street sign correctly.

"Troll?"

"What?" Charles had been looking toward the water, but he turned back to look at her.

"There's a street here called Troll?"

He smiled suddenly. "I'd forgotten about that. Why don't you follow it up the hill?"

She turned the car up the road and thought for a moment the decision was a mistake because the little blue car strained to crawl up the hill, which was even steeper than it had looked from the bottom. The road was narrow and claustrophobic, with the bridge for roofing, its steel feet closing in from left and right.

She was so busy worrying about driving that she didn't see it until they were quite close. The road they were on ended and teed into another road. The bridge overhead plowed into the top of the hill. And in the space between the road and the end of the bridge crouched a giant something.

Without consulting Charles, she parked.

Someone had sculpted a huge humanoid monster out of cement, rising from the sand: a troll for the bridge. Cement hair hung limply over one eye while the other stared over Anna's head at the waterway at the bottom of the hill they'd just driven up. One of its hands, which rested on a real VW Bug, was big enough to engulf the car. The Bug's nose burrowed beneath the troll's beard as if it sought refuge there.

Anna got out of the car slowly and strolled across the

road, Charles at her side. The statue had been attacked with chalk recently, and the bright pink and green colors only enhanced the oddity of the creature. Fingernails and the lines of knuckles had been drawn on the creature's hands. Pink and green chalk flowers followed the contours of the Bug's fender, and on the back window—cement-covered glass—someone had written "Just Married."

Peripherally, Anna sensed they were being watched. Above the troll, in the notch where the bridge met the top of the hill, three or four street people observed them warily. One man set aside a newspaper he'd been reading and started down toward them.

He was a little above average height, though he slumped until he appeared shorter. He wore a battered canvas duster that was liberally splattered with muck. Mismatched Nikes adorned his feet. The right shoe had a hole in the toe and the left another along the edge of his heel, exposing the dirty, sockless foot inside. The jeans he wore were new and stiff, though as mucky as his duster. She caught glimpses of layers of shirts—a red flannel shirt over a yellow plaid button-up that almost obscured a graying white tee.

Anna took note of the man, but with Charles at her side the stranger wasn't a threat—and Anna was more interested in the troll. So she let Charles deal with him as she climbed up the back of the Bug and onto the creature's arm, then higher still until she could rest her hand on his overlarge nose.

"Like my little troll, eh?" the stranger said to Charles, his voice rough like that of a man who'd smoked a pack a day for years. He didn't smell like cigarettes, though. His scent, rising through the air to Anna's nose, was earthy and magical, sharp with a predator's musk.

"Was it a real one?" Anna asked him, safe upon her perch, safe with Charles.

The stranger looked up at her and laughed, exposing ragged, blackened teeth as sharp as he smelled. "Well, now. It might be that the artist saw somp'n. Somp'n he outter not have seen, wolf-kin." He patted the cement arm she stood on, and she took a wary step back. "Happen though, he built me a friend, so we're all happy. Even the Gray Lord, there, she thought it were funny. Didn't hardly hurt me at all for gettin' seen and not tellin' her."

The fae could hide what they were. Could look just like anyone else. But the hunger that shone in his eyes when he looked at her was as immortal as she was and a lot older.

Her wolf didn't like him, and Anna narrowed her eyes at him and let him hear her growl. He should know that she was not prey.

He laughed again and slapped one thigh with a hand covered in a worn fingerless glove. "If'n I forgot meself so bad as to take a bite"—he snapped his teeth together and in the darkness under the bridge she saw the spark when they struck—"she'd chew me up and feed me to them great octopuses that live 'round here, she would." The thought seemed to amuse him. "Though a good meaty bit of wolf-flesh might be worth it."

"Troll," said Charles.

He had been having so much fun with Anna, he'd forgotten about the real threat. Reminded, he jerked around, crouched, and hissed.

Charles took out one of the plain gold studs he wore in his ears and tossed it at the fae, who caught it with inhumanly quick hands.

"Take your toll and go, Old One," Charles said.

"Hey, Jer," came a worried and thin voice from above them. "You don't go bothering them, or the police'll have us outta here. You know they will."

The troll in human guise held the bit of gold up to his nose and smelled. His face twitched, and his eyes swirled with an eerie blue light before they settled down and became just eyes again. "Toll," he said. "Toll."

"Jerry?"

"No troubles, Bill," he called up to his . . . what . . . friends? His roommates, his bridgemates, who were more human than he. "Jest saying good afternoon."

He looked at Charles, and for a moment an oddly noble expression crossed his face, his back straightened, shoulders thrown back. In a clear, accentless voice he said, "Word of advice for your payment. Don't trust the fae." He laughed again, devolving into the man who'd greeted them in the first place, and scrambled up the hill and under the bridge.

Charles didn't say anything, but Anna slid off her perch and followed him back to the car.

"Are trolls really as big as that statue?" she asked, belting herself in.

"I don't know," Charles answered. And smiled at the startled look she gave him. "I *don't* know everything. I've never seen a troll in its true form."

She started the car. "A toll is supposed to be for crossing his bridge. We didn't cross the bridge."

"But we were trespassing. It seemed appropriate."

"What about the advice he gave?"

He smiled again, his face lit with amusement. "You know what they say, 'Don't trust the fae.'"

"Okay." It was a common piece of advice. The first thing people said and the main point of most stories about them. "Especially when they tell us not to, I suppose. Where to now?"

"Back down the Troll road. See those docks down there? Dana lives on a houseboat at the foot of the troll."

*   *   *

HE'ð only visited Dana at her home once before, but Charles had no trouble finding it again: it didn't exactly blend in.

There were four docks; three of them had a number of boats of various kinds secured to them. The fourth had only one. A houseboat two stories tall, it looked like a miniature Victorian mansion, complete with gingerbread trim in every color of an ocean sunset: blue and orange, yellow and red.

Dana brought hiding in plain sight to a new level. None of her neighbors, except the fae themselves, knew what she was. She was powerful enough that she had been allowed to choose to expose herself or not—and she'd chosen to continue hiding.

Charles was powerful, too. But he had no choice.

"This is it?" Anna asked, "It looks exactly like something a fairy should live in."

"Wait until you see the inside," he told her.

For nearly two centuries he had been trekking along happily . . . or at least contentedly, down a straight path. His life had always been about serving his Alpha, who was both his father and the Marrok, in whatever capacity he was needed.

When his father had told him what he intended, had told him he needed wolves to give a public face to the werewolf, wolves Bran could trust not to screw up in public, Charles had agreed to be one of them. Not that it would have mattered if he'd refused; in the end a wolf obeyed his Alpha or he killed him. And Charles knew with an absolute certainty that left him content that he would never be able to take on his father.

But that had been before Anna. Now his life was about

her, about keeping her safe. As much as he agreed with his father about what the proper course of action to follow was, he and Brother Wolf were both concerned that keeping her safe and presenting himself to the public as a werewolf were not compatible.

This week, he couldn't let so much as a breath out that might express his true feelings on this. It was necessary for the wolves to come out. He knew that.

But now there was Anna, and she changed things.

"Should we go see if she's here?" asked Anna, still examining the houseboat from the safety of land.

Dana, no doubt, already knew that they were there—he'd felt magic brush over his skin as they walked down to her dock, but she'd wait until they approached her properly.

Dana, *La Belle Dame Sans Merci*, had conducted this kind of business for his father before. She was being very well paid, but with a fae it was always a good policy to bring an extra gift in lieu of a "thank-you." Saying those words could be dangerous, as some fae took them to be an admission of obligation. The Marrok wasn't the only one bringing her a gift, but his must be greater than the rest combined. Still, Charles could have presented it to her at the first meeting rather than making a special trip.

His da had suggested that Dana might appreciate a visit from him before business—and that Anna might enjoy it as well. So here they were, he with a small, wrapped painting under his arm, and Anna, who, a few steps ahead of him, had taken the first step onto the dock and discovered that a floating dock bounces.

She gave him a happy look as he followed her out on the water-soaked wooden walk. "This could be fun," she said, then turned, took a running step, and did a couple of back flips—like a middle-school kid at recess. He stopped where he was, lust and love and fear rising up in a surge of emotion he did not, for all his years, have any idea how to deal with.

"What?" she asked, a little breathless from her gymnastics. She brushed her wavy hair out of her face and gave him a serious look. "Is there something wrong?"

He could hardly tell her that he was afraid because he didn't know what he'd do if something happened to her. That his sudden, unexpected reaction had brought Brother Wolf to the fore. She threw his balance off; his control—which had become almost effortless over the years—was erratic at best. Sternly, he tried to bring his wolf brother to heel, to bring his own control back.

Anna winced and put her hands to her temples. "You know, if you don't want me to know what you're feeling, you could just distract yourself. It hurts when you block me out."

He hadn't realized he was. Didn't want to hurt her. He began opening himself up, and Brother Wolf took over and opened them both up all the way. It was very much like a man opening an umbrella that had been stored for years. Some parts creaked and groaned and shed dust—others cracked under the sudden stretching and threatened to break.

He felt naked—only more so. As if he'd shed his skin and stood with raw nerve endings waiting to be filleted by the next stray wind. All he was, all he'd been, was there in the broad daylight, where it had never been meant to be seen. Not even by him.

There was a pause, a waiting moment, and then everything hit.

There were too many memories, things he'd seen and done. Pain and pleasure and sorrow: all there as if they were happening now—too much, too much, and he couldn't breathe . . .

And Anna was there, holding him and releasing the spring that held him open, allowing his thoughts and feelings to settle back into private places, but not as hidden as they had been. He waited for the pain to settle, but it dissipated into the sound of Anna's song flowing through him.

His protections, the walls he kept between him and the world, were up again, but Anna was inside them. It felt odd, but not painful, more like someone had pulled the rug out from under his feet. It was intimate as all hell, scary, and miraculous. He was getting used to feeling like that a lot around her.

Anna's face was pressed against his chest, her arms around him, and she was humming Brahms in a low and sweet range.

He ran a hand down her hair and kissed the top of her head. "Sorry, and thanks. Brother Wolf tends to be a little literal, and he doesn't like you hurt." He found himself smiling, even though he was still reeling. "Brahms?"

She gave an uncertain laugh and backed up so she could look him in the eye. "Sorry, I was panicked. And music seems to help me focus . . . whatever it is I can do. Soothing music. And the Lullaby just seemed appropriate. Are you all right?"

"Fine—" he said, then realized that he was lying, so he amended it. "I'll be fine." Yeah, it was a sharp right his life had taken. Having a mate was throwing both him and his wolf off their game—and he wasn't inclined to complain. He smiled to himself. She even sang lullabies to him—and he liked it.

Somehow he'd managed to stay on his feet, thus avoiding a dunking in the cold water, and still had his father's present for Dana.

"Shall we go see the fae?" he asked politely, as if he

hadn't just had some sort of . . . epiphany, metaphysical almost breakdown . . . he didn't have the words.

"Sure." Anna took his free hand, and the touch of her skin was better than her embrace because it was her flesh on his.

Brother Wolf gave a groan of contentment and settled down, even though he was always unhappy around the fae, any fae. They weren't pack and never could be. He himself liked her as well as he'd ever liked any fae. About Dana, he and Brother Wolf agreed to disagree.

THE boat had a door, just like a real house. Anna waited while Charles knocked. She used her eyelashes to hide how intently she watched him. His control was so good she'd had no idea there was something wrong until she'd looked up after a couple of back flips to see his eyes, gold and savage—and then she'd felt him, all of him. Too much to process, too much to see, all she'd felt was his pain. He was rebuilding the walls between them now. She didn't even know if he was doing it on purpose or not.

He seemed to have it all together now, but she kept her hand on his back, tucked up under his jacket, where she could feel the muscles, smooth and relaxed under her fingertips.

Over the smell of brine, vegetation, and city, she could smell turpentine—but no one came to greet them.

Charles opened the door and stuck his head inside. "Dana? My da sent us to bring you a present."

It felt like the whole world paused with interest, but the fae didn't say anything.

"Dana?"

Sound, when it came, emerged from over their heads. "A present?"

Anna looked up and saw that a second-story window was open.

"That's what he told me," Charles said.

Anna could tell that he liked the fae by the warmth in his voice. She wasn't prepared for him to like her; he liked so few people. The wolf inside her, brought out by whatever had happened on the docks, stirred uneasily, possessively, protectively.

"Bring it here, then, dear boy. I'm up in the studio, and I don't want to track paint all over the place."

Dear boy? Anna felt her eyes narrow. It appeared the affection was mutual.

He took her hand absently. Her wolf settled at his touch as she followed him through the door in the side of the boat. Charles seemed to know where he was going, or maybe he was just following the biting smell of turpentine.

She glanced around as she followed him deeper. There were paintings of butterflies and moths lining the hall. The rooms to either side were small and cozy, decorated in purples, pinks, and blues—as if a team of Disney animators had come in and decorated it to make the perfect fairy abode. One room held an artificial waterfall that burbled with manic cheer. A twin-sized bed took up the rest of the space. The whole place smelled of salt water and the same odd smell she'd noticed when they talked to the troll— maybe it was the smell of a fae.

The hall emptied into a cozy kitchen and a narrow stairway lit by skylights and lined with flowering plants growing in various pink, powder blue, and lavender pots. At the top was a large room, one side entirely of glass that looked out over the water. In the center of the room . . . greenhouse, whatever it was, stood the fae.

Her skin was pale, a stark contrast to the thick hair that flowed to her hips in mahogany curls. Her face was screwed up in concentration which made her . . . cute. Slender, long fingers, splattered attractively with paint, played with a small paintbrush. Her eyes were deep blue, like a lake in the high summer sun. Her mouth was dark and full. And she was tall, as tall as Charles, and he was a tall man, over six feet.

Aside from the hair, she was nothing like Anna had expected. There were wrinkles at the side of her eyes, and her face was caught between maturity and old age. She wore a gray T-shirt that had less paint on it than her hands did, and gym shorts that revealed legs that were muscled with the stringy power of age rather than taut youth.

In front of her was an easel holding a largish canvas that faced the other direction, so Anna couldn't see what was on it.

"Dana," rumbled Charles.

Anna didn't want the woman looking at her mate. Which didn't make sense. The fae was not beautiful, and she wasn't even paying attention to Charles. It must still be a leftover reaction to the odd moment on the docks.

Or maybe it was the "dear boy."

Anna's hand had found its way back under Charles's jacket, and she clenched the thick silk shirt he wore and tried not to growl—or drag him away.

Dana Shea looked away from the easel, and smiled, a radiant smile that had all the joy of a mother's first look at her infant, a boy's triumph the first time he hits a baseball with a bat. It was warm and intimate and innocent, and it was directed at Charles.

"Dana," Charles's voice was harsh. "Stop it."

A hurt look slid over her face.

"That magic doesn't work with me," he told the fae—and he was starting to sound seriously angry. "And don't think that my father's favor will allow you leeway with me."

Anna closed her eyes. It was a spell. She breathed through her nose, allowing the sharp smell of turpentine and Charles to clear her head. A spell, but she didn't think it was directed at Charles, not precisely. Dana knew Charles; she'd know he had his own defenses against magic.

Anna knew what this was—a challenge. The fae woman wasn't a werewolf, but she was a dominant in her own territory. And just maybe she considered Charles her territory. As he had certainly once been.

That was what her wolf sensed. This woman had slept with Charles. Anna supposed that in two hundred odd years he'd had sex with a lot of women. But Dana had not been Charles's mate.

Taking another deep breath, Anna leaned her forehead against Charles's arm and thought of the way his scent made her feel, of the sound of his laughter and the rumble of his voice in their bed at night. She wasn't looking for the passion, though there was plenty of that, but for the deeply centered clarity that he brought to her—and she returned to him. Something that she alone could give him: peace.

His muscles softened against her forehead, and his lips came down to brush the top of her head. She opened her eyes and met the fae's gaze.

"Mine," she said firmly.

The fae gave her a slow smile. "I see that." She looked at Charles. "You understand the impulse," the fae told him. "I couldn't resist testing her. I've heard so much about the puppy who caught the old dog in her trap."

"Careful," warned Charles. "That strays perilously close to a lie."

The fae raised an eyebrow in offense.

"You don't want me," he told her. "Don't be a dog in the manger."

She turned up her nose and started painting again, all

but turning her back to them. "Aesop. I'm trying for Tristan and Isolde, Romeo and Juliet, and you bring up that dry old Greek."

"I suppose if Dana is occupied, we can give her the Marrok's gift tomorrow," said Charles without making a move to leave.

The fae sighed. "You know what I like best about you—and hate the most—is that you never have known how to play properly. I am the jilted older woman whose onetime flirt has found a younger, prettier woman. You are supposed to be embarrassed that your new love knows about us." She looked at Anna. "And you. I expected better from you—you are his woman. You should at least be angry with him for not warning you we'd been lovers."

Anna gave her a cool look, remembered that they had come here to make nice with someone who would help them accomplish their task, and didn't say, "You aren't worth getting angry about." Instead, she simply told her, "He is mine, now."

Dana laughed. "You might just do, after all. I was afraid he'd found someone who would always give him his own way, and that would be dreadfully bad for him. Just look what being mated to that whiny fashion plate has done to his father." The fae started to put out a hand, but then gave it a rueful look. "I would shake your hand, but I'd get paint all over you. I am known here as Dana Shea and you must be Charles's mate, Anna Cornick, who was Anna Latham of Chicago." Anna, remembering what Charles had told her about True Names, was a little uneasy with how . . . precise the fae woman had been in naming her.

"I'm not the only one," Dana continued, "who has been curious about the woman who managed to tame our old wolf. So be prepared for a lot of rudeness from the women"—her voice took on a serious warning note as she looked at Charles—"and flirting from the men."

"You've heard something?" Charles asked her.

Dana shook her head. "No. But I know men, and I know wolves. None of them are dominant enough to face you directly—but they'll see her as a weakness. When your father chose to stay home, he gave them an opportunity for challenge. You are not an Alpha—and they'll resent having to listen to you." She took up a turpentine-soaked rag and cleaned her hands. "Now I'll quit lecturing you, and you can come around here and take a look at what I've done instead."

THREE

BRAVE woman, thought Anna, *to thoroughly antagonize us, then show us something that matters to her.* There was nothing in Dana's face to show that their opinion was important to her—but Anna could see it in her body language.

Anna didn't know what to expect, but she drew in her breath when she got her first view of the painting. It was skillfully executed, exquisite in detail, color, and texture. A robust young woman with reddish hair and pale complexion leaned her head against a plastered wall and stared out of the painting at something or someone. There was a yellow flower, delicate and fine-textured, held in hands that were neither.

The colors were wrong, brighter—but there was something familiar in the curve of the woman's cheek and the shape of her shoulder.

"It looks like it was painted by one of the old Dutch masters," Anna said.

"Vermeer," Charles agreed. "But I've never seen this one."

The fae sighed and moved to a table. She began cleaning her brushes with quick, almost fevered movements.

"No one has, not since it perished in a fire a couple of centuries ago. And no one ever will because that painting isn't it." She looked at Anna. "Vermeer. Yes. What is the woman looking at?"

And it was then Anna saw it, the alien beneath the glamour. Alien and . . . recognizable. *She didn't hurt me too bad,* the troll had said. This woman was a predator, a top predator.

Uncomfortable under that strange gaze, Anna shook her head. "I don't know."

Dana made a sharp gesture with her hand. "You aren't looking at it."

True enough. Anna looked at the woman in the painting, who met her stare with clear blue eyes, several shades lighter than Dana's. The only answer that occurred to her was stupid, but she said it anyway. "Someone here in this room?"

Dana's shoulders drooped and she turned to Charles. "No. You see? When he finished the original, he dragged a peasant in from the streets—and even that uneducated fool could see it. Vermeer's students, the ones who were there the day the painter finished it, called it that, what the peasant told the Master: *She Looks at Love.* Vermeer himself titled it *Woman with Yellow Flower* or something prosaic, as he preferred."

Anna looked at the painting, and the more she looked at it, the more was wrong. Not bad—nothing could take away from the skill that caught the luscious texture of skin and hair and the cloth of the woman's dress—but it was like listening to one of those computer programs that played sheet music: perfect technical skill . . . and no soul.

"I don't know a lot about paintings," Anna said to excuse herself.

Dana shook her head and gave Anna a rueful smile, the alien predator nowhere to be seen. "No, it's all right. My people are cursed with the love of beautiful things and no ability to create them." She dried her hands. "Not all fae, of course. But many of those of us who are most deeply steeped in magic give up creative abilities of all kinds. Ah well."

"Dragons are like that," Charles said obscurely.

Did he know a dragon? Anna gave him an interested look. He smiled a little, but his attention was on the fae, who had stopped her scrubbing.

"Dragons can't create either?"

He shrugged. "So my da says. Mostly he only says things he knows to be true."

She smiled, and it was as if the sun came out. "To be like dragons is not such a bad thing. I've only seen the one—out exploring, he said, I think. We didn't have much of a conversation, but he was . . . like the Vermeer. A work of art."

He tilted his head. "Exactly."

Dana tilted her head the same way and looked at Charles, really looked at him. "You are the killing arm of the Marrok. Rude. Dangerous."

"True, enough," Charles said.

Anna found it interesting that the fae thought "rude" more notable than "dangerous."

"I was drawn to that in you," Dana told him. "I would have said that I knew you quite well. But I never knew you could also be kind." She put her hands on his shoulders and, with a grin at Anna, she kissed him on the cheek. Anna could feel the pulse of her magic as she sent it over Charles like a mantle or net. It slid off, but even Anna, who had not been the focus, could feel the fascination and lust she generated.

"There," she told Anna. "A sister could not have been more circumspect. Now didn't you say you brought something for me?"

She didn't lie. Or if she did, Anna couldn't tell—and the fae couldn't lie, could they? The magic could have been involuntary; maybe it happened every time, and the fae didn't even notice anymore.

Charles hadn't seemed affected, but it would have been difficult to tell. His face was doing its usual public thing. Not even the mate bond helped her, because the connection between them told her nothing. But it wasn't possible for a fae with magic like that to kiss him and he not feel anything, was it? Not affection, admiration, or lust? Voluntary or not, the fae's magic had been aimed at him while the merest shadow of it had brushed Anna—who had never in her life been attracted to another woman.

She touched Charles lightly on the arm. He hadn't managed to rebuild his barriers against her because she suddenly knew exactly what he felt toward Dana Shea—wariness. Not desire or fear, but wary respect—one predator to another on neutral territory maybe. And then there was Brother Wolf . . .

She'd heard werewolves talk as if they and the wolves they shared their skins with were one. Some werewolves had nothing more wolfish about them, even in wolf form, than a nasty temper and a need to kill things that ran from them. Other than fighting to keep her sanity in the first few months after her Change, Anna hadn't thought about it much one way or the other.

Charles sometimes talked about his wolf as if it were a separate being who shared his body: Brother Wolf.

For the first time, perhaps springing from that oddly terrifying moment outside when she'd felt everything he was—too much to be absorbed or witnessed—she could feel the wolf inside of Charles. Two distinct souls. And Brother Wolf felt her, too.

Mate, he told her, not unkindly. *Get out of our head so we can deal with She-Who-Is-Not-Kin.*

Not-Kin wasn't the only thing she got from that name. Powerful, ruthless, killer. Bound by rules. Overcivilized. Respected enemy. Brother Wolf's voice was clearer in her head than even the Marrok's. And the Marrok spoke in words—Brother Wolf wasn't hampered by anything so human.

Anna pulled her hand away from Charles as if he'd burned her, and stared at her fingers. Charles's shoulder bumped her with silent reassurance, a casual gesture the fae woman probably hadn't noticed. Or was too polite to comment on.

Later, murmured Brother Wolf quietly, then she was alone in her head. Alone with the remnants of jealousy and . . . hurt at Brother Wolf's rejection. Knowing that she shouldn't feel either didn't help at all.

Charles took the package he'd brought and handed it to Dana.

Dana's eyebrows rose. "Butcher paper and twine?"

He shrugged. "Da gave it to me that way."

The fae shook her head and opened a drawer in a bird's-eye maple desk and pulled out a pair of delicate sterling silver scissors. Setting the package on the desktop, she cut the string and opened it.

And the alien thing Anna had glimpsed earlier was back in full measure. Dana didn't move, didn't so much as blink, but the portent of . . . something filled the space they were in. Every muscle, every hair on Anna's body warned her to run.

She looked at Charles. His attention was on the fae, but he wasn't alarmed. Did he not feel it? Or was he so confident that Dana's threat was something he could handle? But his calm helped Anna regain hers. She waited to see what had caused such a strong reaction.

Even before Dana had opened the package, it'd been obvious that a painting was inside. It wasn't large. Ten inches by twelve, maybe, framed in oak a couple of shades darker than the desk's maple, a waterscape of some sort.

"Da said to tell you it was what he remembered," Charles said. "That he might have gotten some of the details a little wrong, but he thought not."

"I didn't know the Marrok painted." Dana's voice was . . . deeper somehow. Rich and hoary with age. Her hands trembled as she touched the painting. The fae's power that Anna had felt so strongly just a few moments ago was gone as if it had never been.

"He doesn't." Charles shook his head. "But we have an artist in our pack, and he has a gift for painting other people's words—and my father is very good with words."

"I didn't know your father was ever there." The fae sounded . . . lost.

Charles shrugged. "You know how Da is. No one notices him unless he intends it. And he is a bard. He goes everywhere."

Dana lifted her head, and her eyes were puffy, her nose red, though no tears fell down her cheeks. She looked very human. "How did he know?"

Charles lifted both of his hands. "Who knows how my da figures out anything. He thought it would please you."

She looked at it again, and Anna couldn't tell if she was pleased or not—overcome, certainly. Shocked. "My home. It is long gone. Destroyed by magic and geology, the spring dried up centuries ago. The site it occupied is a city street that bears the name of a hundred other streets in a hundred other cities. I thought all memory of it was lost." She touched the painting the way Anna touched Charles: lightly, cautious of pain but unable to resist the draw of it.

She tipped it so they both could see it better. The side of a lake, Anna thought. A deep lake to catch the color of the sky and darken the blue to a near black. The artwork was plainer than the painting Dana had been working on, and the canvas much smaller. But in simple brushstrokes, the artist had captured an unworldly quality that made the small picture a window into a foreign place. A place that held no welcome for Anna—but somehow it matched the alien look she'd glimpsed in Dana's eyes.

"Tell your father," Dana said, returning her attention to the painting, "that I will see if I can return a gift of equal value to him. And my apologies if I don't."

"WELL," said Anna, once they were safely on their way. "That was . . . unsettling."

"You didn't like her?"

She looked at him, then turned her attention back to the road. When the fae's spell had brushed her, Anna had wanted to like her, to fawn at her feet and wait for crumbs of kindness. The rest of the time she'd wanted to kill the fae for flirting with Charles—for having slept with him.

She wanted to crawl in a dark hole so that she never bothered Brother Wolf with her presence again—which she knew was stupid. He hadn't been rejecting her. Not really. But there had been such . . . dismissal in his admonition. His attention had been on Dana.

Dana who was fae, a Gray Lord, confident and powerful. Not a twenty-three-year-old woman with half an education who didn't even know, after three years of being one, a quarter of what she should know about being a werewolf. She was no fit match for Charles.

None of which she could talk to Charles about without sounding like a stupid twit—a complicated, high-maintenance, stupid twit. Fortunately she could answer his question without betraying what really bothered her about visiting the fae.

"In Chicago, at the Brookfield Zoo, they have a reptile house. I took a school tour of it once, when I was a kid. They have a green mamba. It's the most beautiful snake I've ever seen; not flashy, just this . . . indescribable shade of green—and so poisonous that if someone gets bitten by it, there's usually no time to administer antivenin."

"You think she's beautiful?" He considered it. "Interesting looking, I would say, but not beautiful. Few of the fae are beautiful with their glamour on. Beauty doesn't blend in very well. And the fae, like us, spent a long time learning to hide in plain sight."

Anna stared ahead. "She's beautiful. Distinctive. In a room of movie stars, everyone would look at her first."

He was watching her intently; she could feel it even if her eyes were busy with the traffic.

"That's dominance," he said. "Not beauty."

"No?" She passed a couple of boys in a Ferrari, and they took offense, roaring up behind her until they were so close she could tell that one of the pair should have shaved better.

"Beauty isn't always easy," she said. "Take Paganini for instance."

"That's music."

"You know what I mean."

He didn't fall into easy, agreeable conversation, and she liked the way he considered what she'd said instead of just letting her run with it.

"I've seen her without her glamour," he told her finally. "Maybe it blinded me to more subtle things. When we became lovers, I did it because I found her interesting." He was watching her reaction.

That morning she would have told him exactly how hearing him describe a former lover made her feel. But since then she'd had that little glimpse of him, raw and bare—although she'd done her best not to look. No one should stand completely naked before another person. But she'd noticed something . . . unexpected. She knew who she was—and she knew who he was. It wasn't that she didn't value herself; she did. But Charles was . . . a force of nature.

And he worried that she might not ever be able to see who he was and love him—because he looked in the mirror and saw only the killer. It was the reason he kept the bond between them tightened down. He loved her beyond all reason and didn't expect her to love him back. He was just waiting for her to wise up.

She felt terrified—as if she had been given a delicate and valuable glass ornament, and any wrong move would break it. She felt as though it should have been given to stronger, more capable hands so it would not be harmed. Not that she hadn't staked out her claim in front of Dana quickly enough.

When Anna didn't say anything, he continued. "She took me as her lover because, once she knew her ability to make anyone lust after her didn't work on me, she was curious what sex would be like without bespelling her partner."

Anna snorted. "I'm sure the packaging didn't bother her much either."

Charles sighed. "I did this wrong, didn't I? I owe you an apology."

She glanced at him.

"I didn't mean to bog this down in ancient history—but I didn't stop her doing so soon enough either. And then . . . words are not always my best means of communication. Let me make things clear: there was nothing between us except mutual appreciation—and that a century ago or more."

"It's all right," she told him. "I understand." *Humor,* she thought, *it has to be just right. Dry humor.* "You've had a very long time to acquire former lovers I can blame you for."

A warm hand closed over her knee, and a warm, wordless voice curled around her even as Charles said, "I liked it today, when you claimed me in front of her." He hesitated. "I think it hurt my feelings that you were able to talk about her without being jealous."

She took her right hand off the wheel and ran her hand down his arm. "You need to check your nose, Kemo Sabe." If he could be honest, so could she. "I don't like you talking about her. I wanted to rip her face off when she kissed you. And when Brother Wolf pushed me out—"

"He didn't mean it that way." Charles's free hand tapped on the door frame. "He's not . . . not capable of subterfuge, not even to make things easier. He's very straightforward."

The boys in the Ferrari were still on her tail, and she tapped her brakes once in warning.

"Well," she said. *Straightforward.* "I suppose that explains it all." But it didn't bother her anymore. It wasn't Charles's explanation that soothed her, it was the way she'd felt Brother Wolf's *straightforward* agreement with Charles's pleasure in the way she'd faced up to Dana and claimed him at the fae's boat. She couldn't read everything. Not much from Charles at all now—but Brother Wolf, it seemed, was willing to be more forthcoming.

"You two have a great deal more in common than sharing the same body," she said.

Charles started to laugh and slid down in his seat. "I suppose we do, for good or for ill, eh? He doesn't like the fae, not even Dana. And he . . . we are still adjusting to having you. We protect our pack, that's what our job has always been. Especially the submissives who are our heart."

"And he . . . you feel me as an über-submissive," she said. What she was, was Omega, not submissive at all. But she served somewhat the same purpose in the pack. The dominant wolves could . . . relax around her because they knew that she would never challenge them—not because she couldn't, but because she *wouldn't*. Omegas didn't care about pack position, they just cared about the pack.

"You are ours," he said unequivocally, humor gone. "Brother Wolf's and mine. Ours to be kept safe. Dana is many things, but safe isn't one of them. You were distracting us—and if we'd talked to you too long, she'd have sensed it and been offended. It is not difficult to offend most fae, and Dana is not an exception."

"Her reaction to the painting Bran sent her was odd," Anna said.

"Powerful," agreed Charles. "But it would not have done to give her a gift that was less than the gifts others will bring her during this conference. Staying on the right side of the fae is an interesting dance, and I'll leave it to my father to know exactly how to step."

"The Vermeer . . . Why did she copy it instead of painting something of her own?"

"Her own paintings . . . are worse. Do you remember the sad clown paintings? Or are you too young? They were everywhere for a while. Bright-colored and flat-feeling. Empty."

Anna shivered. "My dentist had them all over his office."

"Like that," Charles said.

"Maybe she should paint scenery," Anna suggested. "The background of the Vermeer was very well done."

"I suggested that once, but she wasn't interested. She wants to paint the kinds of subjects she likes to view—lovers and dreamers."

"Do you think the pack has good auto insurance?" Anna asked, looking in the rearview mirror again.

Charles glanced behind them and narrowed his eyes.

The Ferrari suddenly dropped back.

"Jeez," Anna said. "You are handy to have around."

"Thank you."

Anna thought of Dana as she weaved her way through the traffic, her opinion more charitable than she'd been able to manage earlier.

What would it feel like to love music as she did and not be able to sing or play? Or worse, to be proficient but never cross the line between a collection of notes and pitch and rhythm to real *music*? To know that you were missing it by just a hair but have no idea how to take it from metronome correctness to power and true beauty.

She'd known a few people like that in school. Some of them had made the transition, some of them hadn't.

At Northwestern, before her Change had forced her to drop out, she'd been a music major. Her primary instrument had been the cello.

The first violin in the quartet she'd played in at school had been a precise master of technique who was so good he fooled the professors into thinking he was playing music. A regular wunderkind.

She'd thought he was oblivious to it until one night, after a performance, when they'd all gone out to a local bar and toasted the concert in beer and ale. The others were dancing, but she'd stayed at the table with him, worried about the serious way he was attempting to drink the pub dry when it had been his more usual habit to declare himself the designated driver and stick to ice tea or coffee.

"Anna," he'd said, staring into the amber liquid in his cup as if it held the wisdom of the age, "I don't fool you, do I? Those others"—he waved a vague hand to indicate their missing comrades—"they think I'm all that—but you know better, don't you."

"Know what?" she'd asked.

He leaned forward, smelling of beer and cigarettes. "You know I'm a fraud. I can feel the beast inside me, screaming to get out. And if I loose it, it will pull me up to greatness despite myself."

"So why not let it free?" She hadn't been a werewolf then. The world had been a gentler place, the monsters safely in their closets, and she had been brave in her ignorance.

His eyes were old and weary, his voice slurring a bit. "Because then everyone would see," he told her.

"See what?"

"Me."

To make great art, you had to expose your soul, and some things should be left safely in the dark. For a while, after she'd been forcibly Changed, Anna hadn't made music at all—and not just because she'd had to sell her cello.

"Anna?"

She moved her grip on the steering wheel. "Just thinking about Dana and why she can't paint as she'd like to." She hesitated. "I wonder if it is because she has no soul—like some of the churches claim. Or if it's because what is inside her frightens her too much to expose it."

*   *   *

HE'∂ chosen the hotel because he wanted Anna to be comfortable. There were fancier places in downtown Seattle, glittering jewels of steel and glass.

He could afford them.

In other cities, the Marrok's company even owned a few, and they had hefty investments in some others. But he remembered how intimidated she'd been by his house only a few weeks ago, which was not extravagant or particularly large, so he thought she'd be more comfortable in this hotel, which was his favorite anyway.

Sometimes it embarrassed him. This need to show her the things he treasured in the hope that she would love them, too. He was too old to be indulging himself this way: showing off in the plane—taking her to this hotel. He'd have to tell her about the investment portfolio he'd started for her sometime. But he was an old hunter and knew better than to startle his prey. He'd wait until she was more comfortable with him, with the pack . . . with everything.

Anna stopped in front of the curb and he could feel her stress when the parking attendant came to take her keys from her. She hugged herself while Charles gave his name and handed the young man a tip for not looking taken aback by the battered Toyota.

He took their luggage, and, still watching Anna, who was looking down at her feet, refused help with them. She'd feel better without anyone serving them.

Maybe he should have taken her to something more impersonal? Someplace where you parked your own car and no one asked if you needed help? Maybe she was still upset by Dana's attempt to make her jealous. Or maybe she was worried about Brother Wolf.

Brother Wolf had never talked to anyone but him like that. Not even Da. Maybe it upset her? Or maybe it was the way Brother Wolf had opened them to her outside the fae's house. Had she seen something that disgusted her? Frightened her? Maybe the distance she'd put between them when they left Dana's house had nothing to do with jealousy at all.

He wasn't used to the emotional roller coaster he'd been on since he met her. It was a good thing she was an Omega, who could soothe everyone around her—and not a dominant. Brother Wolf was on edge as it was; only when she touched him or when she was happy did he have complete control.

They needed to talk, but not in public.

The hotel was older: brick instead of steel, and eleven stories, not thirty. But it was old-world upscale, decorated with a whimsy that appealed to him, the aim to delight rather than impress in a Mediterranean-influenced Art Deco style. When they walked into the lobby, Anna—who was still quiet—stopped just inside the door. She looked up, looked at the Christmas tree decorated in huge maroon, deep purple, and silver cloth bows instead of bulbs, with an even more enormous gold and deep green bow on top.

Anna smiled at him and took his arm. And he knew he'd picked right. She loved it. Brother Wolf basked in the satisfaction of pleasing their mate.

Their room was on the seventh floor, something that Brother Wolf disapproved of. He'd rather have been able to use the windows as a convenient second exit rather than a risky escape route. But Charles preferred to have a room more difficult for unexpected visitors to enter, and the wolf had conceded the point.

The elevator opened, and in front of them was a mirror to make the hall look bigger and lighter—and a goldfish in a clear bowl on a little table.

"A goldfish?" she asked.

"Tough creatures, goldfish," he said.

She laughed. "No argument. I knew someone who rescued a goldfish from a frat house where it had been living in a bowl of beer. But why goldfish at a hotel?"

He shrugged. "I've never asked anyone. Though if you come by yourself, they put a goldfish in your room for company." He didn't tell her that this was the only time he'd ever been here that he wouldn't have a goldfish in his room.

He'd been alone a long time, despite the pack, despite the lovers he'd taken and who'd taken him. He'd had to be because he was, as Dana said, his father's killing arm. He'd had to be alone: acquaintances were easier to kill than friends.

And now he wasn't. He loved it, he reveled in it—though he was sometimes halfway convinced that the bond between them would be his death. For her sake, he would destroy the world.

Probably it wouldn't come to that.

He opened the room and waited at the door while she explored her new territory.

She wandered through it, touching the table and the couch in the sitting room. She tugged lightly at a tassel on the tapestry drapes that separated the bedroom from the rest.

"It looks like a set from *The Sheik*," Anna said. "Complete with striped wallpaper to look like tent sides and the fabric divider. Cool."

She sat on the bed and groaned. "I could get used to this." Then she turned her warm brown eyes to his, and said, "I think we have to talk."

That he agreed with her didn't stop the cold churning in his stomach. Talk was not his specialty.

She scooted back and sat with her legs crossed on the far side of the bed, patting the mattress beside her.

"I won't bite," she said.

"Oh?"

Anna grinned at him, and suddenly all was right with his world—yes, he had it bad.

"Or at least I'll make sure you enjoy it if I do."

Charles left their baggage in front of the bathroom, blocking the door to the hall, and Brother Wolf didn't even object to the obstruction between them and escape. The warmth in her drew him like a fire in winter, and there was no escape for him or his brother in flesh. And neither of them cared.

He stripped off his leather jacket and dropped it on the floor. Then he sat down on the bed and pulled off his boots. He heard her tennis shoes hit the floor as he stretched out on the bed next to her without looking at her. *Talk. She'd said "talk."* And he'd do that best looking at the wall.

He waited for her to begin. If he started asking the questions he had, Anna might not ask him what she needed to know. It was something he'd learned a long time ago with less dominant wolves.

After a while, she flopped down on the bed beside him. He closed his eyes and let her scent surround him.

"Is this bonding thing as weird for you as it is for me?" she said in a small voice. "Sometimes it's overwhelming and I wish it would shut down, even though it hurts when it does. And when it is narrower, I miss the intimacy of knowing what you're feeling."

"Yes," Charles agreed. "I'm not used to sharing with anyone but Brother Wolf." His mate, he thought. She'd had a rough time, and she needed everything he could give her. So he used the words that he didn't trust himself with to tell her what he could. "I don't care what Brother Wolf thinks of me. You . . . I care. It's . . . difficult."

She moved until her breath touched the back of his neck. Very quietly she said, "Do you ever wish it hadn't happened?"

At that he sat up and turned to her, examining her face for hints of just how she'd meant the question. His sudden move made her flinch, and if the bed hadn't been so big, she'd have fallen off in her scramble to get away from him.

He closed his eyes and controlled himself. There were no enemies here to slay. "Never," he told her with utter sincerity he hoped she heard. "I will *never* regret it. If you could have seen my life before you came into it, you would not ask that question."

He felt her warmth, smelled her closeness before she touched him. "I cause you a lot of trouble. I'll probably cause you more before we're done."

Charles opened his eyes and let himself drown in her scent, in her presence, and kissed a freckle that graced Anna's cheek. Then the one on the side of her nose and another just above her lip. "For a long time, my brother Samuel has been telling me that I needed something to shake me up."

She kissed him—a rare enough occurrence that he held perfectly still and savored it for the gift of trust it was. She'd been tortured by monsters, and sometimes they still held sway over her.

Anna pulled herself away. "If this keeps up, there won't be any talk."

Good, he thought. But he knew there were things she still needed to discuss, so he lay back down and pillowed his head on his hands though there were at least three layers of pillows on the bed.

"I keep feeling like we're doing it wrong," she said. "That this bond between us is meant to be much more than we're allowing it to be."

"There is no *wrong* between us," he told her.

She made a frustrated noise, so he supposed that wasn't the answer she was looking for. Charles tried again. "We have time, love. As long as we are careful to set our feet on the path we want to follow, we have a very long time to get it right."

He could feel her focus her attention on him. "Okay," she said finally. "I can live with that. Does that mean I get to tell you when I think you're walking in the wrong direction?"

He grinned. "Could you help yourself?"

"There is no wrong between us," she repeated his words with more satisfaction. "That means yes, right?"

He looked at her again, "That means yes. Right."

"And you are as confused about this as I am?"

It seemed important to her that they were on equal ground. But he could not lie to her. "No. Differently confused, I think. And possibly more confused. You haven't had the better part of two hundred years to decide who you are and who you aren't. When that all changes . . ." Charles shrugged.

He wasn't used to all of this emotion. He'd taken the feelings and desires of his human half and stuffed them somewhere so they wouldn't interfere with the things he had to do. And now they were all back, and he had no tools to deal with them—and he wasn't stupid enough to think that they would ever allow themselves to be stuffed away again.

"Differently confused," she said. "Okay. That's okay."

She reached out and touched his arm, drawing a finger down. "When I touched you today . . . it feels as though you have two souls in one body. Is that how I am?"

"Anna," he told her. "You are how you are. Brother Wolf and I . . . You know I was born werewolf and not Changed. That has left some differences, I think. To function, most werewolves have to make their wolf obedient if not completely subservient. After a while, the wolf spirit is reduced to a part of the man's spirit. An unthinking, violent part full of instincts and desires but no true thoughts."

He looked at her pale hand on the green silk shirt he wore. "I am not my grandfather, to look into the heart of man," he told her. "I don't know that what I've told you is truth. It is just what I've seen and felt.

"Brother Wolf and I reached a different compromise. In situations where I am better able, he allows me full control—and I extend him the same courtesy."

"Two souls," she said.

"No," he shook his head. "One soul, one man, two spirits. We are one, Brother Wolf and I. Inseparable. If he died, so would I."

"Have I crippled my wolf?"

He rolled on his side, drawn closer to her by her concern. "It isn't something to be mourned. It is simply survival. But if it helps, I think you and your wolf have reached a different compromise altogether." He smiled. "I think that's why Brother Wolf chose you in the first place—before we'd had much more than a chance to say hello. We balance, you know. You to me, your wolf to mine. She's shy unless you are threatened, but she's all there."

Anna closed her hand on his arm. "Okay. I can deal with that better than the alternatives."

"Do you need any more words between us?" he asked, her touch making his voice go husky.

FOUR

BEFORE she could answer, his cell phone rang. It wasn't his da's ring—and if they'd been home, he'd have let the answering machine pick up. But this wasn't home. He was here to do a job, and that meant answering phone calls at inconvenient times. So he snagged his coat off the floor and took his cell out of the pocket.

"Charles," he said.

He was answered by a stream of southern French that flowed by so fast he caught one word in four. But that was enough.

"I'm coming," he said, and hung up while the other wolf was still speaking.

"Did you catch that?" he asked pulling on his boots.

Anna shoved her feet in her shoes. "I don't speak French."

"The Spanish wolves were eating at the restaurant that Jean Chastel decided to bring his wolves to. Matters are escalating—and to add to the fun, the British Alpha is there, too."

"Who called you?"

"Michel, one of the other French Alphas—who'll be punished if Jean ever figures it out. I gather our informant called from the men's room. Hopefully, he'll take proper precautions to protect himself." He jerked on his coat. "Seattle is a big city. Hard to fathom that three factions of werewolves ended up in the same restaurant at the same time. If I find out someone planned this, heads will roll."

"If the restaurant is Bubba's Basement Barbeque, it might be an accident," Anna said, pulling on her own coat. "I had at least five pack members—including your father and Asil—tell me to make you take me there. It's apparently famous for its endless, endlessly good ribs. Asil told me he'd never been, but its reputation was good enough that it had spread all the way to the packs in Europe."

Charles looked at her thoughtfully. "People talk to you," he said. "That could be useful."

APPARENTLY, they were going to jog to the restaurant. Anna was glad of her tennis shoes on the wet and steep hill they charged down.

Charles, cat-footed as he was, slipped and slithered in the pouring rain. His cowboy boots were slick-bottomed, though she didn't think it really slowed him down much. They both ran quietly, but she could feel the attention they were drawing. In the city, people pay attention when you run because it makes you either predator or prey.

It concerned her for a moment, but risk assessment was something she'd have to leave to Charles. She didn't know the wolves involved—or how far they were from the restaurant, exactly. He kept their speed to easily within human limits, so he was giving some consideration to the attention they were gathering.

She liked running with him. Without him, something inside her always worried that she would become the prey. She couldn't imagine Charles being anyone's prey.

After a few blocks, he slowed to a brisk walk, and they turned onto a level street paralleling the Sound. Like Lake Michigan in her native Chicago, the water had a presence, a weight that she'd have felt even if she hadn't been able to see it peeking out between buildings and streets.

A red neon sign proclaiming Bubba's Basement the best barbecue in Seattle had an arrow that pointed down a wide set of steps to the basement of something that might have been some kind of bank or office building—it had that neutral upscale look.

Charles opened one side of the double-door entrance, releasing the heady combination of beef, barbecue sauce, and coffee. The restaurant was dimly lit and, to Anna's quick glance, mostly full. There was a pall over the room like the weight of a thunderstorm, so strong Anna wondered if even humans could sense it.

Charles inhaled and turned left, walking around a wall of shrubbery, through a swinging door, and into a room set apart from the rest of the place. A discreet sign above the door noted that the room could be reserved for large groups for a small fee and could hold up to sixty people. When Anna followed Charles through it, she noted that there were barely a quarter of that many people in the room right now—and it wouldn't have been large enough for them even if it had been four times as big.

Alpha wolves don't mingle well with others. Anna wondered if all of them had congregated here on purpose, or if some misguided person on the restaurant's waitstaff had decided to keep all the potentially problematic clients in one place.

Someone had made a hasty effort to clear a space for

fighting because a couple of tables were lying on their sides against a wall, and chairs had been tossed wherever they landed.

"You don't have the courage of a half-bred mongrel," said one of the two men standing in the center of the room with cool deliberation. He had an accent, but it was so slight she couldn't place it immediately.

Charles looked at her, then at the door they'd just come through. Anna understood. This was private business, and they didn't need any unexpected visitors to complicate matters further. She shut the door and leaned against it.

It also gave her a quick escape—so many dominant wolves . . . Even with Charles, she couldn't help remembering what the dominant wolves in her first pack had done to her. And her heartbeat picked up. Not panicked. Not yet. But not comfortable either.

The room looked like nothing so much as a scene from a reenactment of *West Side Story* or, with slightly different props and costuming, *Gunfight at the O.K. Corral*. Four men stood on one side of the room, six on the other. A few paces in front of either group stood a man, ready to fight. The testosterone level was so high that she was amazed it hadn't triggered the little sprinklers in the ceiling.

There was a thirteenth man still seated in the corner of the room. He had his back to the wall and was cleaning his hands with a damp towelette. He noticed Charles's entrance first and tipped his head in a casual salute. "Ah," he said in a beautiful upper-class British accent, "I was wondering when the cavalry would arrive. Good to see you, Charles. At least the Russians aren't here, eh? Or the Turks."

Action froze for a moment as everyone realized a new player had entered the game.

"You know how to see the bright spot in a cloudy day," said a dark-skinned man in the larger group. "I've always liked that about you, Arthur." His accent made him, and therefore the group of wolves he stood with, the Spaniards.

Which meant that the man who'd been tossing insults could be none other than Jean Chastel, the Beast of Gévaudan.

He wasn't handsome, precisely, but there was a power to his features and in the way he carried himself that made her first Alpha, Leo, look like a half-grown pup. He made an impression, as most of the Alphas she'd met did; he took up more space in the room than he should, as if he were weightier, both physically and metaphysically, than he ought to be.

He was aware of Charles, but his pale eyes stayed firmly on his opponent. Neither tall nor short, Chastel had a lean build. His hair was longish and brownish, brushing his shoulders. His beard was several shades darker than his hair and close-trimmed. But the physical details didn't matter nearly as much as the force of who and what he was.

His opponent didn't stand a chance against him—and the Spaniard knew it. Anna could see it in his stance, in the way he wouldn't look at the Frenchman's eyes. She could smell it in the scent of his fear.

"Sergio, *mi amigo*," said the dark Spaniard who'd spoken before. "Stand down. The fight is over. Charles is here."

The Spanish fighter hadn't noticed Charles's approach, and his startled look was very nearly his undoing. Jean Chastel's right arm shot out and would have connected with his opponent's neck, but Charles had already been moving—as if he'd known what the French wolf would do before Chastel had known it himself.

Charles intercepted the blow and jerked Chastel around, using the other's momentum to propel him into his own people. A quick glance at the Spanish wolves had them all backing up a step, then his attention was focused on the first wolf.

"Fools," Charles snarled. "This is a public place. I'll not have you disturbing the peace while you are guests on Emerald City Pack grounds."

"*You'll* not have us, pup?" murmured the Frenchman, who'd recovered quickly from the unplanned impact with his wolves. He tugged on the sleeves of his long-sleeved, button-up shirt, a gesture that looked more habitual than effectual. "I'd heard the old wolf had sent his puppy for us to feast on, but I thought it was merely wishful thinking."

There was something abject about the way the rest of the French contingent stood that told Anna that none of them liked what their leader was doing, that they followed Jean Chastel out of fear. It made them no less dangerous—maybe more so. Her wolf knew them for Alphas, every one of them, and all afraid.

Beneath all the aggression and posturing in the room, there was an undercurrent of fear: hers, the Spaniard's, and the French wolves', so thick that she sneezed at the smell of it, drawing unwanted attention. Jean Chastel's eyes met hers, and she held them, despite the violence they promised. Here, she thought, here was a monster worse than the troll under the bridge. He stank of evil.

"Ah," he said, sounding almost gentle. "Another story I'd dismissed. So you found yourself an Omega, half-breed. Pretty child. So soft and delicate." He licked his lips. "I bet she's a tasty morsel."

"You'll never find out, Chastel," said Charles softly. "Back down or leave."

"I have a third choice," Chastel whispered. "I think I might take that one."

There was no good outcome for this, Anna realized, the

push bar of the door digging into her lower back. Charles *might* have allies among the Spaniards, and maybe even the British wolf. But even so, if they stepped in, they'd be showing that Charles was weak. She had boundless faith in Charles's abilities to wipe the floor with the French wolf, but even that would be a failure of sorts. This was a public place—a fight would mean police and exposure of quite a different sort than what Bran wanted.

Maybe she could help defuse it. She'd been working with Asil, an old wolf in her new pack, to try to come to some understanding of what she could do. His dead mate had been an Omega just like Anna, so he knew something about how her abilities worked—which was more than anyone else did. Even Bran, the Marrok, had only vague ideas. With Asil's help, she'd managed a few interesting things.

Charles didn't say anything to Chastel. He just stood, his arms loose at his sides, his weight on the balls of his feet, as he waited for Chastel to make a decision.

Only Charles allowed her to put her fear aside—Charles, her wolf, and the door.

She imagined a place in her mind, deep in the forest where the snow lay lightly on the ground and her breath frosted in the air. It was quiet there, and sheltered. Peaceful. A creek full of fat trout trickled under a thin layer of misty ice. In her mind's eye she followed a trout as it slid, a silver shadow, through the fast-moving water.

When she had it clear and perfect in her head, she pushed that feeling out.

Her power hit the British wolf first; she saw it in the relaxing of his shoulders. He recognized what she was doing, raised an eyebrow at her, then took his coffee cup (or maybe he drank tea—didn't the British all drink tea?) and sipped from it. A few of the Spaniards began breathing slower, and the tension in the room ratcheted down a full notch.

Charles turned, his eyes pure blinding gold—and growled. At her.

Leaving Anna standing alone in a room filled with dominant wolves and violence. The smells of it were so familiar that her body flashed with phantom pains, and it hurt to breathe.

She fled through the door she'd been holding closed, fled before her blind terror became the tinder that caused an orgy of violence. She'd seen that happen, too, though never in such a public place.

The Frenchman said something rude as the door swung shut behind her, but she wasn't paying attention. Panic, raw and ugly, made it hard to breathe as her conditioning tried to overwhelm her common sense.

She needed to find something else to focus on. So she looked around.

The patrons in the main restaurant were still unnaturally quiet—and there were a lot fewer of them than there had been when she and Charles first came into the restaurant. Most of them were looking down, an involuntary reaction to so many Alphas, she thought. Even the humans could feel it, though hopefully they didn't know what it was that made them so uneasy.

Even though they were all in the next room, there was a weight to their presence, just like there was a weight to the Puget Sound. While Charles had been at her side, she'd been able to push it away—but now it ate at her. The sound of her heart beat loudly in her ears.

But the wolves were on the other side of the door—and Charles wouldn't let them touch her.

She paused in front of the outside door.

She could go back to their hotel room and wait. The

city at night held no terrors for her—all the bad guys were here. But that would be cowardly. And Charles would get the wrong idea.

Away from the drama and the first impulse to flee attack, she figured out the reason he'd growled at her: he needed to stop her. He couldn't afford to let her quiet Brother Wolf.

Charles might be naturally more dominant—but he was the only wolf in the room who was not an Alpha of a pack. She knew that there were less dominant wolves coming to the conference, but none of them were here.

So many Alphas put Charles in a bad position. They had to fear him, they had to know that he would kill them if they moved against him—or they would smell weakness and attack him together, like a pack of wolves taking down a caribou. She'd been taking away his edge.

There was a battered piano on a small stage in the corner of the room that beckoned to her like an oasis in the desert. She could wait if she found something to think about other than old memories of pain and humiliation. Anna caught the eye of a passing waitress.

"Do you mind if I play?"

The waitress, looking a little stressed, paused midstride and shrugged. "It's fine, but if you don't play well, the cook may come out and ask you to stop. He makes a big production of it. Or the crowd will boo you off. It's kinda tradition."

"Thanks."

The waitress looked around the room. "Play a happy tune, if you can. Someone needs to liven up this place."

The piano was an ancient upright that had been old a long time ago. Someone had painted it black, but the paint had faded to a dull gray, scuffed on the corners and sprinkled with initials carved into it. Most of the edges of the ivory keys were broken, and the highest E key popped up an eighth of an inch higher than the rest.

Something happy.

She played the theme from *Sesame Street*. The piano had a much better tone than it looked as though it should—and it was mostly in tune. She segued into "Maple Leaf Rag," one of two ragtime pieces that every second-year piano student learned. The piano wasn't her instrument, but after six years of lessons, she was moderately competent.

The lively feel and fairly easy music lines of the piece made it tempting to play too fast. "Ragtime is not fast" was a favorite rant of one of her teachers. She disciplined her fingers to keep a steady beat. It helped that she was a little out of practice.

CHARLES watched Anna walk out and knew he'd sent their relationship back to the beginning. But if he hadn't stopped her, it would have been disastrous. He couldn't afford to let himself be distracted. Not by his Omega, and not by the real possibility that he'd destroyed something between them.

Most mates would be angry at being chastised in front of others. But most mates hadn't been brutalized in an attempt to break them. Anna hadn't broken, not quite.

But he couldn't afford to risk that she'd quiet Brother Wolf before she affected the Beast. Brother Wolf's aggression, his willingness to kill, was the only weapon Charles had to control the situation.

Thoroughly tired of Chastel, though he'd only been in his presence for less than a quarter of an hour, Charles called on Brother Wolf, who wouldn't be bothered about the future, to take center stage. Negotiations, as far as he was concerned, were over, had been over the moment he'd had to growl at Anna. Or maybe when Chastel had called her a pretty piece, as if she were nothing.

"You don't want to talk about my mate," he told Chastel

in a very soft voice. Brother Wolf could care less about politics. This one had made him hurt Anna—and it wouldn't bother him in the slightest to kill him here and now.

Chastel lifted his upper lip—but couldn't make himself say anything, not when faced with Brother Wolf. They stood there, eye to eye for a count of four. Then Chastel dropped his eyes, grabbed his coat, and stormed out of the room.

Charles followed him out, intent on trailing the Beast to make sure he wouldn't take it into his head to go after Anna. Charles took two steps into the main restaurant before he stopped, only vaguely noting Chastel leaving the building—because Anna hadn't left after all.

He'd thought she'd be halfway to the hotel by now. Instead, she sat on a short barstool that wobbled under her and played the infamous battered piano, her back to him and the rest of the people in the room. The piece she played wasn't complex, but it was a happy little tune. Familiar. He frowned but couldn't place it beyond the thought that it was some sort of children's tune.

Automatically, he swept the room for possible threats and found none. The only people here were human—and as he watched, they were relaxing into the music. Someone laughed and someone else called for more ribs.

She hadn't left. And that meant he could clean up the mess Chastel had left behind. It would only take a few minutes, then he could come back here and protect her from . . . Charles stopped and took a deep breath. Brother Wolf thought he could fix this by saving her from some danger—he didn't understand women very well. That Anna was still here was a hopeful sign that Charles didn't understand them as well as he had thought he did, either.

*   *   *

SHE glanced out at the audience and saw that the unusual muted quality of the restaurant had dissipated somewhat. She also hadn't heard any sudden noise that would signal a fight, so she was hopeful that Charles had matters under control. She needed something more modern next, something appropriate to the mostly middle-aged crowd she was playing for—which on the piano generally meant Elton John or Billy Joel, both pianists who could also sing. She took the last few notes of "Maple Leaf" into "The Downeaster 'Alexa.'" It wasn't a "happy tune" precisely, but it was beautiful.

It didn't take Charles long to settle the other wolves down. Without Chastel around to prod and push them, no one was interested in a public fight.

He ordered food for everyone—the house special was limitless ribs at a per-person charge—and asked if they would wait for a few minutes while he made sure his mate was all right. The French wolves were a little restless, knowing that Chastel would note how long they lingered without him—but no one objected. Alphas understood about watching over their own.

Anna had gone on to some melodic piece. Without vocals, it took him a few bars to pin down the song. He was a fan of Billy Joel, but "The Downeaster 'Alexa'" wasn't one of his favorites. It reminded him too much of all the people he'd known who were left floundering as time brought change that destroyed their lives. It spoke to him like the names of the dead, sending chills of memories best forgotten—but it was beautiful.

Her hands arched gracefully over the battered keys and pulled music and something more into the room. It was subtle, but he could see it in the chatter and in the way the old one who'd been hunched over his plate slowly straightened, eyes bright as he whispered something to the large young man sitting beside him. The man said something quietly in reply, and the old one shook his head.

"Go ask her," he said, his voice still quiet, but loud enough that Charles could pick out the words over the music. "I bet a gal who can play the ragtime right knows a few more old-time songs."

"She's all by herself, Gramps. I'll scare her. Aunt Molly—"

"No. No. Molly won't do it. Won't want me to embarrass myself—or exert myself. *You* do it. Right now." And the frail old man practically pushed the big man out of his seat.

Charles smiled. That was right. So often people got it wrong, treating their elders like children, people to be coddled and ignored. He knew better, and so did the big man. The Elders were closer to the Maker of All Things and should be deferred to whenever they made their will known.

He tensed a little as the big man made his way through the diners and closer to his Anna. But there was no threat in the human's body language. Charles thought that the big man had spent a long time trying to look less . . . lethal than someone who moved like a fighter and stood six inches taller than most people could. Charles sympathized— though he had learned to take advantage of the effect he had on people rather than disguise it.

BEFORE she'd quite finished, she noticed there was a big man standing miserably beside the piano, hunching his shoulders and trying not to look scary. She judged him to be only moderately successful.

He had a scar on his chin and a few more on his knuckles and was, she judged, an inch or so taller than Charles. Maybe if she'd still been human, she might have been worried, but she could tell by the way he stood that he was no threat to her. People seldom lie with their bodies.

He obviously was waiting to speak to her, so when she played the last measure of the song, she stopped. For some reason she wasn't in the mood for happy songs, so it was probably just as well.

A few people noticed she'd finished and began clapping. The rest put down their food and followed suit, then went back to their meal.

"Excuse me, miss. My grandpapa wants to know if you'll play 'Mr. Bojangles'—and if you'd mind if he sang with you."

"No problem," she said, smiling at him and keeping her shoulders soft so he'd know she wasn't scared of him.

"Bojangles" had been sung by a lot of people, but the very slight old man, leaning heavily on his cane, who stood up and made his way to the piano, looked a lot like the last pictures she'd seen of Sammy Davis, Jr., who'd recorded her favorite rendition of the song—right down to the maple color of his dark skin.

His voice, when he spoke, was a lot more powerful than his frail body.

"I'm gonna sing something for you," he told their audience—and everyone in the room looked up from their meals. It was that kind of a voice. He paused, milking it. "You'll have to forgive me if I don't dance anymore." She waited until the laughter he'd invited died away before she began.

Usually, when she first played a piece with someone she didn't know, especially if the piece was one she knew well, it was a mad scramble to make her version fit with the other person's perception of how the song should feel. But except for the very beginning, it was magic.

CHARLES worried a bit at first as the old man missed his cue, worried more as the beat came up again, and a third time—and closed his eyes when he started singing at entirely the wrong time.

But Anna worked around it in a more clever bit of playing than anything she'd done up to this point, and he knew she was better on the piano than he'd thought from the pieces of music she'd chosen.

The old man's voice was just right. It, the beaten-up piano, and Anna's sweet self all combined in one of those rare moments when performance and music blended to make something more.

"Bojangles" was a song that took its time to get to where it was going, building pictures of an old man's life. Alcoholism, prison, the death of a beloved comrade—none of those things had defeated Mr. Bojangles, who even in his darkest hour still had laughter and a dance for a fellow prisoner.

He jumped so high . . .

It was a warrior's song. A song of triumph.

And at the end, despite his early words, the old man did a little soft-shoe. His movements were stiff from sore joints and muscles that were less powerful than they used to be. But graceful still, and full of joy.

He let go a laugh . . . he let go a laugh . . .

When Anna finished with a little flourish, the old man took his bows, and she did, too.

"Thank you," she told him. "That was really fun."

He took her hand in his own worn hands and patted it. "Thank you, my dear. You brought back the good old days—I'm ashamed to say just how old. You made this man happy on his birthday. I hope that when you are eighty-six, someone makes you happy on your birthday, too."

And that won him a second round of applause and shouts of "encore." The old man shook his head, talked to Anna a bit, then smiled when she nodded. "We just figgered out that we both have a liking for oldies," he said. " Except for me they're not oldies."

And he started singing "You're Nobody 'til Somebody Loves You," a song Charles hadn't heard for forty years or more. Anna joined in with the piano after a few beats and let the old man's trained voice lead her in the dance.

When they were done, the room burst into applause—and Charles caught a waitress's attention. He handed her his credit card and told her that he'd like to pay for the old man's meal and those of his family—in appreciation for the music. She smiled, took his card, and trotted off.

The old man took Anna's hand and made her take another bow as well. He kissed her hand, then let his grandson escort him back to his table in triumph. His family rose around him, fussing and loving as they ought, while he sat as a king and took his due.

Anna pulled the protective cover over the keys and looked up and saw Charles. She hesitated, and it made his heart hurt that he'd made her afraid of him. But she lifted her chin, her eyes still full of the music, and strolled up to him.

"Thank you," he told her, before she could say anything. He wasn't sure if he was thanking her for leaving the room when he'd asked, for staying in the restaurant instead of leaving him, or for the music—which had reminded him that this whole thing wasn't just about the werewolves.

It was about the humans they shared the country with, too.

The waitress, who was coming back with his card, overheard what he'd said. "From me, too, Hon," she told Anna. "It was pretty gloomy in here when you started. Like a funeral." To Charles she said, "All taken care of. You wanna be anonymous, right?"

"Yes," he said. "It'll work better that way, don't you think?"

She smiled at him, then at Anna, before hurrying off on her way.

"I'm sorry," he told Anna.

She gave him an odd, wise look. "No worries. Everything okay?"

He didn't know. Mostly that depended upon her. But he knew that wasn't what she meant. She was asking about the wolves in the next room, so he shrugged. "Mostly. Chastel was always going to be a problem. Maybe by making him back down right now, he'll be forced to play nice. Sometimes it works that way."

THE music helped. Music usually helped. Making people happy helped even more. When she looked up and saw Charles waiting for her with a small smile on his face, that helped the most. It meant that no one had died, that she hadn't messed things up too badly for him—and that he wasn't upset with her.

He escorted her to the other section, where the wolves awaited them. Chastel was gone. Anna hadn't noticed him leaving, and she should have, even with her back to the outside door and music under her fingers. It was dangerous not to notice things like that.

The tables had been moved again until there was one long table in the middle of the room. There were three big plates of food, one full and two mostly gone.

They weren't suddenly all buddies. Spanish wolves sat

on one side of the table, French on the other. The British
werewolf took up one end of the table and there were two
place settings that hadn't been used at the head.

"It seemed a shame to have come all the way here and
not try the food," murmured Charles, one hand light on the
small of her back. She couldn't see his face because he was
just behind her, but she saw the impact of his gaze as the
roomful of Alphas made it clear that they believed he was
the biggest, baddest wolf in the place.

Most of them seemed content with that. Wolves don't
fuss about things they can't change—the only exception,
she thought, might be the British Alpha. Something was
making him unhappy, certainly. But he kept his eyes down
while Charles was looking at him anyway.

"Gentlemen, my mate and my wife, Anna Latham Cornick, Omega of the Aspen Creek Pack." Charles raised his
hand to her shoulder.

"Your pardon, *monsieur*," one of the Frenchmen said.
He had one of those double accents, French with British
overtones. "Perhaps we could introduce ourselves and then
take our leave. We have taken time to eat, and we cannot
linger much longer. Chastel isn't our Marrok, not as Bran
is to those wolves here, but he can make our lives exceed-
ingly uncomfortable."

"Of course."

The Frenchman proceeded to introduce his countrymen
in hurried tones—and as he introduced them, they bowed
their heads. "And I am Michel Girard."

"I look forward to more leisurely conversations later,"
said Anna.

"I also." He smiled with weary eyes. "Until tomorrow."
And they left.

"Anna, this is Arthur Madden, Master of the Isles—the
British equivalent of the Marrok."

"Good to meet you, sir," she said. Not an Alpha then, she thought, or not *just* an Alpha.

"Delighted," Arthur said, as he rose from his place and came forward to kiss her hand. "I am sorry to confess, though Chastel is not waiting to chastise me, we've been here much longer than I intended. My wife awaits me, and I must attend. I would, however, like to issue an invitation before we leave. I've a condo in the University District, and it would be my pleasure to have you two for dinner tomorrow."

Anna looked at Charles. Madden had so clearly excluded the Spaniards that it felt awkward. She didn't know what to say that wouldn't make it worse.

"Thank you," said Charles. "We'll discuss it, and I'll let you know."

Arthur smiled, and she noticed that he was handsome. She hadn't been paying attention until then.

"Good enough." Arthur looked to the Spaniards. "My control is just not good enough, gentlemen, to have more than one dominant in my territory at a time. I am sorry."

"De nada," the dark-skinned man who was the de facto leader said graciously. "We understand, of course."

Arthur excused himself. The whole room fell silent, listening, she thought. When the restaurant door in the other room opened and closed, it felt like the whole world relaxed.

Sergio, the wolf who had faced off with Chastel, tossed a bone on his plate. "Pompous ass," he said.

"Smart, pompous ass," said Charles.

"Deluded, smart, pompous ass," said the dark-skinned man. "Have you decided how you're going to introduce us yet? How about by age?" He looked at Anna. "Charles knows all of us—and probably the Frenchmen, too. Knows everything, your mate."

It was a challenge, less serious, though no less important, Anna understood, than the near fight between Charles and Chastel. *Are we important to you?* was what the Spaniard meant.

"If I manage it, you'll pick up the tip." Charles was as relaxed as she'd ever seen him.

"Fine."

"Sergio del Fino," said Charles. The man he addressed stood, put a hand over his heart, and bowed.

He went through the others without a misstep until he got to the last two: the dark-skinned man and a redhead. He paused and then indicated the darker man with a tilt of his head. "Hussan Ibn Hussan." Then the other man. "Pedro Herrera."

Hussan smiled. "Wrong. I am older than Pedro."

Pedro smiled wider. "*Hijo*, I saw you born. I didn't know Charles knew that."

Charles lowered his head without lowering his eyes. "Asil let it slip."

Hussan slapped his leg. "I think I've been set up. Tell me my father didn't tell you to pull this one on me."

Charles just smiled.

"You're Asil's son?" Anna asked. Now that she paid attention, his skin tone was nearly as dark as that of her mentor in all things Omega, and the nose was the same.

"I have that honor," agreed Hussan.

"Ibn Hussan? My Arabic is nearly nonexistent, but shouldn't you then be Ibn Asil?" asked Sergio.

"Hussan is my father's given name. But for a long time he has used Asil," explained Hussan with a shrug. "He is old. He can do as he chooses." He gave a sour smile. "And he usually does. How is my father? He is still annoyed with me for refusing to kill him when he asked. He will not answer my phone calls or my letters. So I have stopped calling and writing."

"He's fine," said Anna. "Better."

Charles smiled a little. "He'll probably take your phone calls now."

Hussan tilted his head. "Something happened?"

"Yes." Charles pulled out a chair before a clean place setting and indicated that Anna should take a seat. "If we don't start eating, these devils will have it all gone, and we'll have to wait for the next round."

Anna sat, and he pushed in her chair before taking his own. He might sound casual, but he was still acting formal. Maybe it was because these were mostly older wolves, who would expect Charles to treat her this way. She wasn't sure she liked it, but she was willing to play along. Mostly. She used the tongs and dumped a double handful of ribs on her plate: it had been a long time since she'd eaten.

"Asil will be fine," she said. "Unless he annoys Bran too much."

She glanced up and noticed that Hussan was staring at her.

"It is you," he said. "Omega. You saved him."

She shook her head. "Ask him."

"He'll tell you it was her," Charles predicted. "She'll tell you it was not. Still, he will be fine for another century or so—as fine as he ever is."

THEY walked back to their hotel. It was still pouring, but water had never bothered Anna—and Charles seemed to be of a like mind. They walked side by side, not touching.

"Are we going to accept the invitation to Arthur Madden's dinner?" she asked him.

"If you would like. Angus has scheduled some entertainment the next night, but tomorrow is open."

"Is it going to present some diplomatic problem if we go?"

He made an impatient gesture. "As I keep telling them—this is not a negotiation. We've agreed to hear their concerns, and I will address them. But my father is adamant. The first chance my father sees to present ourselves in a favorable light, we are coming out to the public. It doesn't matter if some are offended or feel we are playing favorites. We are not courting them."

Anna kept quiet.

Finally, he said, "Arthur can be charming—and he's interesting." He glanced at her face and then back at the street. "He tells everyone he's Arthur. The king returned."

"What?"

"He's serious. He honestly believes he is *that* Arthur."

"Really?"

"Really. Before his Change, he was an amateur archaeologist—his family isn't royal, but noble and still wealthy enough back then that he didn't have to find real work. It also meant that he didn't have to have any training to pursue his hobby. He claims that shortly after his Change, he found Excalibur in a dig, and when he took hold of her, he was possessed by the spirit of Arthur."

He shrugged. "Afterward, he began taking over all the packs in Great Britain. First he killed the Alphas—but combining packs creates its own set of problems. So he modeled his rule after my da's." He smiled at her. "Da's pretty convinced that it was his decision to use Marrok as a title that sent Arthur to declare himself as *the* Arthur. After all, Sir Marrok was only a knight of King Arthur's."

"So your father thinks he's faking it? How can he do that without everyone smelling a lie?"

"My da can lie so well that no one but Samuel or I can tell," said Charles. He gave her a look—the first time he'd looked her in the face since they'd left the restaurant. "Don't tell anyone—it's supposed to be a secret."

"How old is Arthur?"

Charles smiled. "You mean this time around? I think he was Changed just after the First World War. You think he's not old enough to pull the same tricks an old lobo like my father can get away with? Da says the secret is to convince yourself you aren't lying."

"So he might just be believing his own press as hard as he can?"

"He probably brought Excalibur with him," Charles said. "He usually keeps it close. He might show you if you ask."

"Really?"

"Really."

She tucked her hand in his arm. "That might be fun."

"I'll give him a call, then." They walked another half a block in companionable silence. "I scared you," he said.

"I almost got you killed," Anna returned flatly. "Thank you for stopping me before I ruined everything."

He stopped suddenly, jerking her to a halt. "You understood."

"Not then," she admitted. "I reacted first—which really sucked. Every time I think I might not be a flaming coward, I find myself running away."

He started walking again. "You aren't a coward. A coward would never have survived what you did." But he said it absently, as if he were thinking about something else. "You know I wouldn't hurt you."

He didn't say it as if he believed it. She tightened her hold on his arm. "I do. My instincts sometimes are screwy, but I know you would never hurt me."

He looked at her, a long thoughtful look.

She raised her chin. "I said I know you would never hurt me." Then she had to modify it, so he would sense the utter truth of it. "On purpose." That wasn't strong enough. "And everything you do is on purpose." That wasn't quite right. "You are always careful of what you do. Of me."

"Stop." His shoulders were shaking and his eyes dancing. "Please. I believe you. But in a minute, you're going to talk yourself around to distrusting me again."

After they'd walked a bit farther, he said, "It is beautiful tonight."

Anna glanced up at the rain and the city streets, still noisy with traffic. She liked the way the lights sparkled in the storm. The noises of the city were as familiar and welcome as her childhood home. Somehow, though, she didn't think that Charles would normally think it beautiful. She smiled at the night.

FIVE

"WE are worried about the innocents," said the Russian wolf from the podium. Ostensibly, he was speaking to the crowd, but his words were for Charles. He spoke in English, which was well because Charles's smattering of Russian wasn't trustworthy on serious subjects, and he was distracted by Anna, who sat, very still, beside him.

"We are strong," the Russian said, "and *we* can protect ourselves. But we have mates who are human, families who are human. They will suffer, and this cannot be tolerated."

There was something incongruous about the venue they were in: an elegant auditorium with oak accents, trimmed in fabrics of various brownish gray hues, understated and expensive. A place where Angus hunted the CEOs of large companies and captured them with images of the power his technology could give them. The men and women filling the seats this morning were a different kind of predator. Dressed in their best they might be, but the current occupants of those nice seats made the CEOs look like puppies by comparison.

"If you can't protect your own, you deserve to lose them," commented Chastel from the back quarter of the auditorium. He didn't speak loudly, but in a room designed for sound and populated by sharp-eared werewolves, he didn't have to.

Charles waited. The Russian wolf, whose turn it was to speak, looked at him to enforce discipline. But it wasn't Charles's job. Not this time. Brother Wolf was confident that it would be theirs very soon. Then they would discipline Chastel, and blood would flow. But here, in this room, it was someone else's job.

The morning of the first day of the meeting was a very good time for a demonstration.

"Jean Chastel," said Dana. "You will not speak again in this room until it is your turn to do so."

Charles was probably the only one in the auditorium who wasn't surprised that, when the French wolf sneered and opened his mouth to say something to the fae, he couldn't. In Chastel's own territory, with his pack behind him, she wouldn't have been able to bespell him so easily. But this was Dana's territory (one of the reasons the Marrok had decided to hold these talks in Seattle). Chastel had only his collection of unhappy Alphas who did not share their power with him, no matter how cowed they were, because Chastel would never have let them that close to him. Chastel was not the Marrok.

He could have been—wasn't that a frightening thought. There had been a European ruler equivalent to Charles's da at one time.

After the Black Plague . . . he wasn't old enough to have been there—but Da and Charles's brother had been. It had been horrible. Dehumanizing. Especially to those who weren't truly human anymore. So much death, so many lost. Someone had seen the writing on the wall, knew that humanity would recover—and had come looking for the monsters who had fed upon the dying. So the first Marrok had been created. He hadn't been called the Marrok—that was Da's decision in the New World—but that's what he'd been. Made Alpha of all Alphas and by the power of that, able to take on any other. Or he should have been.

Chastel had killed him—and anyone after him who tried to reestablish rulership. Chastel could have taken it for himself, but he didn't want it. He didn't want the responsibility. He just wanted the freedom to kill and keep killing as he pleased.

Arthur Madden, Master of the Isles, was the closest equivalent to the Marrok that Chastel had allowed in Europe—mostly because Chastel didn't consider the British Isles to be a threat to him.

Even with so much power, Chastel did his murdering more secretively these days than he had when he was first Changed. And that, Charles thought, was because there was one person on this planet the Beast feared. And his da had told Chastel that he didn't want to hear about any more ravaging monsters in France. That had been a couple of centuries ago.

Thinking about it, Charles wouldn't be surprised to find out that Chastel could care less about the Marrok bringing the werewolves out to the public. He'd as near as nevermind done it himself centuries ago. The most probable reason Charles could think of for Chastel's presence at this summit was that he'd wanted a chance to take out the Marrok—which he didn't get.

At least he'd be quiet for now.

Charles turned his head to Dana and nodded his appreciation. She looked frumpier than usual today. She'd given herself twenty pounds more on the hips, lost six inches in height, and wore an expensive but unattractive suit and schoolteacher shoes. He wondered if she'd done it to see if she could get any of the wolves to challenge her—or if, as Anna had said, her other guise had been too distinctive, too beautiful.

"Nice shooting, Tex," murmured the Emerald City Pack's witch in a voice that would, for all its softness, carry into the crowd. She and her mate stood just behind the small table Charles and Anna sat at—honor guards.

The witch was a little thing, the mate to one of Angus's top wolves, a quiet, scar-faced man named Tom Franklin, who was nearly as unhappy about his mate's being in the room as Charles was about his, if for entirely different reasons. The witch was blind, and that meant—at least to her mate—that she was vulnerable.

Normally this wouldn't be a problem for Tom. Charles knew him as a tough son of a gun, but no second was going to be able to protect his mate in this crowd. In other circumstances, Charles would have counted on a witch's being able to protect herself pretty well—but this one smelled clean and pure. White witches weren't nearly as powerful as their black counterparts.

Charles wanted his mate out of this room, too. He tried to focus on the Russian, who'd continued speaking now that the interruption had been taken care of. But too much of him was focused on Anna.

She'd started out all right. She sat close to him and paid attention. But there were more than fifty Alphas in the little auditorium. Fifty Alphas, some of their mates, and a smattering of lesser wolves, over a hundred in all—and most of them were more interested in seeing his Omega wolf than in watching whoever was speaking. And under the weight of all of those eyes, Anna was shaking.

I will kill them all, Brother Wolf whispered, *for frightening her.*

Charles glanced at Anna, but she didn't hear Brother Wolf this time. Why she heard him in Dana's home but not now, Charles put to the back of his mind as a mystery that would solve itself eventually.

Brother Wolf's protective streak aside, it wasn't Anna he was worried about, not directly. She was tough, and she would bear up to a few hours of stress—and he'd make sure that's all it would be. The problem was the wolves.

The wolves nearest Anna were, almost to a man (and a couple of women as well), beginning to focus entirely on her. Her Omega qualities called out for their protection—and these were Alphas and dominants in whom the instinct to protect was paramount. A few of them knew what was happening if not why. Arthur met his eyes and grinned. Bastard. He was enjoying this.

The Russian finished his comments and moved his right foot back, turning his body toward Charles—inviting Charles to address his concerns without asking verbally.

Charles stood up. He could have taken the podium and the mike that the Russian wolf had indicated he would yield to him, but doing so would have left Anna alone (with the second of the Emerald City Pack, his witch, and Dana to guard her) and Brother Wolf was adamantly opposed to that.

It was a good thing this was a small auditorium, and werewolves, like their cousin in the fairy tale, had very big ears.

"I hear you," Charles said, projecting his voice to get his words to the back row. "You are right to have concerns. Almost three decades ago, the year the fae came out, three of our wolves reported being contacted by unnamed government agencies who threatened exposure if they didn't cooperate. One wolf was told that his family was at risk.

"This year, forty-two of our wolves were contacted—by

government agencies, by foreign countries, and by at least three different terrorist organizations. In many cases loved ones and family members were threatened or held under implied threat. My father takes care of his own, and he took care of them. Money, power, and influence mostly, though several people died." He had killed two of them himself.

"But in the end there can be only one way to cope with blackmail." He paused and looked out at the wolves. "Bring our secrets out into the open, and they have no more ammunition. And we must carry the tide of popular opinion when we do. Only then will we be truly safe."

He turned his gaze to the Russian wolf, who did him the courtesy of dropping his eyes at once. "I am not saying that it is a perfect solution—merely that it is the best available to us."

First day, he reminded himself, stick to the script. Today he offered the first of the proposals they had come up with for the European wolves.

"We plan on public opinion keeping the government under control, forcing them to be, at the very least, circumspect in their dealings. My father is aware that public opinion is a much bigger weapon here in the United States than it is in some countries where the governments are less responsible to their citizens. In light of that, he offers this much—for the next five years he will allow any wolf who wishes to migrate to come here." That was a big concession. Usually migrations were only allowed after a lot of negotiation.

"Also, he is willing to consider the migration of whole packs." Now he had their attention. He made sure he wasn't looking at the French wolves, who had the best reason to want to leave where they were. Packs only moved into open territory or territory they had killed to take.

"There will be conditions. They must submit to the Marrok and agree to the rules that we live by here, in his territory. They must agree to go where they are told. In return, they will receive the benefits that all of my father's wolves do—protection and aid."

He glanced at the big clock in the back of the room and noted with some relief that his internal clock was correct. It was eleven—still early for a lunch break but not absurdly so.

The Russian wolf bent back to the mike. "We have had these recruiters you speak of among us as well. Unhappily, our response has not always meant that the only casualties fell among our enemies. I am not as certain as the Marrok or you are that the best answer is to expose ourselves, but . . . given the generous offer of relocation, we are willing to acknowledge that coming out to the humans would be a solution to many things." He bowed to Charles—and offered a lower bow to the fae.

Once the Russian had seated himself in the middle of his fellow countrymen, Charles said, "Our host has had food delivered downstairs. Let us take a break for lunch."

He caught the witch's mate by the sleeve when he would have headed off to some errand—probably having to do with lunch. "Tom, stay a moment. With your mate, please."

From near the door, Angus looked at Charles's hand. A good Alpha protects his own. Charles dropped his hand and gave him a nod to tell him that he meant no harm to Angus's wolf. Tom saw what was going on and made a hand gesture that seemed to have more effect on Angus than Charles's reassurances.

"There was no time for introductions this morning," said Charles when they were alone. "Anna, this is Tom Franklin, Angus's second, and his mate—I am sorry, you were not introduced to me."

"Moira," the witch said. The wraparound sunglasses she wore made her expression difficult to read, but his nose told him that meeting the Marrok's hatchet man wasn't scaring her. Unusual, but then she couldn't see him either. "Nice to meet you both."

"And this is my Anna." He looked at Tom. "There are too many dominant wolves, and she's been"—not afraid; he found a better word and used it—"overwhelmed this morning."

Anna stiffened.

It was Tom who saved him. "Good to meet you. Hell. I'm a little overwhelmed, too. Who wouldn't be?"

"But you aren't an Omega," Charles told them. "Tom—you probably wouldn't notice—"

The witch interrupted him. "Because he was too worried about me being 'overwhelmed' himself"—she nudged Tom with her shoulder—"by all the überwolves. Not being handicapped by overprotective, studly impulses, I could pay attention to other things. By the end, they were all focused on Anna, weren't they?"

Charles felt his eyebrow creep upward as he looked at the witch.

"Hey." Moira shrugged. "I'm blind, not sensory deprived."

"I'm causing trouble for you," said Anna. "I'm sorry. I'll try not . . ."

Under his gaze, her voice trailed off. "Do not," he told her softly, "apologize to me for what was done to you. If it were you who were the problem, I would have no worries. You would stay here and not flinch if the Beast himself leapt slavering in your face. Your courage is not in doubt."

The witch pursed her lips, and said, "Wow. That was a good one."

After an assessing look at Charles, Anna turned to

Moira, and said, in a very serious voice, "He scored a few points, all right." She looked back at Charles. "So what is the problem, if it isn't me?"

"Omega," said Charles formally, "it is the privilege of the dominants to protect our submissive ones, the heart of our packs. Alphas are called upon to protect even more strongly. An Omega calls to us strongest of all."

Anna gave a puzzled nod. She already knew that, Charles thought. She just couldn't see what it had to do with the situation. She was too used to looking at the dominant wolves as threats.

"Sweetie," said the witch, "while you were up here getting the cold shakes from all those nasty wolves staring at you—they were trying to figure out why you were upset and who they needed to kill for you."

"Whoops," said Anna as she comprehended the scope of the problem. "I—" He saw her bite back her apology. "I need to go, then, don't I? I can go back to the hotel."

"Well," said Charles apologetically, "I'm afraid that won't work."

"Why not?" Anna smiled, and asked archly, "So are you renting it out during the day? Stashing ex-girlfriends there?"

He didn't have to bend very far forward to touch the top of her head with his chin. Putting his mouth next to her ear required just a little more bending.

"Because Brother Wolf has been spending the whole morning getting pretty worked up, too." He pulled back and let his brother out just enough so she could see him in his eyes. "If you were in our hotel room, I'd never get anything done here for his fretting." He looked at Tom. "You weren't doing so well either."

Angus's second started to smile. "You want Moira and me to take your lady out to play?"

"If Angus will let you."

Tom pulled out a cell phone. "I don't think he'll have any objection."

Charles narrowed his eyes at Anna. "This is important as well. You have the credit cards. I want you to use them." He watched the refusal in her face—she didn't feel part of him . . . part of *them* yet. His money was not hers, not to her.

She was independent, and she'd spent at least the last three years almost too broke to feed herself. Money was more important to her—and spending someone else's an impossible task. "You need clothes of all sorts. What we could get for you in Aspen Creek is not sufficient for this venue. Your status as my wife means you need clothes for formal occasions. Dresses, shoes, and all the trimmings."

She was still mutinous, but weakening.

Tom put down his phone. "Boss says fine."

"And," he said, "if you go shopping for the Christmas presents, I won't have to."

She grinned suddenly at that—and he knew he had her. "Okay. Okay, fine. What are the limits?"

Tom raised an eyebrow—that Charles handled the Marrok's finances . . . and was very good at it, was pretty well-known.

Charles tilted his head. "If you decide you want to buy a Mercedes, you might have to pull out both cards. Go. Conquer downtown Seattle so I don't have to."

"Banished." Anna sighed, but she couldn't hide the humor that softened her expression as she gathered her jacket and purse. But he took her comment seriously.

"Not permanently," he said. "We'll go and introduce you to Arthur more properly tonight. You'll know Tom and Moira by the end of today. I think that if we keep you out of the auditorium today, everything will work itself out."

"Tomorrow night Angus has invited everyone to our hunting grounds," Tom said.

Charles nodded. "That will be less formal, and everyone will be paying attention to the hunters. Give them some chance to observe you without staring and vice versa."

"Where do you hunt?" she asked Tom. "By the airstrip?"

Tom shook his head. "Angus has a pair of warehouses."

"It's cool," said Moira. "He's turned the whole thing into a maze—tunnels, lots of half stories and walls that can be moved to change it up. You'll have a great time."

"What are we hunting?" Anna's voice had lost the tautness of stress.

"A treasure," said Tom. "The exact nature of which is a surprise. We dragged stuff all over the warehouse yesterday." He glanced down. "Wolves eat fast. If we're going to leave, we ought to get out now."

Anna gave Charles a shy kiss on the cheek and strolled out of the room without a backward glance. Until she reached the doorway, and then, in full view of the curious who'd had the courage or discourtesy to linger in the auditorium after he'd dismissed them, she kissed her palm and blew it to him.

And despite . . . or because of their audience, he caught it in one hand, and pulled the hand to his heart. Her smile dropped away, and the expression in her eyes would feed him for a week. And the expressions on the faces of the wolves who knew Charles, or knew his reputation, would make him laugh as soon as no one was watching. Keeping them off balance wasn't a bad thing either.

SHE wondered that the cards Charles had given her hadn't burned their way out of her purse from the blaze of frictional heat. They'd already dropped one load of shopping at the hotel and had just completed the last bit.

"We're about halfway between the hotel and Angus's offices," she said. "Which way should we head?"

"I'll take you back to Charles," said Tom.

"If you're going to eat with that stuck-up Brit, you need to get ready," advised Moira over the top of him. "Go to the hotel and start on it. You have a cell, your mate has a cell. If he doesn't know where to find you, he can call."

Anna looked at Tom.

He shrugged, his face not looking half as meek as his words. "You think I'm going to argue with her, you've got another think coming."

Moira bumped him with her hip. "Ooo. You're so scared of me."

The big, scary wolf grinned, his mouth pulled a little by the scar on his face. "Truth. Nothing but the truth." He spoiled it by rubbing the top of her head, then he kept his hand where it was so he could stay out of reach as she batted at him.

Anna had quit being nervous around him after the first hour as he patiently led them from one store to another. She'd heard of Pike Place Market for years . . . and at first she hadn't been that impressed. It looked like just another flea market . . . with fresh fruit and fish.

Then Moira began tugging her here and there to this little store and that little booth—for a blind woman she was a heck of a shopper. And Tom was always in the right place to put his arm out to guide her and murmur low-voiced warnings as they dodged around other shoppers and across the uneven floor.

Tom was consulted about fit and color while Moira fingered fabrics and dickered with the shopkeepers. The result was that for less than she'd spent on a couple of pairs of jeans in high school, she had the beginnings of a whole wardrobe. When the booth didn't take credit, Tom paid despite Anna's protests.

"Calm down," he told her. "Charles is good for it." The last statement seemed to amuse him.

She also acquired a whole slew of Christmas presents as ordered. Last year she'd been afraid (and too broke) to send presents to her father and brother. This year she . . . she and Charles had them and all of Charles's family and a double handful of others to buy for.

The conference would run through Christmas—she had the impression that there had been some incident that had stepped up the Marrok's timetable. Charles had been gone for a couple of days and returned even more grim than usual. He hadn't volunteered where he'd gone or what he'd done, and she'd been too intimidated by his oppressive silence to ask. It had been the next day that the Marrok began planning this summit—and he and Charles had begun to fight about it.

She'd found a pair of small gold hoop earrings with round bits of rough amber for Charles—to replace the one he'd given to the troll. And at the same shop, she broke down and bought a cheaper, more dangly pair for herself. She felt guilty about it—but maybe she could pay him back for them. They had been cheaper than they would have been in Chicago.

She came out of a little shop the proud new owner of three silk shirts—and her gaze caught on the display window of a store a few doors down.

"What?" Moira said urgently. "What is it, Tom?"

"A quilt, I think," he rumbled. "Jeez, Moira, if the two of you buy anything more, I'm going to have to help carry stuff—and that makes me a lousy guard."

The quilt was trimmed with narrow strips of red and

green, the colors of the old Pendleton blankets. On the interior, there were four squares and a center section that was round. The square panels were abstract mountain scenes of the same mountain, the top two were daylight, spring and summer. The bottom were night, fall and winter. The center panel was deep mottled green with the red silhouette of a wolf howling.

"I don't think we face anything worse than a pickpocket here," Moira was saying to Tom. "I trust you to handle them with a few bags on one arm."

Moira touched Anna's shoulder. "What are you doing out here? Go in and buy it. Tom, what does it look like?"

Anna looked at the price on a discreet tag pinned to the edge of the quilt and swallowed.

They went back to the hotel after that, Anna the proud new owner of three . . . *three* . . . quilts. One for her dad, one for the Marrok, and one for Charles—the one she'd seen in the window.

"You can put them down on the bed," Tom said, sounding amused. "They won't break—or run away."

"I'm in shock," Anna told them. "Except for the first time I saw Charles, I don't think I've ever lusted after something so badly in my life." Then because Tom, at least, would know that she wasn't telling the whole truth, "Okay. There was that cello at the luthier's in Chicago that cost more than most cars and was worth every cent."

"And she kept finding *more* quilts," said Moira to the air, her amusement evident.

"I couldn't help it," Anna said. Even though she was joking, mostly, she was still shocked by the sheer possessiveness she'd felt. They were lucky she'd stopped at three. "Maybe I'll have to take up quilting."

"Do you sew?" Moira asked.

"Not yet." Anna heard the determination in her voice.

"What do you think? Will I be able to find someone to show me how to do this in Aspen Creek, Montana?"

Tom laughed. "Anna, I think Charles would fly you to England twice a week if you wanted him to. You should be able to find someone to learn from closer than that."

His statement gave her an odd feeling. She touched the package she'd had wrapped for Charles, then turned with a smile when Moira told them both they needed to get moving because there were shoes to be found, and the day was wasting.

Anna pulled the hotel-room door shut behind them and tried to deal with the revelation that she was pretty sure Tom was right.

It wasn't until they were standing in front of the elevators that she found her balance. So he would fly her to England if she asked him to—she'd followed him up a frozen mountain buried in the depths of a Montana winter, hadn't she? It made them equals.

"Hey." Moira snapped her fingers in front of Anna's nose. "Shoes, remember?"

The elevator had opened.

"Sorry," she said. "Revelation, here."

"Ah." Moira appeared to consider that for a moment. "Nope. Shoes are more important. Especially if you're going to have that British snob eating at your feet."

And so Anna girded herself and set off for a second round of marathon shopping. Dark came early in the dead of winter, even if it was just raining. When Moira had done her worst, when Tom was complaining about numb feet, and Anna had shoes—*and* her hair trimmed and styled—Moira finally relented and told them they could head back.

To the hotel, the witch insisted firmly, not the auditorium.

Moira leaned around Tom as if she needed to see Anna's

face when she made her final pronouncement. "Men don't care about dressing for dinner. Men shave and put on a tie and 'poof' that's good enough. Wom—"

They stormed out of the darkness of a basement apartment stairwell and brought a spell of silence and shadow with them. A spell that had hidden them from Tom's sharp senses as well as Anna's less-well-trained sensory abilities.

They hit Tom first, but not by much. Anna heard Tom's gasp, but before she could see what had happened to him, a delicate, strong-as-steel arm snaked around her throat.

Magic moved and settled around them all, a familiar spell, one used by packs to conceal fights or kills or anything else they didn't want the rest of the world to know about. But the attackers didn't smell like wolves.

As she fought to free her throat, she could see one of their attackers, a woman, run into the witch like a linebacker, knocking her down, off the curb and into the street.

A scream cut short, and a body hit pavement hard from Tom's direction. She couldn't see him, but it wasn't Tom who had screamed; she'd be willing to bet Tom had never made a sound that high-pitched in his life. Moira's attacker left the blind witch to help the others with Tom.

"Pretty Anna." Her attacker was a woman, and as she whispered she licked Anna's throat. She wasn't human, though. Nothing human could have immobilized Anna this easily—or taken down Tom in whatever numbers. "Come with me, little girl, and the others will survive—"

And, the immediate shock of the attack over, Anna kicked and broke the enemy's knee. She wasn't a "little girl." She was a werewolf.

The woman screamed into her ear—a sharp, high-pitched noise that deafened and hurt and drove Anna to the pavement to escape it. Hard hands dug into her shoulders in preparation to drag her somewhere. Anna twisted and writhed and hit the woman's jaw with her heel. That stopped the noise.

Her wolf took over then. Not in wolf body but in her human form, Anna taught the woman what she should already have known—Omega didn't mean doormat. It didn't mean weak. It meant strong enough to do exactly what it had to in order to triumph, whether that meant cringing in the presence of dominant wolves or tearing her enemy apart.

Anna was too far gone to pinpoint exactly when she understood what had attacked them: vampires. But she remembered Asil's lessons in how to kill them. When the vampire lay in two pieces—body at her feet and head rather nearer to Moira, who was screaming in incoherent rage—the wolf gave a satisfied snort and let Anna take over. And Anna heard what the wolf had not.

What Moira was yelling was, *"Damn it, damn it—tell me what they are! Tom. Tom. Anna!"*

And, as she sprinted to the pile of bodies that must have Tom on the bottom, Anna told her, "Vampires."

Moira didn't hear her, so Anna ripped the arm off the vampire she'd been trying to pry off Tom, and yelled, "Vampires, Moira. *Vampires!*"

And light exploded around them, warm and brilliant—and the vampires she and Tom hadn't killed stopped fighting and ran. Anna's vampire grabbed his arm off the ground before tearing after the others. Anna took a step after them, then forced herself to stop.

There were still four vampires, and that was probably three too many for her—and she couldn't abandon her fallen comrades.

"Tom?"

"He's alive," she told Moira after a quick-but-thorough

examination—done from five feet away. "But he's going to need a moment before he's ready to believe we aren't the enemy." She knelt beside the witch. "Are you all right?"

"Fine, damn it. Just fine."

Moira was bleeding, Anna could smell it, but not a lot. She saw cuts on knees and elbows, but nothing horrible. The horrible thing had nothing to do with the vampire attack.

Moira's glasses had been knocked to the pavement and Anna saw what she'd hidden behind them. One eye scarred beyond belief, as if someone had ripped it out with a clawed hand. The other withered like a raisin, a sickly yellowish white raisin.

Without a word, Anna found the sunglasses—which were unbroken—and put them in Moira's hand. The witch's hands shook as she shoved them onto her face, then she steadied.

Anna understood about shields and the odd shape they sometimes took.

"He'll be all right," Anna said—glad that Moira couldn't see what Tom looked like. It would be easier to convince her that he would be all right that way. Werewolves were tough.

"Can you shield us from sight? The vampires were doing it—or someone was"—it had felt like pack magic—"and now that they've run, it's gone." She didn't know enough about pack magic to do it herself—and it usually required a pack anyway. Her pack, her new pack, was in Aspen Creek, two states away.

"I can manage for a little bit, but you'll have to tell me if it's working," Moira told her, sounding more like the opinionated woman Anna had been spending the day with and less like the scary witch.

Anna glanced around, but the beheaded vampires' bodies had turned to ash, either from true death or from Moira's sunlight—she didn't know that much about vampires.

"That will work," said Tom, though he didn't make any effort to move. His voice was still growly, and his eyes gleamed yellow in the darkness. "Anna, my cell's in pieces, and Moira won't carry one. You need to call for help—I'm not going to be walking anywhere for a few days."

Dominant wolves didn't deal well with injuries like that. Ones that left them vulnerable. Angus's pack would be set up like most of them. Angus clearly at the head, then two or three near the top, the rest ready to step in when necessary. And Tom had a broken arm, and she was pretty sure there was other damage not immediately obvious.

"You have a healer, right?" Anna asked.

"Alan Choo," said Tom. "But you call Charles and tell him to send—"

Deciding he wasn't going to budge, she turned to Moira, who'd followed Tom's voice until she could touch him. From the look on her face, it was a good thing for the vampires that they were either dead or had fled.

"Moira, tell me about Alan Choo. How dominant is he?"

"He's not." Tom sounded exasperated. "He can't make you safe."

A moment before, Anna had been numb and shaking with the aftereffects of the fight. But when his words registered, Anna was suddenly furious that Tom would put himself at risk for her. Again. Because the vampires had been hunting her.

Power came to her call, and she said, *"I will make myself safe."* When he didn't have anything to say to that, she turned to the witch. "Moira do you have Alan Choo's number?"

"Give me your cell phone, and I'll call him myself," Moira said in an odd voice.

Anna handed it over and turned to deal with the witch's mate—and found him looking at her with a little smile. "Shit, woman," he said, "I haven't been put in my place so well since the last time Charles did it. You'd better call him. Your mate's going to be wondering why you drew upon him that way."

What way? But telling him she didn't have the slightest idea what he was talking about didn't appeal to Anna. She'd learned about revealing weaknesses, too. Even if she liked him.

"He'll have to wait—Moira, tell Mr. Choo to meet us at my hotel room."

"And just how are going to get to the hotel without help?" Tom asked. He tried to sit up and failed. "Shit," he said. "I'm not going anywhere for a while."

Anna waited until Moira was through talking to their medic and took her phone back from Moira. Then she answered his question. "Your mate's going to keep us invisible, and I'm carrying you back to the hotel."

At Moira's astonished face, she rolled her eyes before she remembered the witch couldn't see her. "Werewolf, here. I may not look like a brawny male, but I can carry Tom to the hotel just fine."

Tom relaxed a little. "We don't have any females," he said. "You look pretty scrawny. I forgot." She looked at him, and he gave her a faint smile. "Sorry."

They weren't too far from the hotel, but it seemed like a hundred miles. Tom was not light—werewolves are denser than humans, and she kept worrying about the pained sounds he made no matter how carefully she walked. Then he quit making sounds, and that was worse. And remembering to warn Moira about curbs and broken bits of side-walk was harder than Tom had made it look.

Just when she was ready to call it over, she looked up—and there was the hotel.

Her cell rang. A couple of people coming out of the res-taurant attached to the hotel patted pockets and looked bewil-dered, so Anna thought that maybe Moira's spell was fading.

Anna's hands were occupied, so Moira pulled the phone out of Anna's jacket and silenced it. Tom had lost consciousness a little while back, and Anna worried about blood trail—but it couldn't be helped.

She'd figured out a plan of action on the way back. She'd call Charles and explain the situation. If she understood about pack hierarchy and Tom's danger as a wounded dom-inant, certainly Charles would, too.

"Door," she whispered to Moira, and the witch trailed her fingers from their place on her shoulder to the glass door and held it open while Anna scooted inside with her wounded burden.

"Windy tonight," someone in the lobby commented as the door shut behind them.

By some luck there was no one in the hall by the elevators—or on their floor when it stopped. Anna had to set Tom down to find the keycard for her room. Moira stayed beside him, murmuring softly, when Anna left him there as she tore the bedding from the bed and layered it with towels to absorb the blood.

Getting Tom up again took time they didn't have. He was semiconscious and defensive—and Anna was any-thing but calm. Finally, she just hefted him up. If he bit her, she'd still have time to get him in and shut the door. He was in too rough a shape to do any real damage, not compared to the damage the vampires had done on purpose. And she found that she was willing to risk that.

But he didn't bite her. She got him into the room, on the bed. Moira shut the door, and they both heaved a sigh of relief. Anna's phone rang for the second time. Moira shoved it into her bloody hands.

It was Charles.

"Anna?"

His voice was dark and urgent—and as soon as she heard it she felt him running through the dark streets. Felt his panic and the rising rage behind it like a dark tide of violence.

"I'm fine," she told him—though after she said it, she wasn't entirely sure that was true. In the heat of battle nothing had hurt—but she'd caught a few good punches and given a few, too. She didn't remember it, really. But her knuckles were sore, and so was her right shoulder. And her stomach wasn't too happy with her either. Fortunately, she hadn't taken stock until after she'd told him.

"Angus's healer called Angus to tell him he'd been summoned to our hotel room," Charles said. "Just after I felt your need."

Anna remembered the power she'd summoned to shut Tom up—and his conviction that Charles would feel it. Leah, the Marrok's mate, sometimes used Bran's clout when Bran wasn't even there. Evidently, Anna could do the same thing.

"Yes, well." Anna looked around and took in a deep breath. That secrecy spell, the one the vampires used, had some odd effects on the combatants, too, she remembered, enforcing the need for secrecy. She should have called Charles right away.

"I'd like it if you'd come here, too." She'd like it a lot. "Maybe Angus—but no one else. Tom's been hurt pretty badly."

"Badly enough the rest of his pack needs to stay away,"

said Charles coolly. Her sense of him had faded with his urgency, and she wasn't sure she should trust that coolness. The drop from violence to calm had been too fast.

"Right," she answered, though it hadn't been a real question. "Moira and I got him back here—but I didn't realize how badly he was bleeding. There's probably a blood trail—"

"No," said Moira firmly, though she was as white as the sheet she was sitting on—as white as it was because they were both covered in blood. "I took care of the blood."

Anna had learned enough about witchcraft to know that she didn't want to know any more. The alert beast inside her accepted, provisionally, that they were safe.

"You heard that?"

"I did."

"So we're safe in the room. Tom's not mortally wounded—I don't think . . ." The room abruptly smelled different. "He's changing."

"Best thing for him to do, if he can," said Charles. "You stay back from him. Moira should keep him calm enough that he's safe to be around. I'm coming—and I'll call Angus and tell him that if he values his second, he'll call off the rest of the pack. I'll be there in a couple of minutes, and you can give me the whole story then." Her phone stopped making noise, so she decided that he must have ended the call.

"Have you been around Tom when he changes before?" Anna asked Moira softly.

"Yes," said the witch.

"Good." She let herself sink into the chair opposite the bed. "Just sit still. It'll take a while longer this time—and changing when you hurt really sucks. He'll be vile-tempered when he comes out of it. Maybe not really himself, not for a while. Give him a little time before you touch him. He'll probably let you know when he can bear it."

"They almost killed us," Moira said. "If I could have seen them—"

"That blast of sunlight was impressive," Anna told her. "Next time we're attacked by vampires, I'll cower behind you and shout what they are into your ear." She paused. "It's a good thing you were with us. We'd have lost on our own. Someone knew a great deal about Tom." She remembered the dog pile of vampires who'd been trying to kill him—virtually ignoring her and Moira. "But they discounted you."

"Why would vampires attack us?" asked Moira. "Oh, I know they aren't friendly—but they are practical. Attacking Charles's mate is anything but practical."

"Someone paid them, I expect," Anna said tiredly. "Someone they were pretty certain could and would keep Charles away from them. Someone who knew we'd be out shopping today." She looked down at her hands as Tom growled and wheezed with the difficulty of the change. Then she said the last bit slowly, "Someone who could give them pack magic to mask the noise and the bodies until they were done.

"You think one of the werewolves is behind this?"

"I don't know." But she was afraid she did.

Tom completed his change. His breath came out in harsh, groaning pants. His fur was chocolate brown except where a silvery scar wound around his muzzle—and he was nearly as big as Charles in wolf shape. Charles was a very big wolf.

Moira reached out and touched his neck, and the wolf lunged, sending Anna to her feet. But before she did anything stupid, he settled again, his head in Moira's lap.

Someone knocked on the door, and it wasn't Charles.

Six

CHARLES forced himself to walk. There was no hurry. Tom would have been a problem under other circumstances. But his mate was there to keep him under control. And even mad from pain and weakness, Tom wouldn't hurt an Omega.

He was off balance: Anna's fault. He wasn't used to panicking, and it put him on edge.

There were very few people he'd cared for enough to panic over—and most of them were long dead and forever beyond need of his aid. His father and his brother Samuel he could usually trust to take care of themselves.

Anna left him vulnerable.

She'd said she was fine, and she meant it. He'd heard the stress of survival in her voice, but she was safe for now. And Tom would need calm to deal with his wounds, not some adrenaline-jacked wolf who wasn't one of his pack. But even at a slow, steady pace, Brother Wolf fought against his control, growing more upset, not less.

And the human half wasn't far behind. Someone had tried to hurt his Anna, and he hadn't been there to prevent it.

A young man walking in the other direction jerked his head to stare at Charles—and quickly dropped his gaze when his eyes met Charles's. Only then did Charles realize he was growling softly.

He stopped, sucked in a deep breath—and hesitated as the air he'd taken told him something . . . unusual. Something missing. Something like the usual concentration of city smells.

He stood on a wide swath of pavement that was as clean as it had been the day it was poured. No visible garbage wasn't really strange, not in Seattle, where the rain washed the sidewalks on a regular basis. But no garbage, no scent, no *anything*, that was odd. Odd enough to allow him to hold off the frantic need to find Anna and assure himself she was fine, if only for just long enough to think.

Tom's witch had dealt with the blood trail, she'd said, and he was willing to bet that he was looking at the results: a wobbling stretch of walk two shades whiter than the cement around it. It was still a trail for anyone who wanted to follow it—though he supposed a blind woman couldn't know that. And it was a lot better than the blood that would have sent a slew of human police to the hotel.

He could follow it to the hotel—or he could go hunting. He stood very still and consulted Brother Wolf. Then they turned away from the hotel.

Yes, said Brother Wolf, at one with his human half.

Blood and flesh would be welcome. Anna waited for them. She'd be safe with Angus in a few minutes. Angus had taken his car to the hotel.

So there was time to feed. To rid them both, him and Brother Wolf, of the anger so they could regain their balance.

It wasn't long, only a few blocks, until the unnaturally whitened sidewalk returned to its normally dirty state. Despite the rain, Anna's scent lingered in the air.

It was full dark, though the hour wasn't late—a little after six, he thought. It had been twenty minutes since Anna had drawn upon his power, fifteen since he talked to her. The shadows wouldn't have been so dark then, but still dark enough for a lot of the nastier things to come hunting.

He stepped back into the clean space and looked around. A blackened bit of cloth, wet and dirty, a plastic bag that spilled two pairs of women's shoes with another shoe, hot pink and scorched, several feet away. A little casting about on the edges of the witch's spells—and he smelled vampire.

Vampires in Seattle attacking wolves. He considered it—and clenched his fists at the thought of his Anna going up against bloodsuckers.

The cloth smelled of nothing. The lone pink shoe hadn't been so thoroughly caught in the witch's cleaning spell. When lifted to his nose, it smelled faintly of burning flesh and vampire.

The other four shoes were new and smelled of leather, dye, and, lightly, of Anna. One pair was low-heeled pumps and the other red leather and high-heeled, the kind women wore for men.

Charles could care less about shoes—and he suspected he wasn't alone among men in his feelings. Shoe, no shoe, he didn't care. Naked was good, though over the past couple of weeks he was beginning to think that dressed in his clothes was a decent second best.

Even smiling at the thought of Anna in his sweater, he didn't slow down his hunt. He tracked the edge of the witch's spell until he found the trail the vampires had left—not difficult, as at least one of them was bleeding badly. He let his nose go to work, then he had no smile left in him.

A vampire, he'd thought, or possibly two. His nose now

told him there had been more than that. He caught six individual scents. Six vampires who'd been after his Anna.

And he wondered if she'd been as honest as he thought when she told him she was all right. The pink shoe broke in his hand, and he dropped it. He was growling again as he followed the vampires to a parking garage—space number forty-six.

Four minutes, and a little intimidation—not difficult, the way he was feeling—and he found that the space had been paid for six months but occupied only now and then.

No way to tell if the vampires were connected to the person who rented the space or if they'd just found an empty space to use. He was inclined to suspect the latter. They weren't planning on being there long, and the cars were checked every two hours.

"Yeah," the man—not much older than a boy, really—said. He wasn't looking at Charles now, and not doing so had allowed him to calm down a little. "Someone came boiling out of here like they were fit to be tied. I remember it because it was a minivan, a blue Dodge—not the kind of vehicle you roar out of town in. I didn't notice it coming in, but I did the vehicle check when I started work tonight. I don't remember a minivan except Mrs. Sullivan's parked in here when I did it."

Charles wasn't concerned about that. Mind tricks that work on humans were among the most common gifts of the vampires. If they'd told the attendant not to remember, he wouldn't have.

"Tell me about the minivan."

"Three men and a woman. They all looked like FBI, you know? Expensive and conservative." The man looked up at Charles. "Are you a cop or something? Shouldn't you show me some ID?"

"Or something," murmured Charles, and the attendant

paled and looked away again. Gently, Charles thanked the
man for the information and left.

He could have gotten their faces from the cameras, but
there was no need to traumatize the young man further—
he had their scent, and he would not forget. If not today,
then eventually he would run into them—the world was
not that large to a man who lived forever. When he found
them at last, he would remember this night to them.

When he reached the place where the attack had occurred, he stopped and put Anna's new shoes in the plastic
bag and took them with him. There had been no blood, no
meat at the end of this hunt—and Brother Wolf was not
satisfied. Not in the least.

By the time he made it to the hotel, he'd gotten a sem-
blance of control. It would have to do.

Aɳɢᴜꜱ was sitting on the floor in front of their room, reading a newspaper. He didn't look like much of a guardian,
but there were few other wolves Charles would rather have
guarding his mate's door. There wasn't much that would be
able to get past the old wolf who ruled Seattle.

"Something interesting in the paper?" Charles asked
politely.

"Not really, no." Angus folded the paper back into its
original shape with economical precision, then got to his
feet. He kept his face averted and down. Not slow on the
uptake, was the Alpha of the Emerald City Pack. Charles
might have his game face on—but any wolf worth his salt
would smell the frustration of a failed hunt on him from
twenty feet out.

"Your mate was worried about allowing anyone in before you got here. With Tom mostly down and out, and
Moira—"

"—without enough magic to light a candle," finished Anna, opening the door. "And I'm sorry, but I don't know Angus from Adam—I know we were introduced, but I met a lot of people this morning. And I think that our attack was engineered by one of our own kind. Opening the door just because someone said he was Angus didn't seem smart."

Charles gave her a sharp look—he'd smelled only vampires. Had there been a werewolf, too? He pulled the predator in him under better control once more.

He needed a few answers. And he had to make sure she didn't guess how hard it was for him to appear calm and collected. It was a good thing she was still working on listening to her nose.

"As there was no urgent danger threatening, wisdom dictated that I wait here until someone she knew better came," said Angus, sounding rather pleased with Anna.

"Anna," said Charles, ignoring the urge to inspect her more closely to make sure she was all right. "This is Angus, Alpha of the Emerald City Pack. He would never, under any circumstances, have set Tom up to face a pack of vampires."

Angus gave Charles a sharp look as Anna examined him—and Charles tried to curb his possessive instincts. She was just evaluating Angus. The Emerald City Alpha was only an inch or two taller than Anna, who wasn't overly tall for a woman—and he didn't weigh much more. He was wiry and whip-thin. Sandy hair and dark eyes gave him a casual handsomeness that he used ruthlessly. People who didn't know him underestimated him all the time, which was probably one of the reasons he was so pleased with Anna's caution. The other would be that she had taken it upon herself to protect one of his wolves.

But Anna knew Bran, who was even better than Angus at being underestimated—Bran did it on purpose.

"I'm sorry if I offended you." Anna's apology was sincere.

"No trouble," Angus said. "Do I look offended? Let's all get inside, and you can tell us what happened, so we'll see what's to be done. Vampires, eh?"

Anna backed away from the door. The scent of her distress and the stink of recent fear permeated the room. Her lip curled as she smelled it herself. "Sorry," she said. Her shirt was covered with blood, and the air in the room was redolent with the rawness of open wounds.

Not hers, Brother Wolf told him hungrily. *But it could have been.* He couldn't tell who had thought that last, maybe both of them. It didn't help his control: he was having an unusually tough time keeping it together.

He had to keep his distance, just until he could get himself calm and centered. He allowed Angus to pass between him and Anna, and when it didn't send Brother Wolf into a rage, Charles took a deep breath of relief and allowed himself to examine Anna.

Her freckles stood out on her pale cheeks, but the scent of her fear wasn't fresh. Angus hadn't scared her, she'd just been being cautious. Brother Wolf settled down, but only a little.

"Here," Charles told her, and handed her the bag of shoes.

She looked at the bag blankly before her face lit up in a grin. "You are supernatural, Charles. Absolutely supernatural."

She opened the closet and dumped the shoes in with a pile of bags that hadn't been there this morning. There were a couple of plastic-covered dresses hanging next to the hotel's bathrobes, too. She'd been shopping and back once before they were attacked. The vampires could have been waiting, watching the hotel, and followed them out.

A low growl in the room brought his attention back to the task at hand. The little witch, still wearing her sunglasses, was curled up on the giant pillow at the head of the bed. If Anna was pale, the witch's face was chalk white under the inky blackness of her short hair, and she looked gaunt, as if she'd lost ten pounds since he'd seen her earlier that day.

From the dent in the bedspread, Charles could tell the brown wolf who was Tom had been settled in front of his witch, but the invasion of other wolves had sent him to his feet. One of his front legs was visibly crooked and must be hurting—but that didn't keep him down.

Charles closed his hands on Anna's shoulders before she could get between Angus and Tom, and he brought her back against him. "No," he told her. "It's all right. Angus has this in hand."

There were Alphas he might be worried about, but Angus had been an Alpha for a long time, and he knew what he was seeing: a wolf protecting his mate from an unknown threat. Not defiance.

In a cool voice that held more than a little command, Angus said, "Tom. No harm to yours. No harm." Angus might not be a big man, but his voice, when he chose to use it, was powerful enough to raise the dead.

The wolf's lips curled away from impressive fangs and growled again.

"Down," Angus said, putting serious energy into the word.

And the wolf sank instantly to his belly, his breathing harsh as he dealt with his unwillingness to allow others around his mate when he was injured while meeting his Alpha's demand for obedience.

"Tom?" The witch sounded lost, and Charles wondered what she thought was going on. Damnable to be helplessly blind in a world of monsters.

"He's all right," Anna told her. "Just protective of you. He knows you can't protect yourself right now—and he hasn't had time to gather himself together from that rough change yet. He's hurt and not thinking right. Everyone is going to give him just a minute to calm down."

Slick, he thought with a secret smile. Anna slid that information to Angus as if she were just talking to Moira, so he wouldn't think she was trying to tell him what to do. Then she'd spoiled it all by ordering everyone, Charles included, to leave Tom alone. The white flash of Angus's teeth told him that he'd caught it, too, and had chosen to be amused.

"We'll just do that," Angus said, settling himself on the arm of the chair nearest to the window. "Alan called while I was in the hallway. He's about five minutes out. While we're waiting for him and for Tom, why doesn't someone enlighten me as to what damaged my wolf?"

"Vampires," said Anna. "Six of them—and they hunted like a pack." She glanced at Charles.

"You mean as if they'd hunted together before," he said. Charles knew his calm facade was in place because her nod was matter-of-fact.

"Exactly," she said. "They didn't get in each other's way, not even when five of them ganged up on Tom after they'd knocked Moira over. They were in a basement apartment stairwell and hidden behind a shadows spell. It smelled like wolf magic to me—unless the vampires have access to the same thing. If Moira hadn't brought the sun in, we'd be dead."

Five on one was difficult to manage, especially with a cunning old wolf like Tom, who knew how to maximize others' weaknesses. And a shadows spell . . . Anna was right, that sounded like a hunting pack—except they were dealing with vampires.

"There are vampiric spells that could mimic one of

ours," said Angus. "Tom's old enough to tell the difference. When he can think again, we can ask. That's what made you think that they were sent by a wolf?"

Anna nodded, but Moira said, "Vampires don't lightly take on the wolves, not in this city, anyway. They were trying to kidnap Anna—and what would a vampire want with Charles's mate?"

Angus smiled coldly. The wolves in Seattle had held the upper hand for decades. "If the vampire seethe here found themselves holding Charles's mate, they'd escort her back with armed guards and polish her fingernails before they delivered her to me without a hair on her head out of place. I'll certainly call their Master, but I suspect they are interlopers. He should know about them—and if so, maybe he'll have some names for me."

"One of them was a woman who wore a size six shoe," Charles said. "But I don't think she'll be a problem to anyone again."

Moira's part in the story bothered him. She'd saved Anna—but . . . He frowned at her. "Witch, I've never heard of a white witch who could call sunlight. That's not even something witchcraft should be able to call—witches know mind and body, not the elements."

"I didn't call sunlight," she snapped, responding to his tone of voice, he thought, rather than his words. "Just made the vampire's bodies believe in it—even the dead bodies." She wiggled her fingers. "*Sssst*, and they were dust or running away."

"That's a lot of magic. Vampires have some resistance—and then you made your trail disappear for the better part of a mile."

"She's a white witch," snapped Angus.

Moira grinned fiercely. "I'm a mutant, all right. Poor little blind white witch . . ."

"Sacrifice," said Charles slowly, "is the power that witches pull from. Mostly it is the loss of other people's blood and flesh—but rumor has it that one of the reasons witches have familiars is that they can use them as a higher sacrifice—not just the animal's death but the death of something the witch holds dear."

"You think I kill kitties to power my spells?" Her voice was nasty, and despite the nagging suspicion that all wasn't as it should be, Brother Wolf approved of her.

He couldn't let it be, not with Anna's safety to worry about, but Brother Wolf's approbation gave him pause. There might be a different answer. "I've always heard that self-sacrifice—as when the witch uses her own blood to fuel a spell—has some power, but it's difficult to work with."

The witch pulled down her glasses and he saw his guess had been correct. One eye had been blasted by magic. He'd seen similar results before, and it wasn't something he'd forget soon. Her eye was stained white and shriveled, as if something had sucked it dry. The damage had happened a long time ago because no scent of it clung to her—and when that had happened, she would have reeked of magic for quite a while. The other eye had been destroyed more mundanely, though just as painfully—and likely just as long ago.

Interestingly, Angus stiffened, as if he had not known, and Anna didn't have any reaction at all. Not to the witch's face anyway—she was definitely reacting to him. She was not a bit happy with the way he was going after the witch.

After Moira felt he'd had a chance to look his fill, she put her glasses back on. Tom stared at Charles with intelligent yellow eyes that promised retribution, and Anna looked not much happier with him.

"I don't know Moira," said Charles to the wolf who was Tom, since he understood his reaction the best. "I *did* know that I've never heard of a white witch who could do what she did. And if a black witch is masquerading as a white witch . . . first, the deception implies she is one of the enemy. And second"—he gave the wolf a small smile— "I've never encountered a witch who could hide her nature from me."

"We were nearly killed by a black witch a few weeks ago," Anna told them, though he could tell she was still miffed with him. "It's left us a little skittish."

Moira reached out and touched Tom's flank and let her fingers drift down over his tail, which she tugged playfully. "It's all right, Tom. These are the good guys—even if he's being rude."

She turned her head to Charles. "Fair enough. I've never heard of a white witch that can do what I can either. And I'm not sure how it happened exactly. I can understand being cautious."

"I am sorry I had to push," Charles said, honestly.

"I'm sure I'll find a way to return the favor," she said, showing her teeth in a white smile. "At least you didn't say *ick* and run screaming."

The warm anger at the vampire attack settled a little deeper in his gut, and he let a little of it leak into his voice. "I hope you turned whoever did into a pig."

She stilled, surprised by his reaction, he thought.

"Cowards don't deserve better," said Angus.

The witch clearly wasn't expecting support from that quarter either. Had there been so many repulsed by her scars?

But what she might have said had to wait, as someone knocked tentatively at the door. "It's Alan," their interloper said. "Can someone let me in?"

The minute the Emerald City Pack's submissive wolf walked through the doorway, Charles felt more settled.

Alan Choo was full-blood Chinese, and he looked it: delicate and unexpectedly strong, like a well-made blade.

Except for when he was alone with Anna, Charles had spent his entire life with Brother Wolf raging inside of him, pacing and growling against the trappings of civilization they were forced to bear. That's what it meant to be dominant and ready to kill anything that threatened those under his protection. Kill at a moment's notice.

Today was worse than usual. Brother Wolf was raging, and it was all Charles could do to make sure no one knew how hard he was struggling to hold on to control. He'd thought it only a minor addition that there were two other dominant wolves—wolves not of his pack—in the room with him and his mate.

But that was before Alan Choo walked into the room. He wasn't an Omega like Anna—but he was submissive, and he knew how to deal with raging werewolves. Somehow having him in the room tipped the balance, and between him and Anna, they calmed everyone down—including Charles.

Charles sat in the chair on the other side of the little table from Angus. It was more to give Choo room to work than because he wanted take a seat, but being *able* to sit down with the other wolves in the room was an improvement.

Anna took a quick glance around, so Charles knew she'd sensed the new quiet in the room, too. She caught his eyes and gave him a quick smile and perched on the arm of his chair.

"He's hurt because of me," she told Choo.

Charles shook his head and told her the truth as he saw it. "Not your fault someone decided to try to grab you. Tom did his job, don't be sorry."

"Hey, Tom, man, whatcha been doing to yourself?" Choo's words might have been flippant, but his hands were careful as he handled the injured wolf.

Tom allowed Alan to straighten his leg without uttering a grunt of pain—the little witch did more than enough of that for him.

"Damn it, damn it," she muttered, as Alan worked. "With just a little more power, I could keep this from hurting you. I'm sorry. I'm sorry."

Finally, Angus, *Angus*, who had no use for anyone who wasn't a wolf, said, "Enough, Moira. It's just a little pain. Over in a moment and not worth your fussing. It would be a lot worse if you hadn't been with them—six vampires are more than a match for two wolves and any other witch I've ever seen. If you hadn't used up your magic when you did, no one would be worried about a little thing like a broken leg. Enough."

There was a sharpness in the last word that shut her up and earned the Alpha a glare from his wolf. Angus raised an eyebrow, and Tom dropped his gaze. Angus rolled his eyes. "God save me from lovebirds," he said, and his gaze lighted on Charles and Anna.

They weren't cuddling: Anna didn't cuddle. Charles had the feeling that if life had been fair to her, she would have enjoyed it—and maybe a few years down the line she might. But for now he was grateful that she didn't cower every time he touched her.

Still, she was sitting close enough that the old Alpha grinned.

"All of you lovebirds," he said. "It gets in the way, and I'm not patient by nature. You—" He pointed a finger at Anna, and Charles was up and standing between them.

Reflex. So maybe he wasn't as relaxed as he'd thought.

Angus dropped his finger, but finished his sentence. "Tell me what *happened*. I want more details."

"Native Americans don't like to be pointed at," observed Choo quietly as he wrapped Tom's rib so it could heal properly. "Native witches, skinwalkers and the like, use the gesture to throw curses and disease."

Angus threw up his hands and dropped to his chair. "Oh for God's sake. I'm not a witch. I don't throw curses—I just want to know what the hell went on tonight."

He sounded frustrated and offended—but all the wolves in the room knew the truth: he was afraid of Charles. He hadn't been before, not until he looked into Brother Wolf's eyes and knew the threat of death. Angus was Alpha and old with power, but there was no question as to who was dominant.

There had been no threat from Angus. Charles knew it, but it took more effort than it should have to sit down again. If Angus's quick withdrawal hadn't satisfied Brother Wolf, there would have been blood spilled.

Charles took his seat slowly and reached up to put a hand on Anna's knee, the contact soothing him.

"Well," she said brightly, "hasn't this been interesting." She reached out and put her hand on his shoulder, as if she needed help balancing on the arm of the chair. She and he were the only ones who knew that her touch helped *him* find balance while she distracted the others with her words.

"Okay. What happened." She sucked in a breath. "Tom and Moira took me to Pike Street and we loaded ourselves down with as much as we could carry and delivered it here. I had everything I needed except for shoes—so Moira took me to her favorite shoe place a couple of miles away. We were on our way back when they jumped us. No warning, no sound, no smell, they were just on us." A cold hand folded over his on her knee. She wasn't as calm as she sounded. He turned his hand palm up and held her fingers in his hot grip.

"Four of them attacked Tom, one hit Moira, and the

other grabbed me. I killed mine—" There was a growl of satisfaction under the stress in her voice, and he tightened his grip. His mate was tough. "By that time Tom had killed one of his attackers and Moira's decided she wasn't a threat and was helping the others with Tom. I was just about to throw myself into the fray when my brain caught up with my ears and I finally realized that Moira was trying to find out what had attacked us."

Anna looked over at the witch with a grin. "I can remember thinking, 'Poor thing can't see what's after us. How frightening for her.' And so I told her. Then we were all nearly blinded by sunlight. The dead vamps burned, and the others fled. We called Alan, and I carried Tom and led Moira back here while she cleaned up behind us and kept us out of view."

The witch, lightly petting Tom with clever fingers, gave Anna an innocent look, and Anna snorted. "Poor little blind witch, my aching butt. One-woman demolition crew. They never knew what hit them."

"You think it was a wolf behind it," Charles said.

Anna looked at him and, now that the story was laid out, she hesitated.

"Instinct," he told her, "is most often right."

Her mouth relaxed. "Yes. I think it was a wolf." She closed her eyes while she mulled it over. "The attack felt like a pack attack. Hide in plain sight—enough people to do the job easily. They didn't know about Moira, or they underestimated her." She looked at him and gave him a small smile. "And me. They concentrated their attack on the strongest of us first—werewolf tactics. And they wanted to take me away with them. What would a vampire want with me?"

"Wolves." Charles tried to feel it out. But the spirits were silent as they habitually were in the city. Or any other time they might be useful. "So what do you think, Angus? Could it have been Chastel? We had a run-in last night, and he was angry enough to kill someone."

Angus was sprawled deliberately in his chair, showing how relaxed he was in Charles's presence. "The Frenchman's a beast. A powerful beast—but he's addicted to the kill. He wouldn't send anyone else. He wouldn't want someone else to spill blood that he could feast on instead."

"So who do you think?"

Angus frowned irritably. "I don't know most of them well enough. We could question them—*if* we wanted to start a war. The Europeans are twitchy about their honor. If they only wanted an Omega wolf— I'll call the Italians and warn them to keep theirs close."

Charles's eyebrows raised. "I knew they had one, but not that they brought him here." He looked at Anna. "If he'd have been useful to you, I'd have told you about him—but he's only been a wolf for a year or so and knows less than you do about being a wolf at all, let alone an Omega. Asil, who was mated to an Omega, is a much better teacher— and don't you tell him I said that."

Angus turned his attention to Anna. "He's a young German, actually, who was skiing in the Italian Alps and had a bad fall. The rescue worker who found him was a werewolf and felt compelled to save him any way he could."

"Turned him into a werewolf," Anna said.

Charles nodded. "And the Germans were hotter than blazes when the Italians claimed him as theirs."

"A custody battle, in fact," said Angus. "I expect that's why the Italians brought him—to rub it in the Germans' noses that he chose to stay with them."

Charles was watching the interest in Anna's face. *Yes,* he thought, *you aren't alone.* He should have thought of it himself. He'd see to it she met the young German Omega.

"Maybe that's it," said Moira thoughtfully. "Everyone in the pack has been talking about it—sorry, Anna. But most of them were more interested in you than in all the strange wolves coming in. Maybe it's someone who wants an Omega."

"I met someone like that once," said Anna coolly. "Make sure you warn the Italians."

"Yes," said Angus, with a little amused glance at Charles as Anna gave him another order.

"Don't forget you have a dinner to get ready for," said Moira.

Charles looked at the witch, and he wasn't the only one. She smiled at them all. "We don't know exactly what they were trying to do. Probably they were trying to kidnap Anna. But there is a lesser chance that they didn't want you to get better acquainted with Arthur of Great Britain."

"Besides," said Angus, "why give them the power to change your plans when no permanent harm was done?"

Yes, Charles realized. That was logic he could wrap his head around. He had no desire to go out and do the social thing at the best of times—and this attack made him want to take his mate and barricade her in where she was safe.

"I'll go get another room," he said. "Tom and Moira can stay here until he's healed—and order room service."

"I'll stay here, too," said Angus. "Until Tom's up to taking care of himself."

Charles looked at the Alpha and realized that he wasn't the only one feeling protective. "Good," he told them, and left to do as he'd said.

A collective sigh of relief went through the room when Charles left, but no one said anything until the elevator ding was heard faintly through the walls.

Anna knew Charles had that effect on people—but she hadn't seen or felt any trouble tonight. Except for the pointing-finger thing.

"Well," said Angus, and Tom whined. "There's a reason Bran uses him to scare the bejeebers out of miscreants. I think we all saw it tonight."

"Saw what?" asked Moira.

"Exactly," said Alan Choo, who was repacking the bag he'd brought with him. "Angus pointed—and I didn't even see him move. He just *was*. Standing between his mate and Angus." And then he lapsed into Chinese for a few sentences.

Anna found she didn't like their being afraid of Charles. It hurt him, though he accepted it from everyone. Even if it was safer for him, it wasn't good.

Angus shook his head. "Did you see the faces on some of the wolves when he talked to them today? I suspect they didn't even know he *could* talk—let alone make so much sense when he did. It was as if a shark started speaking the King's English."

Tom raised his head and looked at Angus, and Alan broke off his Chinese muttering to stare at his Alpha.

"*Queen's* English," said Anna with more sharpness than she meant to allow. "And there's nothing wrong with Charles."

"Before God there's not," agreed Angus. "I thought to myself—well look at that, he's conducting a meeting just like everyone else. Maybe the other rumors were exaggerated about him, too. And they weren't. Not a bit of it. I don't ever want to face that man fang and claw."

"If you don't shut up," Anna bit out, "you might not ever have to worry about it."

And Angus sat back in his chair and smiled at her with

satisfaction. "Well, now," he said in an entirely different voice. "Maybe I won't."

She'd missed it, she realized looking at Tom and Alan Choo. She'd mistaken Tom's astonishment for agreement. Angus had been playing her.

"Why the test?" she asked.

Angus shrugged. "I've known Charles a long time. I saw him turn from a quiet boy into the weapon his father needed—that *we* needed. Just because I understood the need, it didn't mean I couldn't regret. I just wanted to make sure that you were able to see below the killer to the man beneath."

"So you set him off on purpose?"

Angus's smile widened into a grin. "With the pointing-finger thing? When he was already thirsting after fresh blood because you were endangered and he'd gone hunting with no results? Do I look that stupid? No, that was just an accident."

Anna looked down at the arm of the chair and rubbed a spot lightly with a fingertip. Now that she thought to test it, she could smell Angus's sincerity. He had been worried for Charles, worried she would hurt him.

"I knew people were afraid of him," she said. "You really think they believe there's something wrong with Charles?"

Angus tilted his head, but it was Alan who answered. "Something off, anyway. Not so much crazy as . . . different. His father's soulless killer, loyal to the Marrok and no one else. Every word that comes out of his mouth put there by the Marrok, like a ventriloquist's dummy only scarier."

Anna thought about the fight Charles and his father had waged, which ultimately Charles had won, and opened her mouth to comment. But then she shut it again. If that was what people thought, it was because Charles wanted them to.

"Charles does it deliberately," Angus told her, watching her closely. She hoped that she gave nothing away, but his words were so close to her thoughts that she must have. He tapped the arm of his chair with impatient fingers. "If the other wolves are all scared of him, they won't be stupid and make him kill them. And they're right, whether they know it or not. There is something off, haven't you noticed? His wolf is completely out of control. It should have turned him into a mindless killer—but it hasn't."

Brother Wolf, thought Anna.

"Why do you suppose that is?" asked Choo.

Angus raised an eyebrow and looked at her, as if he thought she might supply an explanation.

There was a wolf responsible for the attack on them tonight. She didn't really believe Angus was the enemy either. He might even be Charles's friend if she could believe her nose. But she wasn't going to be sharing any insights about her mate—even if she had them—with Angus of the Emerald City Pack.

She gave him a look and relaxed on her seat on the arm of Charles's chair and waited for him to return.

ANGER

He was so angry.

Charles had been all right all the way down to the main desk. He'd focused on the task at hand, gotten a second room, and been fine until he got back into the elevator and considered the attack on Anna. He'd thought he might be able to take what he'd learned from Anna's story and find something new, some hint at why or who.

The control that had always been at his fingertips seemed to be melting away. He watched the floor numbers rise, and they seemed to proceed at a viciously fast pace when he had so much thinking to do.

Two.

Tom had nearly been killed. If Charles had sent Anna with any of Angus's other wolves—and he might have— he'd have lost her.

Three.

Six vampires.

Four.

If Tom's witch had been what she appeared, Anna would have been taken.

Five.

If he locked her to his side, he would lose her. She was not submissive, she didn't *need* his care. Not that way. She needed him to stand back and let her fly.

Six.

And if he was going to do that, he was going to have to get control of his temper. Of Brother Wolf's temper. Not just now, today—but forever. Leash his need to keep her safe so that he could keep her happy.

Seven.

Today, though, she wasn't leaving his sight again.

The elevator door slid open.

Arthur Madden fussed with this and that, moving the place settings farther from the edge of the table, then nudging them nearer.

"My dear," said his mate with amusement, "what *are* you doing? He may be the Marrok's son, but you rule the British Isles. You outrank him—there is no need to be nervous."

She didn't understand. But he was used to that. His wife was human, and there was a lot she didn't understand. He didn't hold it against her. He wouldn't explain that Charles was dominant, that even with the strength of all his wolves behind him, Charles still made Arthur back down with no more than a look. It meant he needed all of his defenses. It meant the dinner must be perfect.

He could trust his mate to make everything perfect.

"You are right, of course," he said. "Dashed silly of me to make such a fuss."

She slid under his arm, as slender as the girl he'd married forty years before. He loved her as much now as he had then, but her age made him sad. When they went out to dinner now, people thought them business associates—or mother and son. When she'd been young and beautiful, he'd never given a thought to her aging, and neither had she.

She smelled of roses. "It will all be fine," she said. "I'll entertain his mate, and you can tell him stories."

He kissed her Saxon-sunlit hair, kept delicately tinted with dyes to the shade it had been naturally when he met her. "And how will you do that?"

"I'll show her my needlework and talk to her about girl things."

He turned and caught a glimpse of them in the huge gilded mirror just inside the entrance of the house. He wore a gold silk shirt that turned his hair a deeper shade of red-gold; his eyes were blue, and the black slacks he wore could have been the slacks he wore to his wedding all those decades ago.

Sunny's deep blue shirt had long, flowing sleeves that showed off the strength of her arms without betraying how her skin showed her age. There was a softness under her chin and laugh lines around her eyes. His Sunny loved to laugh.

She was dying one day at a time. It would take a long while still, he thought, decades, as her skin grew less taut and her muscles stringy and slack. And he had to watch it happen.

She caught his gaze in the mirror. "You look gorgeous as always," she said, hugging the arm that crossed over her shoulders above her breasts.

"I love you," he whispered into her ear, nuzzling at the perfect hair, closing his eyes so he could smell her precious scent.

She waited until his eyes opened and she could look into the mirror and stare into them. Then she smiled the huge smile that had first made him call her Sunny. "I know you do."

SEVEN

THEY were late. Sunny quit trying to contain her husband and sat down on one of the matching pair of Queen Anne couches and watched him instead.

He was magnificent. He'd scorn the comparison, but she always thought of him more like a lion than a wolf when he was in his human form. Even when he was in his four-footed form, he was tawny and gold.

He stood now, gazing out the window with his arms clasped behind his back, giving her a lovely view of his backside. She'd never told him, of course—he wouldn't appreciate it—but she'd always loved his derriere.

She still couldn't believe she'd managed to catch him, not even after all these years. He was everything she'd ever wanted: wealthy, powerful, honorable, and well-bred. He could not claim it, not now, so long after he should have been dead, but he was the younger son of a baron. He was smart and sweet—he still brought her flowers for absolutely no more reason than because he wanted her to have them. She loved to travel, and he could not—not being who and what he was. But he allowed her the freedom to do it on her own.

She still loved his backside.

She hid her smile and tried to look serious when he turned to her. He frowned, and she blinked innocently at him. She'd long ago learned that there were some jokes he could not share, and it didn't do any good to try.

Finally, in a grumpy voice, he said, "I'm going upstairs to get some work done. If they get here, tell them I'm busy." And he stalked up the stairs.

Sunny glanced at the delicate gold Rolex on her wrist and shook her head. They were five minutes late; patience had never been Arthur's gift. She picked up the book she'd brought down—a mystery set in Barbados, her favorite place to be—and started to read.

The knock on the door was quiet, but not so quiet Arthur wouldn't hear it. When he didn't come down the stairs, Sunny set her book down and got to her feet. He'd come out of his snit soon enough. She knew her man: he couldn't stand to ignore an audience for long. Until then it was up to her to make her guests feel welcome.

Nervously, she smoothed out her shirt. She'd heard stories of Charles Cornick, the Marrok's hatchet man, but she'd never met him. She hoped his mate was friendly.

When the knock came a second time, she opened the door—and swallowed her smile.

The man who stood in front of the door was big. Not just tall, but wide. Obviously Native American, with his dark skin and black eyes. His face was still, she couldn't read him at all, but he brought with him an air of grimness, like a dark cloak around him.

Nothing that she hadn't expected from Arthur's descriptions—and his nervousness—nothing unexpected, except that Charles Cornick was beautiful. Not by Western standards maybe, not with his broad and flat features and the amber earrings he wore—and how did a werewolf manage pierced ears?

A man might not even notice the attraction of all that muscle and warm brown skin, but she would bet that he never walked through a room without attracting the gaze of every female there.

Flustered, she jerked her eyes off him and met the eyes of the woman who stood beside him.

Anna Cornick was an inch or so taller than Sunny, which still made her a little shorter than average. She was thin, underweight even, though what flesh was there was hard muscle. Her hair was whisky brown and hung in gentle curls to her shoulders. Freckles dusted her cheekbones, and her eyes were a clear golden brown. She wore a white shirt with a silk skirt that hit her just above the ankles. She wasn't traditionally pretty, but not unattractive, either.

Anna looked tired and outclassed by her more exotic mate, but then she grinned ruefully, an expression that took in Sunny's uncomfortably strong, reluctant admiration of Charles and expressed sympathy for another woman caught in his spell.

It was a warm expression—and Sunny felt all the nerves Charles Cornick had called into being settle back down so she could pick up the familiar role of hostess.

"Hello," she said with a big smile that wasn't as difficult to summon as it had been a moment before. "Welcome." She stood back and invited them in. "I'm Eleanor, Arthur's mate—you can call me Sunny, everyone does. You must be Charles and Anna."

"It's good to meet you, Sunny," said Anna, taking her hand in a strong grip. When her mate didn't say anything right away, Anna bumped him with her shoulder.

He looked at her and she raised her eyebrows—and

Sunny recognized the look from her own repertoire built to deal with a dominant male who didn't always follow the rules of civilization.

"That's a good expression," she told Anna. "Though I've found elevating just one eyebrow is more effective. If that one doesn't work, I've found it's just best to ignore them until they decide to settle down. Why don't you both come in, and I'll get you something to drink. Arthur will be down in a minute. Can I get you some scotch or brandy? Or we have a really nice white wine."

Anna gave her a grin and followed her in while her mate closed the door, gently, behind them. "Ignoring works for you? I just prod until he snaps. Do you have water? No alcohol for me tonight—I'm driving. It might not affect me anymore, but if I get pulled over, I don't want to smell like alcohol."

"He lets you drive?" Sunny asked, taken aback and more than a little jealous. "The last time I drove when Arthur was in the car was the day I met him. I was driving my father's car to Devon, and his car was off beside the road with two flat tires."

"I don't like driving," said Charles. "Brandy would be good, thank you."

His voice was as delicious as the rest of him. Deep and slow with a hint of Welsh and something else altering the usual American accent.

Disturbed because she'd never felt like this around any of the werewolves Arthur had brought to her home before, Sunny took the excuse of his words and went to the bar in the corner of the living room and began getting drinks for her guests.

It wasn't that she'd never looked at another man—but she'd never felt this . . . safe. It was an unexpected reaction to a man she knew was dangerous, and it threw her off her game.

She took down the cut-glass flask she'd purchased a few years ago in Venice—and Anna was there to take it from her and set it on the bar.

"I know," the other woman said softly. "It's all right. You should feel it when the Marrok comes into a room of strange wolves. He'll settle down in a moment, and it won't hit you like that." She looked at her mate, then pulled the stopper from the flask, and the smell of good brandy rose from it. "He's had a bad day, and that makes it worse."

Sunny got a brandy snifter from the cupboard beneath the bar and gave it to Anna. "What happened?"

Anna smiled and shrugged as she poured the brandy. "Same stuff, different day." It felt like an evasion. "He doesn't like cities any more than he likes driving or cell phones or airplanes or—"

"—People talking about him like he isn't here," growled the werewolf as if driven to speak.

When Arthur sounded like that, she knew to leave him alone. His mate just grinned at him. "Come over here and get your brandy—how can you stand that stuff, anyway? I never could drink it, even when the alcohol was the point of it. Quit scaring our hostess."

He took a deep breath and . . . he was just an exasperated man standing in the middle of her living room. He strode over and took the glass his wife handed to him, then turned his attention to Sunny.

"My apologies," he said, and his voice didn't make her heart rate pick up in response. "As Anna told you, I am out of sorts tonight. But there's no reason to take it out on you."

Dismissing his apology as unnecessary seemed wrong, so she tried for the next best thing. "Accepted."

Anna was looking around the room. "This feels more like a home than a place you're renting for a few weeks—you have a nice touch."

Sunny handed her a cold bottle of water from the supply in the fridge. "Oh, Arthur has a few places scattered around. He doesn't come to this one much, but he got it for me for our thirtieth anniversary. I usually come here for a month in the summer. He doesn't like to travel, but he knows that I do."

She stopped herself from saying more with difficulty. Hiding a frown behind a friendly smile, she got out the chilled bottle of her favorite white wine. She never blathered on like that. She was used to keeping secrets. Not that her travels or this condo were secrets, exactly. Still, she hadn't meant to talk about them.

She was saved by the squeak of the stairs as Arthur came down them in an easy rush.

Аηηа watched the British wolf-king descend.

"You were late," he said by way of greeting. "I was worried something might have happened."

"No," said Anna cheerfully. They'd talked about what to say about the attack, and finally came to the conclusion that the best thing would be to warn the other Omega's Alpha and otherwise keep quiet. The attack had nothing to do with anyone else—and Charles said he was not going to encourage copycats. So she took the blame for their arrival time. No one would ever believe Charles would be late for anything, anyway. "It took me a little too long to get dressed. I'm sorry."

Sunny poured a second snifter of brandy for Arthur—yet another werewolf who drank it, despite not being able to benefit from the effects of the alcohol. Arthur's mate poured a glass of wine for herself.

"Dinner will be ready in about a half hour, I believe," Arthur said. "In the meantime, I thought you might be interested in looking at my collection."

"Collection?" Anna asked.

"What I have here isn't very valuable," he explained. "Nor historically significant. We don't spend much time here, and even with a security service . . ." He shrugged. "Still, I have some interesting things."

"Did you bring Excalibur?" asked Charles.

Arthur's eyebrow climbed elegantly up his forehead as he smiled a little. "Never go anywhere without her."

"Isn't that a little problematic?" Anna asked. "Flying internationally with a sword?"

"I fly privately," he said.

"Of course," murmured Anna with self-directed mockery at her sudden elevation to the rich and important. "Doesn't everybody?"

"Poor plebeian," murmured Charles, and she was pretty sure she was the only one who caught the humor in his voice, because both Arthur and Sunny looked taken aback.

"Arthur has trouble with commercial jet travel," Sunny hurried to explain.

"I'm sorry." Anna gave Charles a "help me" look. She couldn't think of another thing to say that wouldn't make the situation even worse.

Charles came to the rescue. "Anna's first pack was . . . troubled and very poor. We've been married less than a month, and she's had a lot to adjust to."

"Living a long time doesn't mean that you'll be rich," said Arthur with an understanding look. "But it doesn't hurt."

"Long-term investments give a whole new meaning to the term 'compound interest,' " added Sunny.

"Tell me about your collection," said Anna a little desperately. And then, because she couldn't help her interest, "About Excalibur."

"I used to be an archaeologist," explained Arthur. "Strictly amateur—which was acceptable to my father in a way that a profession wouldn't have been. Digs weren't as well regulated then, and I was excavating the grounds of an old Cornish settlement conveniently situated on a school-mate's parents' estate when I found her, just dug her up."

He didn't seem crazy—nor did he seem to mind the questions. If they weren't talking about . . . about *Excalibur*, for Heaven's sake, she would be fascinated by the story.

"How do you know it was Excalibur you found?"

He smiled at her. "Tell me, my dear, do you believe in reincarnation?"

No. But that wasn't the polite answer. "I've never heard a convincing argument for it."

His smile widened. "I suppose it suffices to say that I do, and that I believe I am the Once and Future King, who will return in the time of greatest need." Then he winked at her. "I don't insist that others buy into my eccentricities."

If people remembered once being kitchen maids, or farmers who died of nothing more interesting than old age, I might reconsider my stance on reincarnation, Anna thought as she returned the British wolf's smile. She remembered her father once observing dryly, *If fourteen people believe they were Cleopatra in a former life, does that mean that Cleopatra had split personality disorder?*

Then Arthur led them into his treasure hall—probably it had been intended to be an office, or a small bedroom. Three tapestries, flattened between clear sheets of something that might have been glass or Plexiglas, were hung on the wall. There were a couple of display cabinets along the wall itself.

"This is not a proper display," he said. "These stay here all year long, so I can't risk anything of real value. My more valuable artifacts don't leave my home in Cornwall. I acquired all of these in the U.S. This tapestry is fifteenth century, and like many, it has a religious theme. You can see St. Stephen being crucified—upside down, as tradition holds."

Anne looked at the stilted figure, a halo on his upside-down head and blood pouring from his hands.

"Cheery," she observed.

He smiled. "It isn't my favorite, either."

The second one showed a woman sitting on a bench under a tree, sewing, with a large bird perched just over her head. The colors were faded, but brightened as the threads dipped below the surface. *Once,* thought Anna, *this one was a lot more colorful than it is now.*

"This one is Scots." Arthur sounded disapproving. "Thirteenth century or thereabouts."

"Barbarians, those Scots," said Charles with amusement. "My father the Welshman says it exactly the same way."

Arthur laughed. "All right, you caught me. I suppose that no matter how long I live, I'll still, in some aspects, be a man of my time, eh? Just as you are, old friend. It is in unusually good shape, as it has been in and out of museums and collections for about two hundred years, and was well taken care of even before that."

He walked on and made a flamboyant gesture at the final, and smallest tapestry.

"The third is my favorite of the three. It is also probably fifteenth century—I bought it in California from a private collection. It is in rough shape, and has been sewn onto an acid-free muslin to stabilize it. They are all hermetically sealed to protect them from the climate."

Arthur was right, it wasn't in very good shape. Only a section about two feet square had survived. A knight riding a horse who was galloping with all four feet off the ground, its mouth opened around the bit. He had a sword in one hand and it was raised at a slightly more than forty-five-degree angle.

Arthur touched the clear covering over the figure with gentle fingers. "As you can see, it depicts Arthur fighting with Excalibur."

Anna couldn't see why he was so sure it was Arthur until she took a good look at the sword. Of the word that had once been stitched on the blade there were only three letters left. An "x," a "k," and a "u." She had to admit that she couldn't think of many words that someone would stitch on a sword with those particular letters.

"He looks pretty unhappy," Anna commented. "I wonder what he was chasing."

"It might be anything," said Arthur. "He was the Champion of England and fought dragons and other beasts as well as defending his homeland from the Saxons."

The first display case was filled with a double handful of Roman artifacts. Anna suspected some of what he had was illegal. Though maybe a stone from Hadrian's Wall had been okay to take back in the days when Arthur had originally collected it.

The second case held a chain-mail shirt covered with a bright blue tunic emblazoned with three silver crowns.

"That's a replica," Sunny said. "Though it is still worth several thousand dollars. The cloth was woven according to traditional methods and dyed with natural vegetable dyes, the silver thread is real silver, and the mail shirt is hand-made." She touched the case. "It's King Arthur's coat of arms—or at least what he should have worn on his shield, anyway."

"Arthur's coat of arms," Anna said dubiously. She doubted the real Arthur had ever worn chain mail; maybe the British Master had read *Le Morte d'Arthur* a few times too many.

Sunny nodded. "King Arthur, not my Arthur. But my Arthur didn't want to use his own family's coat of arms—"

"A pig," said Arthur over Sunny's shoulder.

"A boar," said Sunny, unperturbed. "There are still some members of his family about who might recognize him . . . a younger cousin and his littlest sister."

"Who is eighty-four, this coming May," Arthur spoke with obvious affection. "I'd visit her, but she's still sharp as a tack and can shoot skeet without wearing glasses. So I chose The King's coat of arms."

He said it with implied capital letters, as if there had never been another king.

"There were no coats of arms back in the era of Arthur," said Charles. "Wasn't he supposed to be sixth century?"

"Or late fifth," agreed Arthur. "The hero of the battle of Mount Badon, and that was in 518 or so. Heraldry and all its trappings were much later. Still, there is a tradition. . . . and I had the whole thing made for fun, anyway." His eyes were dreamy. Anna wondered if he wore it and played with the sword he'd dug up when no one was around to see him.

Her older brother used to sneak downstairs at night and take the old Civil War cavalry sword her father had hung up on the wall over the fireplace and fight invisible foes. And once, memorably, his little sister, whom he'd armed with a broom. She'd gotten sixteen stitches—and he a broken nose. Men, she thought, had a strange yen for long, pointy, sharp things. She kept her smile to herself.

"Now for the *pièce de résistance*." Arthur paused. "I often find that people are disappointed with Excalibur. I think it is because of all the movies. This is not a prop, it is a weapon made for killing."

He went down to one knee and moved the carpet and pulled up a section of hardwood flooring. Underneath was a floor safe. He put his hand flat on the safe, and after a moment it beeped and opened in a slow, steady motion. Inside was a narrow wooden case a little more than three feet long.

He picked it up and set it on top of the display table. The case itself was beautiful, a handcrafted blend of light and dark woods.

He opened the latches that kept the case closed and took the top completely off.

And she understood why a man might think that this . . . this was Excalibur. It bore as much resemblance to her father's cavalry sword as a jaguar to a lion—both very effective predators.

Arthur's Excalibur was shorter and wider than her father's blade—and it was sharp on both sides. The blade was dark down the center, where it was indented, and she could see the patterns in the steel as if it were Damascus—and perhaps it was. The edges were smooth and bright, though, running parallel to each other for most of the length of the blade. The grip was made of steel and, in comparison to all those Excaliburs of film and TV Arthur had mentioned, was very utilitarian—and short. It was a sword meant to be swung with one hand, a sword meant to kill.

"Did they have steel in the sixth century?" she asked.

"They had steel swords, in some places, at least a thousand years before that," answered Arthur. "Toledo steel swords were mentioned by the Romans back in the first century B.C."

"It is—" She was going to say beautiful, but that wasn't right. Her father's sword had been long and graceful—a weapon designed for beauty as well as function. This was different. "Powerful."

"No gems, no gold or glittery parts." Arthur sounded pleased.

"It doesn't need them." The impulse to touch it was strong, but she kept her hands behind her back.

"The sword wasn't the only weapon that Arthur carried," Arthur said, his voice fervid with passion. "Just the most famous. There was the Sword in the Stone, which recognized Arthur as rightful king. That is probably also the sword known as Clarent, which was used to bestow authority—such as kingship or rank. Some of the early Welsh tales mention the dagger, Carnwennen, with which he slew the Very Black Witch."

A buzzer sounded. Sunny let out a squeak, checked her watch, and ran out of the room ranting about timers and burnt offerings.

"Your mate is lovely," said Charles.

"She is," Arthur said. "She brings me joy." He touched the handle of his sword. "Excalibur is over fifteen hundred years old, and she will be with me another fifteen hundred years. My Sunny . . ." He swallowed. "My Sunny is dying slowly every day."

It was late when they left. To Anna's relief, the evening had passed mostly without incident. She'd been worried that Charles's earlier mood would continue, but he'd been perfectly civil over dinner.

He hadn't said much, but when Arthur ran out of King Arthur stories, he managed to get the British wolf talking about the difficulties the CCTVs—the cameras that Great Britain was installing all over the place to keep an eye on her citizens—were causing the werewolves.

"Well," she said, as they approached the battered Toyota, "that was almost civil—"

The man who'd been sitting behind the shrubbery rose

a little stiffly. She recognized his scent a moment later and swallowed the sound she'd been about to make.

"Michel," said Charles.

She'd met him in the restaurant last night, but without the others around, she read him better. Alpha, but not very dominant. In her old pack, the Chicago Pack, he might have ranked halfway up, but no more than that. His face was battered and his blackened eyes said that someone had broken his nose. He was healing, but for some that happened more slowly than others. He hadn't straightened all the way up and had an arm over his stomach.

"Charles," he said in a low voice. "The Beast took my cell phone, and I wasn't sure how else to contact you."

"What do you need?"

The Frenchman shook his head. "Came to deliver a warning to you. Your mate, he wants her. You understand? He kills women and the innocent—and he has fastened on her as a victim. He thirsts for her. You must keep her out of his way if you can."

"Thank you for your warning," said Charles. "Come, we'll give you a ride wherever you need to go."

But the French wolf took a step back. "No. If I return smelling like you, he will kill me."

"But not if you smell like me," said Arthur.

Anna hadn't heard him, but neither of the other wolves were surprised.

"I found you hurt by the side of the road," continued Arthur, glancing at the street that ran past the end of the driveway. He made a soft sound between his teeth. "For shame, Jean, not taking better care of your wolves." He looked at Charles. "By the time I finish with him, Jean will be so enraged with me he will forget about hurting Michel."

"He hates you, too," Michel warned him, even though his acceptance of the plan was evident in his face.

"He always has. I am not afraid of him," said Arthur. And no one told him that they knew it was a lie. Even Anna could tell he was afraid.

He looked at Charles. "You go to your hotel. I'll feed him something that bleeds to help him heal. Then I'll get him back to his den unharmed."

With a sharp nod, Charles rounded the car to get in the passenger side. Anna opened her door, then said, "King Arthur was said to be a brave man, too."

He feared, but took care of the weaker, less dominant wolf—even though Michel was an Alpha in his own right.

"A good man, our Arthur," said Charles softly, as she backed onto the street. "Even if he's quite mad north-northwest. At least the wind is usually southerly."

Shakespeare. "He usually knows a hawk from a hand-saw?" she threw in, so he'd know she recognized his allu-sion. "You don't believe he is Arthur?"

He smiled a little. "Most of the old wolves are mad about something. For our British monarch—it is King Arthur. A relatively benign madness. I much prefer it to Chastel's."

"Arthur's not as old as you," she was certain of it.

"No. But he is old enough."

8HE wasn't pouting. Anna sucked in her bottom lip, crossed her legs, and wiggled her toes. She'd agreed to wait someplace safe during the next round of meetings. Charles didn't want to risk sending her out on her own again—and she didn't want to risk anyone else's life. Tom would be fine, but he was still stiff and sore this morning—and Moira had still been sleeping, utterly exhausted, when Anna checked on them.

She'd tried again to sit beside Charles and relax, but there were so many strangers who were staring at her . . .

She'd flagged down Angus, who took her upstairs to his own offices, a floor up from the auditorium. He'd ushered her into his private sanctuary, then shut the door, having instructed her to lock it. Dead-bolted, the steel door probably wouldn't keep out a determined werewolf, but it would give her time to use her cell phone and call for help.

Angus's office was far from Purgatory. There was a TV and a couch in addition to his desk and his ridiculously luxurious office chair. There were magazines, and she had brought a book to read.

So why was she sitting in Angus's very comfortable leather chair *not* pouting?

No reason at all.

Someone knocked at the door.

"Who is it?" she called.

"Angus. I have a guest for you. Ric, the Italian's Omega."

She unbolted the door and it popped open about six inches. A blond head with a short red beard stuck itself in the narrow opening. "Presto. Your entertainment is here." He slipped all the way into the room and shut the door behind him. "Tame and safe." His voice owed as much to Britain as it did to Germany.

"Frankly," she told him, "I'd have welcomed a pack of villains to rip to bits—it is boring in here."

"Alas, I am not a villain," he said grandly, snitching a handful of nuts from the bowl on Angus's desk. "Although I could be if you wished." He wiggled his eyebrows at her. "Your mate decided my Italian buddies and the Germans would settle a bit better without my presence. Though he didn't say precisely that." He grinned at her. "I believe the total of his words were 'Omega.

Go.' Angus decided he meant here." He canted his head to the side as if that would give him a different view of her. "You're the first Omega I've ever met."

"Likewise," Anna agreed. "I thought you *were* German?"

He shook his head and sauntered over to the window. "Austrian."

His choice to join the Italians suddenly made a lot more sense. He must have read it in her face because he laughed.

"Yes, Italians are a lot more effervescent and cheery than the Germans. Even werewolves." He thought about that a second, then added, "Maybe especially the werewolves."

"Why didn't the Austrians want you?" she asked.

His face sobered. "There aren't any Austrian packs anymore. There were only two, and four years ago Chastel got bored and hunted down both Alphas. He—" The other wolf drew in a sharp breath. "But that is no conversation for today. So I must be Italian or German. And I choose Italian. My Alpha says that if they knew how much I talked, the Germans would be happy for it."

"Your English is very good." Anna sat back down in Angus's chair. It swiveled so she could keep track of Ric's exploration of the room without pacing beside him.

He turned his back to the window so he could look at her—or so she could look at him. He put both hands to his chest in a flamboyant gesture that looked very Italian to her, not that she'd met that many Italians. "Scholar," he said. "That's me. I had most of a doctorate in psychology before my Change. I can speak English, getting much better at Italian. My French friend tells me that someday, if I work at it, I may no longer be flattering myself when I say I can speak a very little French." He sat on the sill of the window, which was wide enough to make a pretty good seat. "My Alpha says that you haven't been a wolf long."

"Three years."

"That is two years and six months longer than I. So you can tell me exactly what an Omega is—something that my lads haven't quite managed to explain satisfactorily yet. I would like something more than 'you make us happy,' which is the best they have managed so far. My lovers tell me that, and it is good, no? My wolf pack—who are mostly men, and I do not swing that way—tell me such things, and it doesn't sound too good to me. 'You bring us joy' is even worse, so I stopped asking. I need to know more, yes?"

His pained look was so exaggerated she couldn't help laughing. "Disconcerting." She tried to imagine what Charles would do if another man came up to him and said, "You bring me joy."

"I don't know all that much," she confessed. "My teacher is a man who was married to an Omega for a couple of centuries before she died. The problem is, there aren't many of us. We're not as rare in the human population, but seldom Changed." Sunny, she thought, might be a human Omega—or perhaps just very submissive. "Even enraged werewolves seldom attack Omega humans, and I understand that even if the Omega desires to be Changed, it is difficult to find a wolf willing to do it."

"So I understand," he said. "I had a skiing accident and was lucky the man who found me, a friend and a member of the ski patrol, was a werewolf—a secret he had kept for all the time of our friendship. I was dying, and he Changed me to try to save me." He gave her a tight smile. "Me, I thought it was because we were friends—but he told his Alpha it was because he knew I was Omega and would be a treasure to his pack, and this the Alpha accepted as truth and did not discipline him for Changing me without permission."

"Is he still your friend?"

He sighed and rocked back, the motion making his head hit the window with a soft thump. "Yes."

"Then maybe he only gave the Alpha the truth he needed. A person quite often has more than one reason for doing something—particularly something so . . . big as Changing a mortal human into an immortal wolf."

Something in his face loosened, and he nodded once. "Just so. I had not thought of it in that way." He gave her a quick glance from under his lashes. "Truthfully, I had not noticed it bothered me so much until I spoke here with you. How were you Changed?"

She looked away.

"I am sorry," he said, and he was suddenly a lot closer than he had been.

He'd abandoned his seat on the window and crouched on the top of the desk. From the speed of his change of position, he must have jumped there.

"It was a bad thing?" he said gently. "You do not have to tell me of it." He settled, sliding one leg under the other so he rested on a hip. "For many it is not something they care to discuss."

"A mad wolf will attack anything," she told him hoarsely. If she closed her eyes, she knew she would see Justin's face, so she left them open. "An Alpha's mate was going mad, and he thought an Omega would help her maintain control. So he found me. He couldn't force himself to hurt me, though, so he took a wolf who was blood-mad, moon-mad, and sent him after me." And he'd hunted her and taken his time over the brutality that was a necessary part of the Change. "I don't think I was the first he'd tried it on. But the others he failed with, they died."

He held her eyes, his own intent. "Rough."

She shrugged with a nonchalance she didn't expect him

to believe. But she didn't want to cry on his shoulder. Though she suspected he wouldn't have minded, Charles would.

She smiled, and it was genuine. "Things are a lot better now. Charles rode in like a white knight and rescued me."

He returned her smile. "I met Charles. A very scary white knight."

She nodded. "Yes. But that was exactly what I needed. So you want to know more about being an Omega?"

"Yes, *bitte*. I get that I am the bottom of the pack—but how am I different from the submissive wolves?"

"Did they tell you that you were on the bottom?"

He leaned a chin on his upright leg. "Not exactly."

"Good," she said. "Because you aren't. You are outside of the pack structure. You're the only one who can defy the Alpha." She hesitated. "That doesn't mean he'll let you get away with it . . . but a submissive wolf, even a wolf who is a lot less dominant than the Alpha, would have trouble standing up to him at all. Most werewolves have a . . ." She fought with an exact explanation, then decided not to worry about it. He was a werewolf, he'd understand. "A built-in meter that tells them whether a wolf is dominant to them or not. If the meter doesn't tell them right away . . . well, they usually fight it out."

"This I have seen," he said.

"Right, then. That's something you and I are missing. I mean, I can still tell—even with humans—who is in charge and who isn't. But it doesn't have anything to do with their relationship with *me*."

"Ja," he said jerking his head up and slapping the desk. "I thought there was something wrong with me, that I did not feel this. That I did not feel the need to drop my eyes or bow my head."

"They probably didn't even think to tell you," Anna told

him. "And . . . it is still *safer* to drop your eyes around the more dominant wolves."

He took a deep breath and leaned forward. "I thought they had trouble hurting ones such as you and I."

Anna pulled back. "Yeah, well, there's always the crazy ones."

"Isaac, my Alpha, he told me that there was a problem, yesterday. I saw it, but I couldn't decipher it myself. He says something scared you, and every wolf in the room was ready to defend you—and they were all looking at the wolves next to them to see who the problem was. That is to do with being Omega, too?"

Anna sighed. "I told you something about my first pack—they left me with a few issues. Too many dominant wolves, and I turn into a chicken. What do you know about the difference between the dominant wolves and the submissive ones?"

He shrugged. "They tell me nothing. These wolves, they don't talk much. Me, they will tell you, I talk all the time. Or maybe you have noticed. How can we solve things if we do not talk? Talking is useful. But I watch, too. The dominant wolves fight with each other and take care of the submissive wolves. The submissive ones, they are no threat. They need to be taken care of, though—a pat on the head. A reassuring touch is necessary for them."

"I had it explained in very simple words," said Anna. "*Dominant wolves*"—she deepened her voice to a passable baritone, but she couldn't quite get Asil's accent—"their instincts tell them to protect with violence and control their environment. They are ready to kill. The more dominant the wolf, the quicker he is to kill. Less dominant wolves cede the authority to protect to the more dominant wolf. An Alpha is the ultimate control freak, ready to kill anyone who threatens his pack. He protects the weaker from the strong and suffers no defiance of his will. There's other stuff, magic stuff, but that's the gist of it."

"Yes," he said. "I have seen this."

"Submissive wolves are the kinder, gentler wolves. They are missing the killing instinct. That doesn't mean they won't kill under the right circumstances, just that it is not their first answer to every problem. They don't need to control everyone around them. With a submissive wolf, a dominant wolf will relax because the lesser wolf is no threat."

"All right. Yes."

"An Omega wolf is an Alpha wolf who is extremely zen."

There was a little pause as he absorbed that. She grabbed a handful of nuts and came up with a bunch of Brazil nuts and a peanut. Angus, evidently, didn't like Brazil nuts.

Finally, Ric said slowly, "An Alpha is the most dominant wolf in the pack, the most prone to violence."

Anna nodded. "No one gives him crap, and his job is to protect his pack. No one gives Omegas crap either, and our job is to protect our packs, even from themselves. The zen part comes because we don't have to kill anyone to get our way."

"Alpha," he said it again, to get the feel of it. And there was a little punch behind it. Anger, even.

"Alpha," said Anna, eating a nut. She didn't mind Brazil nuts, though she preferred almonds. "Minus most of the tough stuff, and our magic stuff is different. With our magic, we make our pack happy."

Ric grinned at her.

"While the Alpha can pull strength, even magic, from all the pack, the Marrok—and this is only the smallest part of what makes him scary—can pull from all of his Alphas. I don't think we have anything like that. But yeah, you don't have to listen when the big bad wolves want to boss you around. Omega doesn't mean weak."

Evidently he could be quiet, too, because he tilted his head toward the ceiling and thought for about ten minutes—long enough that Anna had time to think over what she had told him. She hadn't been acting like an Alpha with zen; she'd been acting like a submissive wolf . . . No, because even a submissive wolf didn't usually put her tail between her legs at the first sign of a dominant wolf, as she had been doing. She had killed a vampire. She had killed a witch so scary that she'd chased Asil out of his home and kept him on the run for two hundred years. Asil, the Moor, whose name was whispered with awe (or, sometimes snarled) wherever he went.

Grumpily, she picked up her book and stared at the page.

"Anna," he said, at last.

"Yes?"

"I would like to teach my pack this truth of yours. That I am not a child, a plaything they may find convenient. An über-submissive wolf, yes? They must see me for the zen wolf that I am."

Zen wolf. That had a bigger punch than Omega.

"And how have you decided to do it?"

He smiled at her, his face lit with mischief. "I have an intention. Tonight there is to be a feast, yes? And after that, a hunt. Anyone not a submissive wolf may join in the hunt. That exclusion is for their protection, with so many dominants about. Anyone. I think that I should hunt."

EigHt

CHARLES was most comfortable by himself or, if that wasn't possible, with his pack in the wild. Talking for hours in a crowded auditorium was not on any list of things he enjoyed—or things he was good at. At least no one had died. Yet.

The Germans had settled down as soon as the Italians' Omega had stalked off with offended dignity. The Italians, for their part, did a good job of concealing their glee and got down to business. Deals were hammered out.

By two in the afternoon, Charles and the Finnish delegates were finally bringing to fruition a complicated dance of issues further confused by translation problems. They claimed to have no one who spoke English. He didn't speak Finnish. So they translated through a Norwegian wolf who spoke Finnish and Spanish, and a Spaniard who spoke English. He suspected it was a ruse to give them time to think—and he had no objection.

He agreed to a no-interest loan for the Finns to use for positive publicity, fronted by the charitable arm of the

Marrok's company. Though Charles himself would be in charge of the distribution and would expect results for the money—it was still a good deal.

The Finns weren't the only ones smiling as they finished up. Everyone had been following the negotiations closely, many of them even taking notes as they finally decided to believe that the Marrok had no intention of leaving them high and dry—and was willing to sign contracts, legal contracts that could now be taken to courts just like anyone else's: a benefit none of them had thought of until now. Gradually, as the day progressed, a spirit of cautious optimism had begun spreading through the wolves.

"We are agreed?" Charles asked the man who'd been acting as the Finnish lead.

As the translation worked its way through the language barriers, and the Finn began to nod, Jean Chastel stood up, and said, "No."

The Frenchman waited until the Finn, who had come to his feet in the middle of negotiations, slowly sat down before he continued. "We won't accept guilt money for this betrayal of all the treaties we've signed with the Marrok in which he agrees to keep his nose out of our business."

And damned if he didn't open up a slick briefcase and start piling up paper—and parchment that looked as though it might have been older than Chastel, and was ancient enough to smell of dust rather than lamb. "We do not need the Marrok's money. We are not under his 'protection.' He has no jurisdiction in our territories."

There was a grim triumph in Chastel's face. The French wolves—including Michel, bruises and all—looked stolidly supportive. They had no choice.

Quiet settled over the room, an uncomfortable quiet as they focused on Chastel. The Beast couldn't keep the Marrok from bringing the wolves into the open. But he could keep him from helping the European wolves cope—and in the end that might be disastrous for everyone.

Chastel ruled the European continent when he chose, and he'd just marked it as his territory, leaving Charles the choice of letting Chastel's claim stand or challenging him outright.

"Yes," said Dana in a motherly voice. "Thank you for that, *monsieur*. You have been heard." The fae smiled congenially at Chastel, then raised her eyes to the rest of the world. "On behalf of the Emerald City Pack, I have an invitation to all of you who have gathered in Seattle for this conference. As a part of our hospitality, we have organized a hunt tonight on the pack's own hunting grounds. There will be no blood—the Marrok asked me to extend his apologies. But since there is more than just one pack hunting, we felt that no blood would keep the threat of violence down . . ."

Charles might not be comfortable or particularly good at public speaking, but Dana was. When his father had asked her to moderate, Charles had worried because she didn't know wolves. His father had smiled. "She knows men," he'd said. And he had been right.

Everyone already had the information about the hunt. She was robbing Chastel of his limelight—and his power— and everyone knew it. Without her, Chastel could have taken the meeting over, leaving Charles . . . and maybe, just maybe, Arthur to face him down or back off and let him run with it.

And if they had challenged him and killed him, Dana would be honor-bound to destroy them. He wasn't sure she could manage it, not if he and Arthur were working together. But he didn't know that he and Arthur would be working together either; Arthur could be very difficult to predict.

And none of it would have worked if she hadn't already proven herself more powerful than Chastel before them all. The Frenchman let her take over because he was afraid to challenge her. And as she droned on with information everyone already had—Charles had e-mailed them all the details of the hunt a week ago—every wolf in the room understood what she was doing.

Chastel stood up and stormed out of the room, leaving his papers behind. Angus took a step to the side and blocked the door.

It was a foolhardy thing to do. If Chastel chose not to remember that Angus was under the Marrok's protection, Angus's life could be forfeit. And maybe, just maybe, he counted on it. If Chastel spilled blood first . . . But the Frenchman held his temper. Just.

"Madame?" Angus said diffidently.

The Beast turned his head toward the fae. "I need fresh air. Something stinks in here."

Dana's smiles were weapons, even when they were gentle. "By all means," she said. "Leave."

Angus stepped aside and opened the door for him.

And the Beast retreated. But he retreated triumphant. None of the foreign wolves would challenge Chastel's right to make this decision for them. And, just as when the Marrok revealed the werewolves, it would reflect on Europe—so, too, would the failure of the European wolves to persuade the human population that they were no threat reflect upon the Marrok's territory.

Charles couldn't help but wonder if matters would have been different if his father had been here.

Angus had over a hundred channels on his TV: sports channels, news channels, comedy channels, cartoon channels, science channels, and about fifty shopping channels. The only thing either Anna or Ric could stand to watch was a *South Park* marathon.

The kids were being chased by the Nazgûl fifth graders—and the station switched to a commercial for male enhancement products.

"So," Anna said to distract herself from the silly grin on the face of the man on TV, "you think entering the hunt will be useful how?"

The man must have bothered Ric, too, because he jumped up from the couch and turned off the television before settling back on the desk again. "I don't think that my Alpha understands the difference between submissive and Omega. Now that I do, I would like him to also. I think the hunt will help—a game where I can face down the dominants with impunity."

"You think that would work? Charles would just strangle me and put me out of his misery."

He leaned back and waved his hands. "Hello, *psychologist*, yes? Or almost. *Of course* I don't know. I believe it will help me—and I *think* that participating in the hunt will help you with this issue you have with dominant wolves."

"Like throwing the kid who is afraid of water into the deep end to sink or swim?"

He grinned. "Not so bad as that. *I* think that if you have something to do, some task—like finding this bait that the fae lady and Angus have hidden in the pack's hunting grounds—I think you won't be so afraid. And if you are not afraid, they will not crowd you. And by the time you have a moment to worry about them"—he snapped his fingers—"they will have been surrounding you, hunting with you, and it will seem silly to be afraid."

She looked at him. Charles had suggested something

similar, she remembered. Though he hadn't intended her actually to participate. "The ocean. Like throwing a two-year-old into the ocean. With sharks."

He laughed. "Look. I am not long a wolf, but I observe. My mentor at the *uni*—university to you—he says I am a genius. I will give you his number, and he will tell you so." He paused, and he grinned a little self-consciously. "Of course he will also tell you I died tragically in a skiing accident. Anyway, it means this: you should listen to me.

"We wolves are more resilient than when we were human. The wolf is always in the present, it does not worry much about past or future. Your wolf will keep you from panicking if she can. The hunt will give her the help she needs. By the end, you will be better because she will help you."

"Unless they *do* kill me," Anna said.

"No blood," Ric said. "It is in the rules. Did you see the way that fairy made the Beast shut his mouth yesterday, or was that after you left?"

"Before," Anna said. "And they prefer fae. A fairy is a specific kind of fae whose actual form is about twelve inches high—and I'm pretty sure that Dana is not one of those."

"And she will be on hand to keep things safe: they will behave themselves."

She knew Charles wouldn't be happy if she chose to be in the hunt. Accidents happen. Especially when they are on purpose. Charles had enemies, and it would do her no good to be avenged after she died. She didn't want to make Charles unhappy with her.

"Look," said Ric seriously. "Isaac, my Alpha, will be in this hunt, too. I think he'll agree to bodyguard you with me. No one else is going to be working together. Can you imagine Alphas cooperating with each other? The three of us, we stand a better chance at winning. And we can keep you safe."

"I had two people get hurt trying to defend me yesterday," Anna said. "And that was on a shopping trip."

"Someone tried to hurt you?"

She knew Charles had called his Alpha last night to warn him about the possibility that the vampires had been targeting her because she was an Omega—rather than because she was Charles's mate. Apparently he'd decided not to pass on the news.

"You should have been told," she said—and then she took care of it.

"We are viewed as weak," Ric said grimly when she had finished. They'd decimated the nuts, eaten the lunch delivered by a pair of Angus's wolves, then found a secret stash of trail mix. Ric picked through the bag and took a couple pieces of dried peach. Then he threw them up into the air, catching them in his mouth on the way down in two quick snaps. "Maybe it is not just my wolves who need to be told but everyone else as well. It is not safe in our world to be seen as weak. It makes us prey."

"If your Alpha didn't look at you as some sort of supersubmissive, he'd have told you about the threat of the vampires, and you'd have been alert to the danger," Anna agreed.

He tossed her a couple of banana chips, and she snatched them out of the air without her hands as well.

He saluted her. "Though, mind you, I think that's a pisspoor way of protecting even the submissive ones. They are not children—they are werewolves."

He closed his eyes, tossed a cranberry into the air, and ate it on the way down. "You say we are like submissive wolves who do not obey. I wonder if there are dominant wolves who do not protect?"

"*Yes.*"

Anna looked up, but Ric had to turn all the way around to see Chastel standing in the doorway.

"They call us *beasts*." He smiled at Anna, his eyes hungry. "Are you afraid of me, little girl?"

Ric might as well not have been there for all the notice Chastel took of him. His focus was all on her, his eyes wide and golden. A faint flush over his cheekbones told her that he was excited—he looked just as Justin, the wolf who had Changed her, had looked before—

She swallowed that thought. This man was looking for prey. And she would not be sport for him. Nor for anyone. Not ever again.

She called up her wolf, not so much to start the change but to borrow the wolf's courage and let it settle into her bones. When she was certain her knees wouldn't shake, she stood up as the silence gained weight like a brewing storm. She took her time before answering—he displayed the patience of a good hunter.

"You're the one who should be afraid," she said finally, letting her matter-of-fact voice carry the message she wanted to give him—that she wasn't afraid of him. Because she *was* afraid of him, she couldn't tell him she wasn't. But she could lie with the truth and make it stick.

"If you touch me, Charles will hunt you down and eat your marrow while you are still alive to scream." She called upon her two acting classes and let her mouth turn up. "I'll be happy to watch." She licked her lips.

The smile dropped off his face, and he growled.

She wasn't helpless, not like she'd been in Chicago when Justin hunted her down—or later, when the pack helped subdue her to his will. Here, the only other person in the room was Ric—and he would help *her*, not Chastel. Chastel would best her, probably best them both. But she would make sure he was hurt—and then Charles would kill him. Her wolf approved, and her fear slid away, leaving her balanced lightly on the balls of her feet and ready for blood and death.

There was only now, between this breath and the next— and that left no time for fear.

"Your vampire was lovely. She died too quickly." Anna imitated the motion she'd used to snap the woman's neck. "Hopefully you'll make a better show."

"My vampire?" He dismissed her words with an impatient hand. "You are a fool, and your mate is a thug, lacking in intelligence. Nothing but his father's lapdog, who fetches and kills on command."

She let her smile bloom. "Is that what you think? How foolish of you."

With the hand that the Frenchman couldn't see, Ric gestured sharply, trying to get her to stop baiting the Beast. She knew it was stupid, but Ric couldn't know that her alternative was cowering in a corner. So she baited him.

"*Salope,*" Chastel snarled.

She knew that much French. "Thank you."

And suddenly, because she had neither seen nor heard him, Charles was there, standing directly behind Chastel. "Be careful whom you call a bitch, Jean, *mon cher,*" he said in a voice that was too calm to be believable. "Someone might feel it was an insult."

Chastel turned around, giving Anna his back so he could face the more dangerous one. "Ah, here he is. Your woman tells me you will hunt me down and eat my marrow while I live."

"Did she?" Charles looked at her, and she saw the approval in his face. She doubted anyone else would have read anything at all. His voice was a caress, just for her. "Would you like that, love?"

She clasped her hands under her chin in her best silent-film-star pose. "Only if I can watch."

Charles laughed and, on the tail end of the sound, rounded on Chastel, using the motion to place himself between the Frenchman and Anna—and he wasn't laughing at all. "Go."

She couldn't see her mate's face, but she saw Chastel flinch and drop his eyes. His hands fisted, but it didn't keep him from taking a step back. With a low oath, he turned and stalked away.

Charles tilted his head, obviously listening to Chastel leave.

"While he was still alive?" he said.

"Women are the bloodthirsty sex," said Ric sadly. "We get the reputation, but it is only because the women stand behind us, and say, 'Kill it. Squish it.' "

Anna thought it was time for formal introductions. "Charles, this is Ric—I'm sorry, I didn't catch your last name."

Ric hopped off the desk, where he'd been crouched and ready to pounce if needed, and held out his hand. "Postinger. Heinrich Postinger."

Charles shook his hand. "I am Charles Cornick."

Ric looked at Anna. "Your defiance is admirable, but it was not the most brilliant thing I've ever seen anyone do. He's going to come after you now. He must do this."

"Ric is a psychologist," Anna explained.

"He was going to go after her no matter what she did," said Charles.

Anna grinned. "There's a certain satisfaction in knowing that I deserve it, you know? Better than thinking he's coming after me because I ran like a chicken."

Charles kissed her. "Yes," he said, pulling his mouth away. "There is that, isn't there? I have to go back—

everyone is still in the auditorium waiting on me. Would you please *lock* the door this time? It doesn't do you any good hanging open so anyone can walk in, O-Woman-Who-is-Not-a-Chicken."

"Of course." And with a sudden burst of confidence, she rose on her toes and kissed his chin—which was as high as she could manage. He didn't help, but his eyes were smiling when she finished.

"Good," he said, though whether to the kiss or to her agreement to lock the door he left deliberately up in the air.

He'd reached the door when she remembered there was something he should know. "He didn't know anything about the vampires."

When Charles looked back at her, she said, "I told him I killed one of his vampires, and he didn't have any idea what I was talking about."

"Chastel never was a good suspect for bringing in vampires," Charles said. "But it is good to know for sure."

He smiled at her. Then, with a nod at Ric, he left, shutting the door behind him. She waited a moment.

"Anna." Charles's voice carried through the metal door, and so did the exasperation.

She grinned at Ric and turned the dead bolt. Charles tapped the door and left. She couldn't hear him, but she could feel him move farther away from her.

It had felt good to defend herself against Chastel, even if it was only with words. She was tired of being afraid of her own shadow—and for a little while she hadn't been afraid at all. She liked it.

With the fae supervising the hunt, not to mention Charles observing (he wouldn't join the hunt; like Angus, he was one of the hosts), she would be as safe there as she would ever be surrounded by Alphas.

She turned to Ric. "If your Alpha agrees to help play bodyguard, I'd love to join the hunt tonight."

He nodded. "I'll ask him."

Sᴜɴɴʏ frowned at the nail she'd chipped as she took the elevator down to the parking garage. Arthur was tied up in werewolf functions tonight, so she'd taken the opportunity to have dinner with some friends.

She didn't have any close female friends—it is a hard thing not to tell a friend that the reason your husband looks so young is because he's a werewolf. And friends you have for a long time tend to notice things like your husband's not aging at all. So she had condos in various cities, and when she'd lived in a place off and on for a decade or so, she would uproot and move somewhere no one knew her. She'd write letters or e-mails for a few months, then let the friendship drift away.

These women she'd known for a couple of years, casual friends who liked to go out without husband or boyfriend once in a while and talk girl stuff. She'd met them at the gym, and they shared no real interests, but they were smart, funny, and easy to talk to on a superficial level. They made her feel connected, not so alone.

She'd left them before dessert, though, because she didn't trust herself not to indulge. The restaurant they'd chosen was justly famous for its exotic cheesecake. She hadn't kept her figure by allowing herself to sample food she might like too much—and she'd noticed it was getting dark. Arthur didn't like it when she was out too late, he worried about her.

The elevator opened onto the right level for her car. The light next to the elevator was out. She hurried through the darkness until the next light, then felt silly for her anxiousness.

Someone on the other side of the garage was arguing with his girlfriend. Neither of them was very upset. Probably foreplay, she thought. She and Arthur indulged, and she recognized the tone.

She looked, but she couldn't see the couple because an SUV was in the way. Before she got a clear view, the sound of car doors shutting cut off the sound of their bickering. A car engine started, and a silver Porsche passed by, its lights momentarily blinding her.

She dropped her keys and started to kneel and pick them up. Someone's hand was there first.

"Allow me." The man was taller than her Arthur, though not as wide through the shoulders. For a minute she was worried—as any woman alone in a parking garage with a stranger would be. But then she saw the cut of his wool coat: thugs wouldn't wear expensive coats and white linen shirts.

"Thank you," she said as she took her keys out of the leather-gloved hand that held them out to her.

"No troubles," he said. "You'll forgive me the question— but what is a lovely woman like you doing out here all alone?"

Part of her preened under his obvious admiration—she knew her aging distressed Arthur. The honest appreciation in a handsome man's eyes soothed a growing wound in her heart. This man looked to be a few years older than she, and his manners were gallant.

"I was dining with friends," she told him. "My husband is waiting for me."

"Ah" He opened his fingers as if he'd held something precious he had to let go. It was so artfully done that she was certain he had to be an actor or maybe a dancer. "I should have known that such a lovely woman would not be left free—but a man lives on hope. Your accent is charming—you are British?"

"Yes. And so is my husband. Thank you for the keys and the compliment." She smiled at him and headed for her car with brisk strides that would let him understand that, although she appreciated his admiration, she was not available. The smile stayed on her face, warmed a little, as soon as she had her back to him.

She pressed the button that unlocked her car and opened the door—and a hand closed around her mouth.

"Forgive me a little harmless flirtation," he said in her ear. "It seemed a kindness I could give. I regret that your death will not be so kind. My employer failed me—and so I no longer have to follow his so-explicit instructions. My friends are sad, and a little play will make them feel so much better."

She screamed, but the faint noise that escaped his hand wouldn't travel far.

His free hand petted her face as he whispered, his breath smelling like peppermint, "I'll see to it that your husband knows that you didn't flirt with me. That you were faithful to him unto death. Will that soothe him, do you think?"

He was strong. He controlled her struggles effortlessly even though she worked out on a daily basis. Werewolf. He must be one of the werewolves.

"Come, my children," he said, and she realized he wasn't alone. She heard people move behind them, but the only one she could see was the woman who hopped onto the roof of her car. A beautiful woman with honey-colored hair caught up in a ponytail.

"We can play with our dinner?" the woman asked, and terror made Sunny's knees give way. The woman had fangs.

Not werewolf. Vampire.

"We're going to see if she is his mate—or merely his wife, Hannah," her captor said.

"That means yes." The voice came from her left, but she couldn't see the man who said it. But she felt him pull her arm straight and sink his fangs into the inside of her elbow.

It hurt.

THE Emerald City Pack's hunting grounds were in a warehouse district that had seen better days. Those warehouses nearest the water were lit up and, if not hives of activity, still obviously running with a full shift of people. As the ground rose away from the water, the warehouses began to look less and less prosperous.

Following Charles's directions, Anna continued up the battered asphalt road to a pair of huge buildings surrounded by a twelve-foot-tall chain-link fence, hospitably topped by razor wire.

The whole property looked as though no one had done anything industrious there for fifty years—and none of the other warehouses in the immediate area looked any more occupied. Adding to the general disreputable air, the metal roof of one of the buildings was missing a sheet or ten of roofing material.

The people at the gate must have recognized the car because they had it opened for her to drive right on through. As she drove closer to the warehouses, the buildings looked bigger and bigger, and, as she passed between them, they shut out the night sky until it was a narrow ribbon with the Hunter's Moon, just a sliver of silver, in the sky above them.

There were thirty or forty cars in a space big enough to park a hundred. Most of them were parked next to the larger of the two warehouses, so that was where Anna parked, too.

"You're quiet tonight," said Charles.

She looked at her hands and flexed them on the steering wheel, easing her grip when the wheel creaked.

She'd meant to keep quiet about joining the hunt, but as the time approached, springing it on him in front of everyone seemed more and more stupid. "I have an idea—and you aren't going to like it."

He looked at her for a long time, long enough that she finally looked back.

"I am dominant," he told her, as if she didn't already know. "And that means I am driven to take care of those who are mine."

She met his gaze, held it, and realized slowly that it pleased him that she could do so. It pleased her, too.

"You want to go into the hunt."

"Yes."

She expected him to forbid it outright—and realized that part of her had been counting on using that as an excuse to bow out.

Instead he simply asked, "Why?"

"Because Ric thinks that it might help with this . . ." She dropped her eyes and then raised them again and firmed her voice. "With the baseless fear that had me shivering in my seat yesterday when the auditorium filled up with Alphas—who were ready to kill each other to *protect* me. It made me feel stupid and weak. I was less frightened when Chastel came into Angus's office—and I had a lot more reason then."

His eyes flared gold, and he said, in a voice that was lower and rougher than his usual tone, "It's because you fought Justin once, and your pack caught you and held you for him."

Anna nodded jerkily. It hadn't been just for Justin, and

it hadn't been just once—and she wasn't about to tell him that with Brother Wolf looking out through his eyes.

"How does Ric think this will help?"

"Because I'll be focused on the hunt. He thinks that my wolf will help, that she'll keep me from panicking."

"He is a psychologist?"

She couldn't help but smile. "Almost, he says. But not to worry, his mentor thinks he's a genius."

"I cannot join the hunt," he said heavily. "If I won, it would be a political disaster. If I lost, it would be worse. If you hunt, there are those who will be hunting you rather than the prize. Because you are my mate and because you are an Omega."

"Chastel."

"Chastel is not the only enemy my father has here—and I have a few myself."

"I actually thought about that possibility. Ric is hunting tonight. He says that he will keep an eye on me, and thinks his Alpha—someone named Isaac—will agree to do so also."

Charles nodded and opened his door.

"Charles?"

He bent and looked back into the car.

"Can I join the hunt?"

His eyebrows went up. "That was never up to me. You've assessed the benefits and the possible problems. It is up to you." He closed his door.

Anna unbuckled herself and got out of the car. "So what happened to 'I am dominant and I protect those who are mine'?"

He propped a hip on the front of the car. "If it would benefit you, I would kill every wolf here. But there are things that you need to do—and interfering with that is not protecting, not in my book. The best way for me to protect you is to encourage you to be able to protect yourself."

He gave her a sudden, rueful smile. "I admit it doesn't make me happy. But with Dana and me on watch, and Ric and his Alpha on the floor, you are as safe as you are going to be in a hunt full of dominant wolves. You've killed a vampire and a witch—you are hardly helpless."

She straightened her shoulders as his confidence lent her courage. So she walked to him and put her arms around him, burying her face in the sweet-smelling warmth of his chest. He wore one of his favorite flannel shirts over a plain red T-shirt and the cotton was soft against her skin. "You are a remarkable man, Charles Cornick."

He wrapped his arms around her shoulders and put his chin on the top of her head. "I know," he confided lightly. "And often underappreciated by those who don't know any better."

She poked him with a finger and looked up at him. "And funny—though I expect that is another facet of your character that goes unappreciated even more often than your remarkableness."

"Some people don't even notice," he said in a mock-mournful voice.

THE main room in the bigger warehouse was more than twenty feet tall and large enough to swallow all the wolves who had chosen to hunt and leave room for twice as many more. The rest of the wolves—a strong majority—stood on a platform ten feet above them. Everyone was still in human form. One wall of the room was covered with flat-screen TVs, which were off.

Dana stood in the center of the raised platform and spoke. "The rule is no bloodletting—which rule I will enforce. The walls and floors of these buildings and the earth beneath will tell me if there is blood. You will start out human and change when the bell is rung. There are three leather bags, hidden several days ago, containing a handful of pig sausage each—and one of them also holds a two-carat star-ruby ring provided by the Marrok."

As she spoke, the last the monitors all turned on to show a woman's hand holding a ring in its palm. The setting was plain enough so that the ring could be either a man's or a woman's ring—it was the gem that made the ring beautiful. The ruby was a deep semitranslucent red, with a star that was almost white.

It was beautiful and doubtless valuable—and Anna was pretty sure there wasn't anyone standing on the wooden floor with her who was here for the prize. The hunt was all that was important. How often did an Alpha get a chance to pit himself against other Alphas without risk to those they must keep safe?

Angus spoke while the ring was still on display. "Our hunting grounds encompass both buildings, which interconnect via layers of underground tunnels. This building has between two and six layers of maze aboveground, the other three and four, and both have three basement floors original to the structures and two more beneath those that we have added. The three bags are hidden here, and one contains the ring."

Anna glanced at the people around her. Chastel was there, and she recognized Michel and several of the Spanish wolves she had met at the barbecue restaurant. Arthur, though, was standing just behind Dana, with the ones who had chosen not to hunt.

Angus's instructions continued. "Once you find a bag, bring it here. The rules are finder's keepers—no thieves. Any wolf carrying a bag is untouchable. We have monitors, we have people hidden, and Dana has given the bags a little extra fae magic to ensure this is the case. Anyone interfering with a wolf carrying a bag will be eliminated from the competition and the bag will be returned to the finder. You will not be able to open it—Dana has made certain of it. When all three bags are here, we will sound an alarm that you can hear from anywhere on the grounds. Return here—and when everyone is accounted for, Dana will open the bags, and the winner will be announced."

After Angus conducted a brief question-and-answer session, it was Charles's turn. He looked at her, then at Ric and his Alpha, who stood beside her.

"The hunt," he said, "is on."

There was a metallic chunk, the lights went off, and Anna had her shirt halfway off before the last of the light died. On the wall, the monitors switched their display from the ruby ring to black with small red letters on the bottom right-hand corner of each, which abruptly provided the only light in the room.

Clothing ripped and soft, pained sounds echoed as several dozen werewolves began the change from human to something more. Laughing, breathless, she stripped off her pants and shoes, socks and underwear before she began her own change.

Shards of agony spread over her, beginning at the base of her spine and spiraling out to her fingers and toes. Wet pops announced the reshaping of joints and bone as her wolf slid over her skin. Claws and fangs, muscle and fur— wet tracks slid down her face as her eyes watered. Strength surged like the tide rolling in, and she came to all fours with a grunt of effort.

The room was too full of others for her to pick up a scent, and her eyes were blind with the last wave of white-hot pain. She stood shaking, then threw her head back and sang.

Alone.

Because she was the first to change—it must have been a gift from Brother Wolf and the mate bond they shared. She'd never been able to change that fast before. She could have started her hunt, but Ric and his Alpha were still caught in the change. So she stood over them, ready to protect them if they should need it.

By ones and twos, other wolves rose. When they got too close to her, she displayed her fangs, and they let her be.

Ric's Alpha, Isaac, now a winter white wolf who was only a little larger than she, stood up, and they both waited for Ric, who was finished only a few minutes later. He wobbled like a newborn lamb when he came to his feet, not experienced enough yet to wait for brain and muscle to reconnect. She put her shoulder against him and let him lean on her.

In his human form, he was average height and build—maybe even a bit lean. His wolf was on the large side, certainly bigger than she or Isaac. In the dark her eyes gave her shapes, but not colors. He was darker than his Alpha but several shades lighter than she, but she couldn't tell if he was gray, brown, or red.

He shook himself as though he were wet and, as if that were a signal, his Alpha surged forward leaving Anna and Ric to follow. They ran first through a hallway and into a narrow stairway that led down and down, and the scents changed from fresh air to musty and moldy.

AFTER a minute or two the stygian blackness resolved into something more fathomable to Charles's wolf-enhanced vision. A hole in the ceiling let in some starlight, and the monitors began to show orange and red and gold as wolves passed by the infrared cameras scattered throughout the maze and lit the big room with the warmth of their bodies.

Even though he couldn't see her, Brother Wolf told him she'd already completed her change. The first to do so, he thought. He expected her to run immediately, but she waited.

For her guards, said Brother Wolf approvingly. He wasn't happy about Anna running this hunt while they were stuck with the wolves who chose not to go. He wasn't especially happy about missing the hunt himself—particularly with Chastel out there somewhere. Only the knowledge that Anna had allies kept Brother Wolf under wraps.

Groans of pain turned to howls and the sound of claws digging into wood as the last of the wolves entered the hunt, and finally silence descended upon the room. Charles heard a rustle and a click—and a bank of dim lights illuminated the room.

"Lights are still off everywhere else," said Angus. "It'll be a while before we see any of them again, and we might as well be comfortable. Come, my wolves are setting up tables and chairs on the main floor, where we can watch the action.

It took a while, but most of the watchers caught the trick of identifying friends and enemies even on the infrared. Hoots of laughter as traps were sprung and wolves fell into water or garbage or foam packing peanuts. Nets dropped unexpectedly, and one caught six wolves in a net meant for one. When they were finished with it, there wasn't a scrap bigger than eight inches long.

"Way to kill a defenseless net," said Arthur dryly, his crisp English voice carrying over the crowd.

Charles stood in the back, his arms folded and his eyes tracking the heat-trace image of three wolves as they left one monitor only to reappear in the next.

Arthur stood up suddenly, and staggered, knocking over the table next to him. The occupants turned on him with surprised snarls, but he didn't seem to notice them.

"Sunny?" he said, his voice cracking like an adolescent boy's.

The wolves who'd been knocked about stilled their protests. And when his eyes rolled up in his head, and he fell, one of them caught him before he hit the planks of the floor.

ΠΙΠΕ

WHICH way? Which way? Anna, her tongue lolling out to absorb the coolness of the air, decided to let the others choose. Her breath sang out of her throat, and exultation made her shiver.

The hunt.

It didn't matter that the moon's song was only a will-o'–the-wisp chime in her heart, or that the prize was a bag of pork that had been spoiling for two days and might or might not also have a ring inside. For the first time ever, she loved the hunt even when Charles wasn't running beside her.

Because we are with you, Brother Wolf told her. *That is what mating means. You are never alone. Never so long as we live.*

Good, she told him.

They'd followed Angus's scent for a long time before it ended in a note propped in front of a very small battery emergency light. It read, "I didn't hide any of them—Angus." They weren't the first ones there—she could smell the scents of several other wolves—and another wolf showed up just as they were leaving.

Then Ric had picked up another scent—presumably belonging to another of Angus's pack, though she didn't recognize it. And she'd been hot on his tail when his Alpha threw his weight against her and she stumbled sideways against the wall as a net snapped up and jerked Ric off his feet in a nicely packaged bundle.

Between her jaws and Isaac's, it had taken them only a moment to get it off—after they teased him a little. Five turns later they'd come upon a wolf hanging upside down in a tall shaft that ran all the way to the open air some four stories above their head.

Isaac made a noise in his throat that sounded sympathetic and probably wasn't. The trapped wolf snarled as they left him behind, and Ric's Alpha appeared extremely happy for a while after that.

Anna caught Moira's scent and led them through a tunnel no more than two feet around that was such a tight fit Isaac was very unhappy—and Ric had to drop to his belly to squeeze through.

It dumped them off into a small, almost airless chamber. They were coughing with distress by the time Ric managed to destroy the two-by-six wooden wall lined with a moisture barrier that had kept the air out. Anna and he had to drag Isaac by the scruff of his neck into a place with better air—though it was smelly (not in a good way) and stale.

"ANYONE here have Arthur's mate's cell phone number?" Charles growled. No one answered, and so he took his own cell and dialed his father for it.

"What's wrong?" asked Bran when he answered on the first ring.

"That's what we're trying to find out. Do you have Sunny . . . Arthur's mate's cell phone number here in Seattle?"

"Yes, give me a second." As good as his word, Bran was back on in a moment and read him off the number.

"I'll call you when I know what's happened," Charles said, and hit the END button.

He called it, but was unsurprised, given Arthur's distress, that she didn't answer. Then he called another number. "I need to know where this cell phone is: 360-555-1834. GPS location, then an address for that if there is one." He didn't bother waiting for a reply, just hung up.

Arthur was pale and sweating, his skin chill to the touch. His body twitched, but he remained unconscious.

It would take a while before his man could track the phone. Hacking a system without leaving a trail took time. He could have done it, given a computer, Internet access, and a few days—his man was better. But time was not Sunny's friend.

Twenty minutes passed, maybe twenty-five, before his phone rang.

"Charles?"

"Yes?"

"That phone is about a quarter mile from yours, and it isn't moving."

He looked at Angus. "I have to check this out. You'll watch over her for me?"

The Emerald City Alpha nodded. "I, my pack, Isaac, his Omega, and the fae, we all will watch."

THEY found Sunny just outside the fence, a hundred yards from the locked gate: naked, broken, and dead. Just in case they didn't spot the body, a sky-blue Jaguar that he presumed was her car was stopped a couple of body lengths away, with the driver's side door hanging open.

Sunny's body was still warm, and her eyes were open, fogged with death.

A spirit knelt beside her, one of the forest folk. He seldom saw them, though he could tell when they were about. The spirit's slender brown hands petted Sunny's cheek as it crooned to her—so he knew that Sunny had been alive when they dumped her here. The spirit was a shy thing, slipping away as men, who didn't notice its presence, surrounded the corpse. It brushed against Charles, and he felt its sorrow pull his own spirit.

Poor thing, it told him. *She was so scared, so scared. Alone. She was all alone.*

Distracted, Charles barely remembered to stop the others before they could touch her.

"Let me catch the scent," he said. "So I'll know her killer." It wouldn't help to question the spirit. They told him what they wanted to, whether he wanted to hear it or not.

The other wolves backed away, and he set his nose between her neck and jaw, where scent would linger. And he smelled, not unexpectedly, a familiar villain. How many things could there be running around in the night targeting werewolves and their kin?

He didn't touch her as he moved from one pulse point to the next. Where the vampires had fed, the flesh was torn, but there had been no time for bruising. And they had fed everywhere.

He smelled her fear, her suffering, and stood her witness. He was thorough, making sure they hadn't added to their hunting party. But he found no surprises: there were just the four vampires who'd attacked Anna.

Brother Wolf went wild as he understood that this could have been *her*, this could have been their Anna lying here.

Charles closed his eyes and forced his body to stillness. Long, cool fingers stroked his face and sang to the wolf—which didn't help. What a forest spirit was doing out here in the middle of the city, he didn't know—and he seized upon the distraction of the mystery it offered.

He opened his eyes and looked around. There were any number of abandoned warehouses nearby—and blackberries, the infamous weed of the Pacific Northwest, were taking over their empty parking lots, creating a sanctuary for those who didn't mind their thorns.

One mystery down. Charles let the sound of one of his grandfather's songs run through his head, bringing clarity and peace—despite the spirit that patted and petted him. If he'd been alone, he would have knocked the spirit away—Brother Wolf didn't like to be touched by anyone except Anna. But no one else could see it . . . and he had enough of a reputation for oddness. He didn't need people to know that he saw things no one else did, too.

When he could be reasonably sure that Brother Wolf would allow him to behave in a civilized manner, he stood up.

"Vampires," he said. "Bring her into the warehouse for Arthur." It wouldn't help the British wolf—except as confirmation that she was out of the vampires' hands.

FRUSTRATED, Anna looked at the bag dangling twenty feet over their heads, up one of the long shafts that occasionally perforated the ceiling of this level—after their near disaster with the airless room, Anna was pretty sure that the shafts were useful.

As she stared at it, a wolf snatched victory out of their reach.

It was too dark to be sure who it was, even if she had known all the other wolves in their furred form. The wolf leapt out of an opening a story above the bag, snatched the prize, and disappeared into another opening a floor lower, still well over Anna's head. Watching helplessly as their prize was stolen out from under . . . okay, above their noses, was maddening.

Isaac snorted in disgust.

And Brother Wolf was . . . surrounding her, his anxiety, his fear and love making her stagger against Isaac—which Brother Wolf did not like at all.

Something was wrong. But when she asked, Brother Wolf couldn't or wouldn't tell her.

She had to get to Charles. Now. The problem was, Anna didn't know precisely *how* to get back—oh, she could have backtracked, but they had wandered all over the place and would have had to go through the narrow tunnel again.

Up would be good.

She was running full speed ahead when a white wolf pushed in front of her. A second wolf was hard on her tail—Isaac and Ric.

It was Isaac who found the first set of stairs headed up. They emerged on the ground floor of the smaller warehouse, and when they made for the door, a werewolf in human form stopped them.

"If you cross the outer door, you are officially done," he said.

The Alpha wolf stared coldly at him and the man dropped his eyes, throwing up his hands as he backed away. "Just saying what I'm told, man. You go outside, that's out of bounds."

They ran past him and out into the fresh air. Ric, his fur gray in the light of the yard, sneezed his pleasure at leaving the underground labyrinth behind. Anna took in a deep breath and smelled—vampire.

She stumbled to a halt, examining their surroundings

for the enemy. At last she saw him standing on the other side of the chain-link fence a hundred yards away.

It took a moment for her eyes to link the spiffily dressed older man to the vicious killer she'd last seen sitting on top of Tom. But her nose had already made the connection. She'd gotten two good strides in when she hit the side of the white wolf, who'd run in front of her to stop her, his attention on the vampire as well.

The dead man laughed and motioned with his hand. A blue minivan drove up, and he climbed in. It took off before he'd finished closing the door.

Isaac growled low in his chest, an echo of the noise she was making, too. He'd known what that one was, all right. Ric gave them both a puzzled look—but Anna had never run into vampires before yesterday either.

There didn't seem to be much point in sticking around here, so Anna turned and made for the main room of the bigger warehouse, where the lights were blazing, Brother Wolf's presence an ache in her chest.

Inside the warehouse, all of the wolves who had stayed in human form were gathered in a tight group, focused inward. There were too many of them for her nose to tell her anything.

All of the clothes had been pushed against the wall, and it took her a while to sort hers out. By the time she had them collected, Charles had found her. His eyes were all for the gathering in the center of the room, and there was an odd stiffness to his body that worried her.

She changed, her body protesting the shift even more than it had when she'd taken wolf form. She, like all the wolves, had been well trained not to make much noise while she shifted, but, damn, it hurt.

"Ow, ow, ow," she whispered as her hands slowly, gratingly, reluctantly re-formed as wholly human. She tucked them under her arms and squeezed, the pressure helping the pain. Every change was different, but she hated the ones where her hands were the last thing to make it to human. There are so many nerves in a hand, and all of them hurt. It left her light-headed.

Charles growled at her pain.

She looked up, but there was no one anywhere close to them. Ric and his Alpha were still caught up in their change on the other side of the pile of clothing. She glanced at him and let her body grow still. His eyes were yellow, and the corner of his mouth twitched, then twitched again, as if he had a nervous tic.

"Charles?" her voice was still hoarse from the change.

"Sunny's dead." His voice was guttural, and she knew that he was on the verge . . . of something.

Anna worried about it for all of a half second before his words registered. "Arthur's Sunny?"

He nodded a quarter of an inch, his eyes locked on her face. "Vampires. We found her body just outside the gates."

And the vampires had hidden, waiting for the wolves to find Sunny. When he—the vampire in the suit—saw Anna, he made sure she saw him, too. Staring into those wild gold eyes, she decided it was something she would tell Charles in a while. The vampires were gone. She had the plate number, but it wouldn't matter: probably the van was rented anyway.

A wolf howled, a wild mournful cry, and a half dozen other voices lifted in song to show their sympathy for one who had lost his mate—all of them from human throats.

Charles held out his hand, and Anna let him pull her to her feet. She was a little stiff still—and he looked as though he needed something to do.

He used his body to shield her from the sight of anyone

in the rest of the room, as if he knew she didn't really like being naked in front of a bunch of strangers. Most wolves got over that in the first year of being changed. For Anna, it was still an effort. Not because of modesty, but because clothing gave her the illusion of safety from the attention of the males of her first pack.

She grabbed her clothing and put it on as quickly as she could, shoving her feet into her tennis shoes while she tucked her socks in her pockets.

"Is Arthur all right?" she asked.

Charles closed his eyes and pulled her to him, pressing his nose into the crook of her neck, breathing in like a marathon runner.

"No," he said. "And neither am I."

Her skin hurt, her bones ached, and she wanted to be held as much as a person who'd fallen asleep on the beach for four hours without sunscreen would want to cuddle. But because he needed it, she relaxed against him.

Sunny had been killed by vampires.

"Sunny would have been an Omega if she'd been turned." She made it a statement, but she meant it as a question.

"Yes."

Anna shivered, and his grip tightened. Her change-sensitive skin protested, her sore muscles complained, but her wolf wanted to burrow inside of him, to keep him safe.

SHE was here, she was safe. He let the reality of her, of her scent, push away the need to make something bleed.

He was holding her too tightly, he knew it. Just as he knew she needed time to recover, and he couldn't give it to her. The sound of her pain as she changed had stirred the wolf up again. Brother Wolf wanted blood or sex, and he wasn't going to get either. No blood—and no sex, not until he calmed down a lot. Brother Wolf wouldn't hurt Anna, but he might scare her.

Holding Anna was the next best thing. Gradually, as she softened against him, Brother Wolf consented to settle down a bit. It would be a long time before he calmed enough to cede Charles full control again. It was too easy to see Arthur's agony and understand that it could have been his own.

The attacks were odd. Too focused on the wrong things, the wrong people, to accomplish anything. The attack on Anna could have been an attempt to kidnap her for ransom or hostage. But Sunny's death accomplished nothing. Anna's death would accomplish nothing. He couldn't see why Omegas would be targeted—especially since one wasn't a wolf. So maybe they had targeted the mates of two of the three most powerful or dominant wolves at the conference. What would that accomplish? Especially given that the talks had done all that they could.

He couldn't see the shape of what the vampires, or whoever hired them, were after yet. Nothing fit.

Omega.

Anna thought the vampires were working for a wolf. Her personal experience with the enemy gave her instincts weight, and he would trust her insight—Brother Wolf did, and that was good enough for him.

Whatever the ultimate goal, Charles could think of at least one reason why a wolf might hire someone to murder Sunny and attack Anna. A wolf, especially a dominant wolf, would have a hard time deliberately hurting an Omega, even a human Omega.

Maybe even Chastel wouldn't have been able to do it.

Charles made himself let Anna go and stepped back to give her space. He tried to ignore the relief in her body posture—it wasn't a reaction to him. It was the feel of the change still lingering on her flesh that made her want to stand alone.

"You're the first ones back," he told Anna. "What brought you in so early?"

She gave him an odd look. "Brother Wolf told me you needed me here."

He had no idea what to say to that. Should he admit that he had no idea what Brother Wolf had been up to? Would that worry her? Before he had to make a decision, Dana broke free of the group around Arthur and approached Charles.

"There is some concern for Arthur's sanity," she murmured softly as soon as she was close.

And there were no other wolves here who would stand a chance of controlling Arthur if he lost it, she meant. They needed him to be on watch.

"I'm coming," Charles said.

"I'll come over, too," Anna told him. "It can't hurt, right?"

He didn't want her anywhere near the other wolves. There were too many of them. If they all attacked her, there was no way for him to protect her.

But an Omega wolf could be useful.

"Thank you," he told Anna as he argued silently with Brother Wolf. "That would help."

Arthur was sitting on the ground, cradling his mate in his arms and whispering to her while the others held a wary vigil. His face was streaked with tears and his nose ran. "Sunny girl, my sunny girl."

He looked up, and his eyes focused on Charles. "She is gone."

"Yes," Charles said.

"Vampires did this," he whispered. Then he roared, his voice echoing in the tall room. *"They hurt her!"*

"I know. I will find them."

"Kill them." Arthur's face was ravaged, almost unrec-ognizable in his grief and rage. In his pain.

"I will."

Arthur tightened his hold on his wife, tucking her head against his shoulder. "She hated growing old," he said, rock-ing her. "Now she won't have to. My poor Sunny girl."

Angus said to Charles, though he made no effort to quiet his voice, "He'll survive. If the madness was going to take him, it would have already done so. That being so, it might be a good thing to remove our fallen and wounded from the hunting grounds altogether." He looked at Arthur a moment. "Arthur, would you let us take you home? The others will be here soon, fresh from the hunt." A dead body smelling of fear and pain was not, probably, going to send any of these wolves into a frenzy. But there was no use in taking the chance.

"Yes." Arthur stood up, his wife cradled in his arms. Charles thought that Angus might be a little too quick to pronounce Arthur well. He swayed a little and looked shocky—still, it would be better to get him away from the hunt.

But he couldn't go alone. He hadn't brought any of his pack—a statement of strength and, maybe, trust. But that left him alone in a foreign county with his dead wife.

Angus met Charles's eyes briefly, maybe he saw the panic in them—Charles wasn't up to comforting Arthur tonight. Offering comfort wasn't something he was very good at on his best day.

The Emerald City Alpha looked over his shoulder at one of his wolves. "Send someone to find Alan Choo. Bring me Tom." He glanced at Charles, not long enough to be a challenge, just enough to indicate he was talking to him when he said, "Alan's cousins own a funeral parlor. His family takes care of our dead, they know what we are, and they can help Arthur now. And if Tom and his witch can fight off a pack of vampires—they should be able to keep Arthur on track."

"You wanted me, Angus? I was just outside." Tom's usually easy glide was a little stiff—the only thing that showed he wasn't fully recovered from his fight. His calm gaze took in the distraught werewolf and Sunny's corpse. "I see. You send someone after Alan, too?"

"Yes. Gather a couple of more pack members, your witch, and Alan—he'll be here in a moment—and see if you can settle Arthur in for the night at his house."

Charles pulled out his wallet and extracted one of Arthur's cards—he had two, one from his father and one from Arthur. "This is where he's living in Seattle. Someone should take his wife's car back to his house as well. It's the blue Jaguar parked just inside the gate—I don't know what he drove here."

"I do." Tom took the card. "I'll see to it." And within a few minutes he'd extracted Arthur, the body, and a handful of Angus's wolves as skillfully as a surgeon.

And the first victor of the hunt came into the room just as the door closed behind Tom. Charles looked around for his Anna and found her talking to Ric and Isaac, her face solemn.

Better that she talk with them than with him at this moment. He wanted to take her away, fly her home, where the vampires and whoever was behind them would never be able to come. Lock her in his house and bar the door.

Yes, it was better that he not talk to her just yet.

THE wolf who came in was carrying their bag. Anna could recognize the scent of it, of Moira's hands on it, even in human form. The wolf who brought it in paused in front of their group, and she caught his scent. This was the wolf they'd found trussed up in the net early in their hunt.

"Yes, Valentin, dear," said Isaac. "I see that you got it. Congratulations." Under the biting sarcasm, Anna heard Isaac's reluctant amusement. "Get it away from here, it stinks."

The smell of rotten pork *was* a little overwhelming.

The wolf grinned around his prize and continued to where Dana and Angus awaited him. The bag was taken and tagged with a marker.

"So the talks are doomed," Anna said, continuing the conversation the wolf had interrupted. Charles hadn't told her about today, maybe he hadn't admitted defeat yet—but Isaac seemed pretty certain.

Isaac shrugged. "Anything is possible—except defying Chastel outright. I expect everyone will go home without accepting anything the Marrok has offered." He smiled at her, though there was darkness under the expression. "Then they'll call him and make quiet deals. Nothing as good as what we could accomplish openly—but maybe, just maybe, enough for our survival."

"Why doesn't anyone go after Chastel?"

"Because he's as good as he claims. The fields of Europe are graves for a good many of our dead who have tried to kill the Beast. Maybe the Marrok could take him on—but in Chastel's own territory, I would not bet on the Marrok. Here?" He shrugged. "But the Marrok is not here, and I do not think that Charles is his match."

"He made Chastel back down," she said, "twice."

"When Chastel hunts, you don't get a chance to face him down." Isaac's face was grim. "That's not how he takes his prey unless they are children or human women." He looked at her. "In the first hundred years he lived, he killed three *hundred* humans that we know of, probably more. Many, many he took in broad daylight in front of their friends and families. They shot him, hit him, and nothing happened.

"Late in the eighteenth century, Chastel concentrated his killing in Gévaudan, France. It was so bad there that the peasants—those who worked the land—would no longer go out into their fields. Frightened, the nobles organized hunting parties, hired wolf-hunters, and killed every wolf in the region—and many werewolves, too. The king of France was bestirring himself, then history tells us a man named Jean Chastel, whose wife had just been killed by the beast, took a silver musket ball made from a melted heirloom cross. He had it blessed three times by the village priest and went out with a small party to hunt the animal down. A great Beast appeared before them, and Chastel shot it once and killed it—and so died the Beast of Gévaudan."

"What really happened to stop him?"

"The Marrok happened," said Ric.

"He wasn't the Marrok yet," Isaac corrected. "The story I think is most likely is that Bran Cornick hunted the Beast down and told him unless he put an end to things, he would see that Chastel ended up in the hands of the witches." He smiled a little. "The witches were more powerful in those days—and would have liked nothing better than a were-wolf to torture for blood, meat, and fur for their spells. Chastel was a hundred years old—and Bran was . . . *Bran*. It was a very good threat, then. Now Chastel is stronger than he was then, smarter, too—and he hates Bran like any dominant hates the one who humiliates him."

"He's doing this to get back at Bran?"

Isaac shook his head. "Many reasons, I think. That is one. So is what he said about keeping the Marrok out of his territory."

"Does Sunny's death change anything?" She was still trying to figure out a reason for the woman's death, but she couldn't find one.

Another wolf came in, weary and limping—but he had a bag in his mouth. He paid no attention to them, and only Anna seemed to notice his passing.

Isaac shrugged in answer to Anna's question. "If anything, it adds a final straw to the issue. Arthur is perceived as Charles's strongest supporter: the only one of us far enough from the Beast to risk displeasing him. I'm not sure that is true, except in 'the enemy of my enemy' sort of sense. Arthur and Bran . . . don't see eye to eye about a lot of things. That doesn't matter, though. Arthur won't be any good for weeks after this. Losing your mate is . . ." His face twisted a little, then, with effort, regained its usual good-natured expression. "He won't be of help to Charles, that is for certain."

The first victorious wolf had already changed back to human and, naked, was searching through the piles for his clothes. Which reminded Anna that she still had her socks in the pockets of her jeans and her feet were uncomfortable. She toed off her shoes and put the socks on her feet where they belonged.

She was kneeling to tie her shoes when the third winner came into the room. She'd never seen his wolf form before, but his scent told her exactly who he was: Chastel.

As soon as he walked into the room, someone set off the alarm and the whole of the warehouse sounded with a low hum for a count of five. Then again for another count of five: the signal that the third bag had been found.

Anna hardly heard it. Chastel was the most humongous werewolf she'd ever seen. Ric was larger than average; Charles was bigger than he; and Chastel made both of them look like half-grown puppies. He looked like a Saint

Bernard in a roomful of German shepherds—the statistical outlier. His coat was mottled in various shades of brown: the perfect color to blend with a forest.

He met her eyes, his own yellow and mad, and she backed away, bumping into Isaac, who steadied her with a hand on both shoulders and pulled her upright. Chastel trotted from the doorway he'd come through to the place where Anna stood with her hunting comrades.

He stopped in front of her and dropped the bag, taking a step back—an invitation.

"I have a mate," she said. Ric had been right about her participation in the hunt, she realized. She'd been in this room, with all these wolves, and not felt a lick of fear. Here, where Charles was, where her friends were—however new they might be—she wasn't afraid. "And I want nothing from you."

His jaw dropped and let his tongue loll out as he smiled at her—creepy bastard. He took the bag up again. He took a pace beyond them, then turned and lunged at her, dropping his bag on the floor to free his jaws. He was fast, so fast. She pushed herself backward and hit Isaac, who was just standing there, not moving at all.

She had no chance to get out of the Beast's way and she waited for his fangs to sink into her. Blood rushed to her head, and she had time to understand that he was going to kill her. In front of all these wolves, he was going to kill her, and no one would be able to do anything about it until it was too late.

And she was not afraid. It had never been death that scared her—it was being helpless.

He stopped his own attack, pulling back at the last moment and snapping his jaws just short of her throat, which he could have reached with both front feet on the floor. Too late, Isaac jerked back, pulling her with him. Chastel gave

them all a satisfied look, turned back to retrieve his bag—
and Brother Wolf blindsided him.

The attack was swift and silent; Anna was as surprised
as Chastel. She hadn't even seen Charles move—hadn't felt
him change to wolf.

Chastel snarled and growled, but Charles was dead quiet
and all the more frightening for it. There was an intensity
to his attack that Chastel was missing: Charles was aiming
for the kill, and Chastel was still trying to figure out what
was going on.

Anna had seen Charles fight before—but he'd been exhausted and wounded or reluctant—and mostly in human
form. Brother Wolf on the offensive was an entirely different thing. There was no intelligence, no science to the way
he fought here.

The other wolves backed away, clearing room for the
fight. There were no cheers or raucous comments. The
witnesses, like Charles, were quiet, intent, as the battling
wolves dug in deep with claws and fangs. This wasn't a
game, and no one treated it as such.

If the size difference worried Charles at all, Anna
couldn't see it. Once Chastel settled in to battle it wasn't
nearly as one-sided as it had been at first—and it was
brutal. Fur made it difficult to tell how badly either was
wounded, but they were both bloody. When they broke
apart and stood, heads lowered, fangs bared, blood dripped
off their bodies and made little puddles on the wooden
floor beneath them.

Chastel dove under Charles and snapped his teeth closed
on Charles's hind leg. Before the French wolf's grip was
sure, Charles jerked the leg forward, twisted like a contor-
tionist at *Cirque du Soleil*, and set his fangs into Chastel's
nose. Anna could hear the crunch from where she stood.

Chastel forgot everything but getting Charles off his

muzzle—releasing Charles's back leg, then pulling, pushing, shaking—anything to get the other wolf off. Brother Wolf, who was Charles, held on like a bulldog while the French wolf's struggles became more and more feeble. Until his eyes closed and his body twitched helplessly.

Something tried to direct her attention away from Charles. A soft *look here, look here* from inside her—but Anna was busy trying to see how badly hurt he was.

Angus stepped forward. "Let him go, Charles."

Brother Wolf jerked his head around—bringing Chastel's massive and limp body with him. He looked Angus in the eyes and growled. Angus paled and backed up half a dozen steps until he bumped into Dana—who was watching the fight, looking far too pleased.

Cold chills chased up Anna's spine as she looked at the fae whose job it was to ensure order. *Yes, here. Look. Look. She means him harm,* whispered Anna's wolf.

The intent was written in the fae's body, not her face, which showed only worry. But her body gave it away, the eager flex of fingers, a shift of weight—she was ready to spring for the kill. A hunt was up and, for the fae, Charles was the star-ruby ring at the end of it.

Anna's wolf told her, *We will stop her. No one hurts the one who is ours.*

"Yes," whispered Anna.

Dana spoke, "Charles Cornick, you have broken the peace here. Release him."

Brother Wolf didn't even bother to look at her. What had he called her? She-Who-Is-Not-Kin, who thought she ruled him here in the place that belonged to the werewolves. Anna could all but touch his thoughts from his body language. Chastel tried to fight again and her mate sank down lower to increase his leverage. After a moment, the French wolf lay still again.

Anna had no trouble with Chastel's death—the consequences for Charles were another matter entirely. If she'd
thought Charles would fight the fae, she'd have been less
worried. But her mate was, in his heart of hearts, a man
of order. If Chastel died because he was trying to terrify
Anna, and the fae decided to call it a break of the truce,
Charles might just concede the point. She didn't know what
the fae would do to him, and she didn't intend to find out.

Anna pulled away from Isaac's slack hold.

"Charles, let him go," she said, walking to the middle
of the cleared area. She'd almost addressed him as Brother
Wolf, but somehow that seemed too intimate, too private
to be shared.

It was certainly Brother Wolf, not Charles, who turned to
look at her, his eyes glazed with rage. She tried to open the
connection between them wider, but Charles was holding
himself apart—trying to protect her from what he was.

She went to him and tapped him on the nose, ignoring the rage that, finally, made him growl full-throated and
angry.

"Open up." She hadn't been afraid, but his growls and
the smell of blood and other things made her remember
too much. Remember when the blood, the desperation, had
been hers.

Her hands were shaking, and she was breathing through
her nose like a racehorse at the end of the Kentucky Derby.
But she stuck her thumb in his mouth and pulled, his canine
sliding along the edge of her hand and slicing it open.

As soon as he tasted her blood, he dropped his hold, letting the other wolf's head flop on the ground, and backed
violently away from her. She didn't know if Chastel was
alive or dead—couldn't bring herself to care, though she
knew it would be important in just a minute. Right now, all
of her attention was on Brother Wolf.

The red wolf who was both Brother Wolf and Charles stared into her eyes, and she saw him grasp just one thing out of all the things he could have seen in her. She was scared to death—of the fae, of the blood and anger, of her own audacity—but all he let himself see was the fear, not the reasons for it.

He held her eyes for a moment more, then trotted out the door—which opened for him, though no one held it, and slammed as soon as he was through.

"After him," said Dana in a voice like cut glass. "He drew first blood."

Her voice provided impetus to men who had been immobile observers, and they started toward the door.

"Stop," Anna said . . . and then did something she'd never done, not quite like this. But the wolf knew how to do it, she'd used Charles's power to change faster than she ever had before—and she used it now to put strength into her voice. *"Stop."*

And the wolves, on two feet and four, who'd begun to move for Dana, stopped where they were and turned to look at her.

The fae turned to her, too, and *her* voice had power as well. "He drew first blood. I am fae, I cannot lie. My word is that the one who drew blood during the hunt would be punished: blood for blood. The walls cry out for my word to be fulfilled."

She left her eyes on Anna but touched Angus, who stood nearby. "Liam Angus Magnusson, son of Margaret Hooper, son of Thomas Magnusson. By your true name, I tell you to fetch me Charles Cornick."

Angus took a step toward the door.

"No," said Anna, and her wolf made it stick.

Angus turned back to her, a slow smile on his face. "Yes, my lady," he told Anna. The smile grew. "You are forgetting something, Dana Shea. The hunt was over. The bells rang before Charles attacked, and the rule of blood no longer applies."

Dana's face froze, and for one instant Anna read in her eyes a lust for Charles's death, for any death. A lust that rivaled anything she'd ever seen in a werewolf. But the fae regained control, and she smoothed her hands over her suit jacket as if it were wrinkled. "Ah. You are right."

"Chastel threatened Anna, Charles's mate," Angus continued briskly. "Outside of the hunt, such a thing justifies the attack under our laws."

He was right. Anna had been so wrapped up in how Charles felt about the situation that she hadn't pulled back enough to see the full truth. Even though Chastel hadn't harmed her, the threat was enough to justify Charles's in-the-heat-of-the-moment attack. Charles might not feel that way, but the wolves would—and it was enough to force Dana Shea to change her position.

"Not to the death," said Dana.

"He's not dead," parried Ric, who knelt beside the fallen Frenchman with Michel, the French Alpha. Someone, maybe Michel, murmured, "More's the pity."

Angus strode to the wolf on the ground and took a good look. "Not even badly wounded," he said, sounding a little disappointed himself. "Charles just cut off his air, he'll be fine in a few minutes except for a very sore nose."

"Good," said Anna. She walked past Angus and Dana, but stopped at the door. "Finish up here," she said. "I'll go talk to Charles."

HE hadn't gone to the gate, which was what she'd expected him to do.

Anna didn't have much experience at tracking, and most

of what she did know needed snow. The gravel would have defeated her if her quarry hadn't been bleeding like a stuck pig. Impossible to miss that the trail went in exactly the opposite direction from the gate. All that blood worried her, and she picked up her pace. Gravel changed to mud—and mud wasn't a bad second choice to snow. Charles had big paws, and his claws dug in deeply as he headed toward the water that edged the warehouse district they were in.

He hadn't been running—rather a steady trot that made her hope that he hadn't been too badly hurt despite the blood. His tracks took her to the fence at the back of the compound. Twelve feet of chain link with razor wire—and wounded, he'd managed to jump it. She wasn't sure she could have, even in wolf form. And she wouldn't change again so soon unless she had to. In twenty minutes, maybe. But she wasn't going to wait that long.

There had been something wrong in Brother Wolf's gaze. Something mad . . . maddened. As she contemplated the fence, she remembered a challenge he'd issued to her as they went to see Dana Shea for the first time. They'd both forgotten about it.

"What kind of a fae is Dana Shea?" she muttered to herself as she searched for a way past the fence. Dana was something strong enough to frighten a troll, certainly, strong enough to be a Gray Lord—though Anna had no real idea how strong that would have to be. Something that ate people—the hunger the fae'd shown was unmistakably predatory. Something to do with water—she lived in a houseboat and still had a water fountain and pond inside.

La Belle Dame Sans Merci. The beautiful lady without mercy, who lured men to her river or stream and drowned them. Made them believe something that wasn't.

Made them believe something that wasn't.

Charles had proven himself immune to Dana's spell

of desire. Maybe he wasn't immune to all of her magic, though.

Charles had been kind of on edge tonight. But he was smart, he was quick-thinking—and he attacked after Chastel had withdrawn. That was very uncharacteristic. She'd been worried about the consequences of that—how Charles would feel about his actions. She hadn't stopped to think that was because his actions had been so far out of the ordinary for him.

Her mate knew more about Dana, he'd told her so—and presumably Bran knew even more than Charles. She'd ask him about it, tell him about what she'd seen in Dana's face—as soon as she found Charles.

She went to the nearest fence post and pulled the chain link until she'd popped all the retaining clips that attached it to the post. Then she jerked it up, feeling the bite of it in her shoulders and biceps. It wasn't something a human of her size could have done: there were a few benefits to being a werewolf. When she was done, she had a big enough hole to crawl through—she'd have to remember to tell Angus he needed to fix his fence.

She followed Charles's trail, not hurrying because he wasn't. She didn't know what she'd find at the end of the trail, but she was pretty sure it would be better if she didn't find him too soon. Or too late.

Would he expect the hunt that Dana had been so quick to send out? Was he ready to face dozens of the toughest wolves Europe had to offer? Did he expect Angus to come after him? Or Dana herself? Had he felt it when Anna had drawn upon his power to stop the fae woman? Could he feel her coming after him now? The bond between them sang with strength and tension, but that was all she could sense through it.

Except . . . she found that as she thought about it, she

could tell where he was. He was releasing his hold on their bond, not hiding so hard. Anna stopped at that thought. Was that what he was doing? Hiding from her?

He was not a violent man by nature. She knew that, had felt his gentleness herself. He had made himself into the man his father needed, his pet killer, his sword arm. He was very, very good at his job.

But Brother Wolf craved blood and flesh. Her own wolf didn't: it was one of the differences that being Omega gave her. She remembered Charles's stopping in front of his father's house when it smelled of blood and pain. He'd asked her what she smelled, then told her that if she were not Omega, the smell would have made her hungry.

He'd been hungry, though he hadn't told her that.

In her wolf form, she could eat raw meat and like it. But when she was human, blood smelled like blood, not food.

Anna started walking again and noticed that he was headed downhill, toward the . . . she squinted and wasn't able to figure out if it was the Sound, or just another of the saltwater lakes that were everywhere she looked in Seattle. She hadn't thought to ask when they drove here; she'd been worried about the hunt.

There was a narrow path next to an equally narrow freshwater stream that slid through the blackberry brambles, now barren of berries and full of dead leaves and thorns. The path was mud and sucked at her shoes, half pulling them off, as it threatened to give way entirely and dump her in the creek.

Charles's paw prints stuck deep, where he'd stopped to drink. Bleeding made you thirsty, she knew. The blood trail had been less and less easy to follow. She hoped it was because he was healing. The more dominant wolves healed faster—as long as you didn't combine wounds with silver, exhaustion, or magic.

Couldn't help but worry about him anyway.

So it was with great relief she made it down to the beach, a rocky, wet, and cold stretch of land, and saw Charles shaking himself off. He'd been in the water, cleaning the blood off. "Brave of you," Anna told him. "That water is too freaking cold for words." But she'd never had cause to doubt Charles's courage.

Amber eyes watched her as she slid down the last ten feet of slope with more grace than she'd expected, only to stumble as her shoes hit the better traction the small rocks of the beach gave her.

"So," she told Brother Wolf, "I have some things to talk to you about when you're ready. But we're safe enough for now. I left Angus in charge, back at the warehouse." Had she? Maybe Angus had left himself in charge at the warehouse.

The rocks were only high and dry in a strip about six inches wide. She looked at her muddy shoes and, deciding there was nothing she could do that would make them worse, she stepped out into about six inches of icy water. The air left her in a startled hiss. "Very cold," she told him, then started off down the shoreline because her body didn't want to stand still.

TEN

CHARLES stood where he was, the icy water covering his paws and a few inches beyond. He'd been waiting for the goon squad and gotten the beauty instead, and it left him oddly defenseless.

She walked along the shoreline, her muddy shoes splashing in the water that covered the rocks. Above them, beyond them, and to both sides, docks stretched out into the black water. Four or five docks down there was a ship being loaded, and he could hear the men talking in the grunting rhythms that working men have. They were far enough away that they would not see a woman and her very large dog walking along the water's edge.

He decided she was getting too far from him, and so he followed, padding behind her to make sure she was safe. He hadn't killed the Beast who threatened her . . . a growl rose in his chest at the thought. He should have killed him. Should have torn his head off so he would no longer hurt the weak and helpless ones. Not hurt his Anna. No matter that she was proving to be neither weak nor helpless.

Brother Wolf scented the air, but the scent of the other wolves was distant. Ahead of him Anna had found a log that had washed ashore, now a throne for his lady. But first she had to climb all over it.

He detoured around it, making sure it would stay stable—and found it difficult to close the distance between them.

She had seen him in action before, had seen him kill, and she had not flinched from him. But this had been different, Charles knew it. This had been . . . not unprovoked, but certainly not necessary either.

Chastel thought too much of his own hide to try anything while in the middle of a pack of enemy wolves. He wouldn't have hurt her, not right then. None of that had mattered to Charles, though—all he could see was those fangs buried in Anna's throat and him all the way across the building and too freaking slow.

He looked at her, just to make sure his vision hadn't happened. She'd found a comfortable spot and stretched out on it, her face tilted toward him, resting on her extended arm.

Anna had said she wanted to talk about some things. She hadn't sounded angry or, worse, disappointed.

And there were things he needed to know. Like why there weren't dozens of wolves bringing him in—he'd heard Dana call for his hide, had expected them. Why Anna said *she* had left Angus in charge—though he expected that it had something to do with the pull he'd felt from her shortly after he'd left the warehouse.

If Brother Wolf hadn't been foremost, he'd have simply waited for the other wolves, acting for Dana, to attack him in the warehouse. But Brother Wolf had demanded the chance to choose the battleground. That meant down to the shore, so the deep water at his back kept him from being flanked—werewolves don't swim, they sink.

And Dana's element was freshwater, not salt.

But Anna had pulled the rug out from under his battle plans. They weren't coming after him—and Angus, not Dana, had been left in charge. Anna, who was all alone on her log, watching him out of the corner of her eye while he paced.

He kept his distance for a while longer. While he was wolf and Anna a good distance away from him, she couldn't tell him that . . . what? She was disgusted by his attack on Chastel? That he'd scared her? Or, possibly even worse, she enjoyed watching? She wouldn't say any of it, and he knew her well enough to understand that.

So he didn't know why he came to her as wolf and not man. She sat up and patted the log in front of her. He hopped up and she hugged him, long fingers playing with his ears and the sensitive spots on his face.

She leaned against him. "Love you," she said.

That was what he'd needed. He took a deep breath and changed. She backed away, giving him space.

"How come you don't have four dozen red or blue T-shirts and fifty pairs of boots?" Anna asked when he was finished. "And do you think this mate thing would work well enough that I could change back to human with clothes instead of stark naked?"

He glanced down at himself, fully clothed as usual. No other werewolf he'd ever heard of could clothe himself coming out of the change. He didn't know if it was were-wolf magic or a bit of the magic of his shaman grandfather. He only knew that it had started happening when he was fourteen or fifteen and being naked was considered shameful in his mother's tribe. Then it had been buckskins—he could still do those if he thought about it.

Charles turned around so he was facing her, looked hard at her grinning face, and took it in his hands and kissed her as if he could fill himself with her. She opened her mouth and let him in, welcoming him with warm touches and small sounds. They had not been together long enough for even the most basic touches to become routine—but he didn't think he could ever take her kisses for granted, the touch of her tongue, teeth, and lips.

When he pulled away, he left his face against hers as he said, "I don't know. We'll just have to see—keep a count of the red T-shirts, maybe."

"Why red?" she asked. "Why not green or blue this time? I've seen you do blue. Do you pick?"

He laughed, needing this, small intimacies he'd never had before Anna. "I don't know. No one ever asked, and I never paid attention."

She put her mouth against his ear, and the feel of her breath in his ear certainly made him pay attention. "I bet they wondered, though. Too scared of the big bad wolf to ask."

He laughed again, the relief of her presence—not just Omega but his Anna—making laughter necessary, whatever the excuse.

She pulled back, her eyes still smiling. "Dana is a water fae, isn't she? The ones who lure men into the water and drown them."

"Yes."

"How did she do it? Was it compulsion—or was it some sort of manipulation?"

He couldn't read anything in her face. "I don't know. Why are you asking?"

"It's not like you to freak out like that—not without planning it better. And Chastel. He is how old? His modus operandi is more subtle than it was tonight, right? He takes out little kids and human women in front of people too weak to hurt him. You, he would never antagonize like that, not where you would be justified in attacking him face-to-face."

With Anna here, Brother Wolf settled down into a contented presence. Charles could think more clearly, consider tonight's oddities.

"Not quite true. He is reckless sometimes—and no coward, really. He likes to play games: his lunge at you that would have been fatal if he'd wanted it to be—that is very much the Beast of Gévaudan." But she was right in that the Frenchman's behavior had been odd. "But that moment when he laid the bag, his prize, at your feet, *that* was unusual." He thought a moment. "Romantic, even. I don't know that I've ever heard Chastel had a partner. Women, mostly, he kills. Children, too. It's as if their fragility calls out the worst in him."

"He told Ric and me that he was the opposite of the Omega. All the violence, none of the protective spirit."

Charles felt his eyebrows go up. "That's perceptive," he said. "I would have just called him a sociopath. My father calls him evil."

" 'Evil' works for me," Anna muttered. She played with the bark of the tree: mostly rotted from its immersion in the water, it virtually dissolved under her fingers.

"But the thing with the bag wasn't typical of Chastel," Charles said. "And . . . what I did wasn't usual either. Not like that. It felt like he had done it, ripped your throat out— even though I knew very well that he hadn't touched you. You think the fae had something to do with it?"

"I think I read bloodlust on her body when you attacked Chastel. The first thing out of her lips was an accusation— of something you actually hadn't done. Stupid fae hadn't remembered that once the bells sounded, the hunt was over." Anna's nails dug into the tree as if she had claws, and her voice was hard. "She wanted you as her prey."

And he knew, suddenly, that the reason Dana hadn't gotten him was sitting beside him on this log. She didn't look tough, his Anna, with her freckled face and body that could still stand to gain ten pounds even though it was considerably more sturdy than it had been the first time he'd seen her. But she was tougher than old shoe leather, and what was hers, she took care of.

"Dana didn't know who she was messing with," he murmured, charmed and awed at the same time.

"Damned right," Anna said. "She was hunting tonight. I don't know who was her initial prey . . . it might be like when a dominant comes into a new pack and looks for the nastiest brute around to fight and so establish his place. I don't know if it was a planned thing or if it just happened."

Charles caught a scent and turned his head. "Angus," he said, as the other wolf walked up to them.

"Let you scent me," Angus said, a little defensively.

"Thank you." Charles decided that wasn't enough as Angus still looked uneasy about interrupting them. "I appreciate it. What do you know?" Because the wolf had been there a little while, and likely would have ghosted back up the hill without saying anything if he didn't have something to contribute.

"I heard a bit of that," said Angus. "Anna's right. I tasted fae magic at work, but I didn't realize what she'd done until you attacked Chastel. She attempted to make you kill Chastel."

"I thought they couldn't do that," Anna said.

"Obviously it's not impossible," said Charles. "And I don't know why they don't. Just that they don't. Ever. They don't break their word, and they don't lie. *Can't* is how I've always heard it. Always. But she did."

"Ask the Marrok," suggested Angus.

Charles reached for his cell phone, then stopped. "No cell phone," he told them.

Anna giggled. "All those red T-shirts and no cell phone? I don't have mine either, left it in the car."

Angus handed his over to Charles. "Red T-shirts? Do I want to know?"

"Probably not," Charles told him as he dialed and put the phone to his ear. Then his da answered and he busied himself laying the whole story before the old bard. Bran listened all the way through without comment. When Charles was done, there was a small pause as his father sorted out what he wanted to discuss.

"Six vampires hunting together," he said finally.

It wasn't a question, but Charles answered it anyway. "Yes."

"I'll look into it. There've been a few stories—I'll check them out more thoroughly. They sound like mercenaries to me: assassins for hire. Angus hasn't had trouble with the Seattle vampires for a good long while—and Tom would have recognized them if they were local. Vampires in a minivan says rental to me—"

"I have the plate numbers," said Anna. "But it looked like a rental car to me, too. American minivan less than five years old." She rattled off three letters and three numbers.

The joy of phone calls with sharp-eared werewolves was that *all* phone calls ended up being conference calls whether he wanted them to or not. At least Charles didn't have to repeat everything anyone said.

He could hear pen running across paper as his da wrote the license-plate number on a piece of paper. "I'll check it out," he said when he was finished writing, "but I suspect she's right. We'll find them faster by other methods. You think they're trained by a werewolf?"

"They fought like a pack," Anna said. "Made their choices like a wolf pack would. Brought in magic that felt just like pack magic."

"That was Tom's assessment, too," Angus said. "Tom's been in a few fights—and can wield pack magic with the best of us."

There was another pause, then the Marrok said in that light pleasant tone that warned everyone who knew him that all hell was about to break loose. "Can you prove Dana caused the fight?"

Charles looked at Anna.

She shook her head. "No. You had to have been there."

"That's so," said Angus. "I saw it, but I doubt anyone else was looking who would recognize what they saw. She would have sent me after Charles, you know, after I refused to go. Bespelled me with my true name. I haven't answered to that name for nigh on a hundred years—and a hundred years ago I was no one. Not Alpha at the time, not even in this country. Be interesting to know how she found out what my birth name was. I doubt there are ten people who'd know after all this time."

"True-named, and you didn't follow orders?"

Angus threw his head back and laughed. " 'For God Almighty himself, Bran. I got my first look at the shivering little thing that is your daughter-in-law quaking in her boots in an auditorium filled with predators and thought your son had found a wererabbit."

"Thank you," said Anna with a nasty edge to her voice.

Not intimidated in the least, Angus grinned at her. But when he talked it was directed at Bran. "I thought she wasn't up to his weight. But that was before she killed a vampire and set that old fairy on her heel. Here's me bespelled by that fae—'Stop,' Anna told me. And damned if I didn't have to listen to her, fae compulsion or no fae compulsion. Broke Dana's hold just as certain as if you had broken it your own self."

"You should have seen her kill the witch a couple of weeks ago," Bran said affably. "*Asil* had been fleeing from this one for two hundred years, and my son's little 'rabbit' killed her while in human form and armed with nothing more than a knife."

"Asil?" asked Angus, suitably taken aback. "*Asil* the Moor?"

"That's the one," said Charles.

"Suddenly I don't feel so bad at being rescued by a rabbit," Angus said cheerfully.

Anna narrowed her eyes at him. "One more rabbit comment, and you'll regret it."

The Marrok spoke into the silence that followed Anna's threat. "If I come now—"

"No," said Charles in instant rejection.

His father sighed. "You did note the 'if,' didn't you?"

There was no good answer to that, so Charles just waited.

Satisfied that his son had been properly brought to order, Bran said, "I do not think it would help at this stage. It certainly wouldn't make any difference to the negotiations. Chastel did exactly as he intended—and we'll work around him."

"I am sorry, sir," said Charles.

"Not at all. It would not have mattered if I had been there. Until one of the Europeans decides to rid the world of Chastel, we'll all have to work around him. It would have been . . . very unexpected had he played ball with us."

"He's not an anti-Omega," said Anna. "He's an anti-Marrok."

Charles explained the reference, and his father laughed easily. Some people might think that would mean he wasn't angry—they'd be wrong. "I suppose both are correct."

"Why don't you take him out?" asked Angus suddenly.

"Not my place," Bran answered. And then said, proving he'd thought of it, "And then I'd have Europe to take care of, too. I can assure you that my plate is more than full. I do not need anything more to do. Are you looking for a job, Angus?"

"Hell, no." The Emerald City Pack leader grinned appreciatively. "Not that I could take on Chastel, anyway. Your son is a nasty, infighting, rat-bastard. I've seen him fight cold before—you should have seen it when he's enraged. Took him all of two minutes to have Chastel on the ground."

"Charles's fights are always fast," said Bran. "Most serious fights are. We aren't cats to play with our food."

Charles heard his father draw in a deep breath as he changed the subject. "So. *Your* job, Charles, as I see it, is to find the vampires who killed our poor Sunny. Eliminate them and find out who hired them. Conduct business as usual tomorrow—and understand that no one can agree to accept help, but they will listen to what you have to say. And we'll help them as we can. This is the only way we can let them know that we'll do so. And keep Dana from making you kill anyone you don't intend to."

"She's broken her word," Anna said.

"We can't prove it," Bran answered.

"What happens when a fae breaks her word?" Charles asked his father. "All I've ever heard is that they don't."

"I haven't the faintest idea," said his father. "I'm not fae—and we have nothing on the fae for keeping secrets. I've never known a fae to break his or her word—bend it, twist it into a pretzel, yes. Break it, no. I would have expected lightning to strike her down from on high. Since that hasn't happened, your guess is the same as mine." He paused. "Be careful. And you might consider wearing your crucifix and finding something that would work for Anna. It's not foolproof, but it is helpful when you're dealing with vampires."

And he rang off.

"You know," Anna said thoughtfully, "I'm kind of disappointed. I thought he knew everything."

"Not everything," admitted Charles. "He's just very good at giving that impression."

"And ad-libbing," said Angus. "Though I've never really caught him at it." He paused. "You know, I'm thinking that he might be that lightning bolt. Hope I'm there to see it."

Charles yawned. "So, tomorrow is one more meeting. I'll pull out some of the more creative things Da kept for last, then . . . perhaps an early end to the negotiations, which are useless now."

"Sunny's death," Anna said. "It seems wrong to let her death be . . . useful to us, but Sunny's death would be a good reason to close the meetings early."

Angus nodded. "No one will be fooled—they know what Chastel has done—but it will allow us to save face."

Aɴɴᴀ burrowed under him and grumbled when Charles laughed as cold toes made it to places cold toes should never hit an adult male. He rolled over on top of her, and she sighed happily, her eyes slitting open and glittering blue in the darkness of the hotel room.

"Well, hello," he murmured to Anna's wolf. "Were-wolves," he informed her solemnly, "are warm-blooded. Very warm-blooded. We don't get cold and stick frigid toes and fingers into places cold things shouldn't go."

She blinked at him a couple of times. "Warm," she said, her voice husky.

"Yes," he answered. "But you could have pulled up the blanket before you got that cold."

She arched up off the mattress and kissed him hard, gripping his jaw in her hands.

While he kissed her, he rolled over until she was on top. Anna's wolf sometimes did things that Anna wasn't comfortable with. He'd learned to make accommodations for that—and one of those things was to make sure that unless Anna was in charge, she got the top. If she woke up underneath him, she had a tendency to panic.

He couldn't communicate with Anna's wolf the way he—and Anna—could talk to Brother Wolf. She tended to come out when Anna was asleep and usually spoke in one-word sentences.

She nipped his ear, tugging on the amber earrings she'd gotten for him.

"Gently," he told her. "I like those earrings."

He ran his hands up the small of her back, and she arched into him with a happy sound. He let her play as she would for a while before catching her hands.

"Hey, lady wolf," he said breathlessly. "We need to wake up your other half before we take this any farther." He didn't actually know how much Anna knew about what her wolf did at times like this—whether she was along for the ride or still asleep. But it didn't seem right to do anything serious unless he was certain Anna knew what her wolf had been up to.

She stared at him, and he watched the change happen, just in her eyes. Blindingly blue eyes warmed to root-beer brown in a few heartbeats. She didn't seem surprised to find herself braced on top of him, just smiled and flexed her hands on his shoulders.

"All right?" he asked.

In answer, she wriggled her hips and pushed herself

down. He groaned at the unexpectedly aggressive move. Anna's wolf did things like that—Anna was usually more temperate. She set a hard and rapid pace, and he let her do as she would.

"I'll just lie back and think of England," he huffed to make her laugh.

It backfired on him because she rose up—and then stopped, holding his hips down by tucking her feet over his thighs. "If you are thinking of England," she said, "I must not be doing this right."

And she did a few things that turned his brain right off.

Afterward, she lay across him like a sweet-smelling blanket—only blankets didn't usually drop kisses down the side of his neck.

He said, "Do you remember when I told you that you were my mate—and you responded by telling me you didn't like sex?"

She giggled at his smug tone. "I thought it only fair to warn you."

"Rabbits like sex," he said blandly.

She sat up and nipped his nose. "I'll *rabbit* you. I know where your ticklish spots are."

Someone knocked on the door, a quick, urgent sound. "It's Angus. Let me in."

Anna squeaked and dove out of the bed, putting on last night's clothes. Charles pulled on his jeans and strode to the door. It was a little after 2:00 A.M.—something urgent must have come up. Especially since Angus hadn't called.

As soon as Anna was decently covered, Charles pulled open the door and invited Angus in. The other wolf hesitated on the threshold but made no other comment on what Charles and Anna had been up to—though even a human nose would probably have picked it up.

"Brought sustenance. Take one," Angus said. He had

a cup holder with four steaming cups: two cocoas, two coffees.

Charles took a cocoa and Anna, who usually drank cocoa with him, abruptly grabbed the coffee.

"Need to wake up," she told him, so he must have looked surprised.

Angus set the holder on the table and took a seat, the other coffee in hand. "Chastel's dead," he said flatly.

"I thought his wounds weren't enough to kill him." Charles actually couldn't remember how much damage he'd done.

"Not from the fight." Angus took a swig of coffee. "Someone shot him with silver buckshot and then . . . It looks like they filleted him. Beat the hell out of Michel, poor bugger. Do you know him? Fractured skull, broken jaw, broken ribs, and other trauma. It'll be a while before he's in any shape to tell anyone anything."

"Who killed him?"

"That's the problem; your scent is the only one present besides Chastel's and Michel's."

"He was with me all night," Anna said indignantly.

Charles gave her a pleased smile. "I didn't kill him, nor had I hand in it."

Angus nodded glumly. "Figured so. But needed you to tell me."

"Filleting a person takes time." Charles supposed that was something he shouldn't admit to knowing. "How professional was the job?"

"I couldn't have butchered a hog as well," Angus said. "And I worked as a butcher for twenty years." He hesitated, then sat on the chair. "Look, I know it wasn't you. This is . . . not your style of kill. Whoever did this was fricking crazy. You'd have just ripped him to pieces and been done with it. But that fae . . . she can't recognize the truth when she hears it. Not like we can—the fae don't accept our word as good enough." He sounded a little bitter.

"As soon as Dana gets news, she's going to be after you—who escaped her clutches before." He gave a little nod to Anna. "I saw it, too, when she focused on Charles as her prey. Outside of truth saying, you look good for this. The fight. His stonewalling the conference. Stalking your mate. Tom's been a policeman off and on for most of his life. He says that what she has on you would get you arrested in human courts—and quite likely convicted." He raised his eyes to Charles, who allowed it. "She doesn't have to convince us or your father, remember. The only higher authority among the fae is the Gray Lords—and good enough for human courts is what they'll look for."

He took a strong swallow of his coffee. "Her word. And she's a Gray Lord. She'll have every fae in the States on your tail. If you resist, if your father resists—and you know he will—it would be war."

"Would she do that?" Anna asked.

"Yes," Angus bit out without hesitation.

"We have to find out who killed him before she hears Chastel is dead, then." Charles said it as if it was no big deal.

"Right."

"Call your minions and have them cancel the dog and pony show for today," said Charles. "Arthur's mate's death is a good enough excuse for now. We need to check out Chastel's death scene, then I'll talk to Michel."

ANGUS was a good guide, stopping at yellow lights so Anna, behind him in the battered Corolla, didn't have to run red lights or risk losing him.

He'd told them that the French wolves had stayed in

a private residence, rented in the Queen Anne district, a neighborhood of well-kept houses on the side of a hill not terribly far from their hotel.

She saw the house before Angus turned on his signal. It was thoroughly modern, standing out from its more traditional neighbors like a sore thumb. And the reason she knew it was the right house was because of the werewolf drinking beer on the front porch.

Ian, their greeter from the airstrip, sat on a metal rocking chair with a can in his hand. The beer was camouflage, she thought. It was cold enough out that a man sitting on his porch at two thirty in the morning for hours was odd—and the beer can made it a little less . . . remarkable. Like he'd been kicked out and was waiting to be let in.

Anna followed Angus's car and parked in the driveway instead of on the street. It was a tight fit—there were already two cars in it—but the Corolla was a tidy little car.

Anna opened her door, and she could smell blood. She glanced at Charles, but he didn't show any sign of noticing. The hunger for raw meat was no new thing to him. He knew what he was and, usually, was able to accept it; accept it well enough that he and Brother Wolf could work together in a way no other wolf did.

At the top of the stairs, Ian held the front door open—while he stood a little to the side, protecting himself as much as possible from the smell of murder. He kept his attention firmly on his Alpha.

"Sir," he said. "No one in since you left. We've guards front and back as you requested. The other Frenchmen are settled in at the hotel as you requested."

"Good."

"Yes, sir." Ian appeared a little stressed. Impulsively, Anna touched his hand.

He took a couple of deep breaths and stared at her.

Angus tapped him on the cheek affectionately. "Omega wolf, my boy. Spreading peace and happiness, it's what they do."

He gestured, and Anna let go of Ian and followed Charles into the house.

"If Dana set this up, she'll know already," said Anna, when the door was shut behind them.

"Yes," Charles said. "Still, no sense advertising it if she doesn't." He paused in the hallway and looked at her. "You understand people better than I do. Do you think Dana would hire vampires? Do you think the vampires could be operating on their own?"

He underestimated himself, she thought, but put her instincts to work anyway.

"She's a Gray Lord. She enjoys playing games—she . . . takes pleasure in making herself look . . . unattractive. Which probably means she's either horribly ugly or stunning without the illusion." She closed her eyes, trying to make it fit. "No way she'd hire a vampire. She wouldn't trust them with her secrets." That was right. "She . . . she'd be okay having someone else do her dirty work—but not for money, I don't think. Someone who owes her—fae minions, maybe. Blackmail. But not hired guns."

"Agreed," said Charles.

"As far as the vampires are concerned . . . When they came after us, there was no emotion, no personal involvement in it. Just doing a job. But then we killed a couple of them, and that made it personal, right? So when they killed Sunny, they messed her up and left her where they did to . . . to count coup on the werewolves."

"Angus?" Charles asked. "Dana lives here. You'll know her better than we do."

"I don't understand women at all," disavowed Angus.

"Add fae to that, and you can count me out." There was a little pause. "But I think Rabbit's got her nailed. Sounds right about the vampires, too."

"Anna," said Charles mildly before Anna could protest. "Not Rabbit."

Angus tilted his head. "Term of respect," he told Anna. "That's all. Anna."

"If you please." Charles didn't dwell on it, he just went on to the next thing. "The vampires have some way of masking their scent from us. Keeps us out of their daytime sleeping places."

Angus froze. "You think this is a vampire kill? Four vampires against Chastel and Michel?"

"The Beast was hurt." Charles avoided saying the names of the dead, usually. Referring to them by a nickname was apparently okay. "Michel . . . is much less dominant than your Tom. His heart is in the right place, but he is no warrior. Otherwise, the Beast would have killed him long since. Where were the rest of the French wolves?"

"At an all-night LAN party."

"A LAN party?" Anna sort of knew what that was. "Isn't that where geeks meet up and play the same game together on a lot of computers?"

Angus nodded. "Alan thought it might be interesting— let them get their aggression out without actually killing anyone." He paused. "And no one actually did—not there, anyway. Anyway, he and a few members of his family, several of my pack, and . . . I think one of the Spaniards took it upon themselves to arrange a LAN party with some first-person shooter game."

"Who would know that there would only be two wolves here?" Anna asked.

"Anyone who read the sign-up sheets—which are on our

semiprivate site on the Internet. That means all of my pack and any of the wolves who came to the conference and took time to check out the welcome materials we provided."

"Assuming our vampires are working for one of us," mused Charles, "they would have known."

"If it's the vampires, they're moving awfully fast," Anna observed. She realized that they were all trying to avoid moving forward, into the house, closer to the smell of blood. "Tom, Moira, and I were attacked the day before yesterday, Sunny yesterday, and Chastel later last night." She didn't want to see it, to go near the evidence of all that pain and death. She thought that maybe the others were fighting exactly the opposite battle.

"Assassins with multiple targets taking them out as fast as they can," suggested Angus. "Strike before the enemy has a chance to pull their pants up and fire back. Busy as little bees."

"The question is, what are they doing? And why?" Charles sounded thoughtful, as if he were talking about a game of chess instead of discussing murder in a pleasant little sitting room that reeked of death. "And is Dana a part of this? Or is she a separate matter altogether?"

He looked at Anna. "You can stay here."

"But you want me to come." She knew she was right, and it surprised her.

"You bring different eyes," he said. "Angus and I—we can decipher the battle. You tell us about the person. Who we are hunting for and what that person is trying to accomplish." He gave her a tight smile. "You see things, why people do things. Vampires who act like wolves. I want you to stay here, but I'm afraid we might need you in there."

She took a deep breath. "Okay. But if I throw up, I'll blame you."

"Granted."

She bent to retie her tennis shoe and caught a glimpse of Angus's face. "He is very protective," she told him. "In a very Nietzschean 'that which does not kill us makes us stronger' sort of way. At least there won't be twenty feet of snow here."

Charles laughed.

No one was smiling when they walked into the room.

Blood soaked the carpet, and the walls were sprayed with it. It was getting old; in a few hours it would start to smell rotten. The walls looked brown rather than red. She didn't look at the two piles of meat and bone and body parts yet. One small step at a time. What did all the blood tell her?

"'Who would have thought the old man to have had so much blood in him,'" murmured Anna.

"I thought you did Latin quotes," said Charles.

"I can't do Shakespeare in Latin." She thought about it a little because that meant she didn't have to look more closely at what was in the room yet. "*Cui bono*, then. Who benefits from this?"

"I can't see how it could possibly be money," said Angus. "Or not only money. Or love, either. Sunny, maybe—but Chastel?"

Anna stepped all the way into the room, and the carpet squished just the way the carpet in her friends' apartment did after a keg of beer had broken open (some bright person tried to open it with a screwdriver and a hammer when the tap quit working).

She could tell where Michel had been because there was a person-shaped place where the blood hadn't saturated the tan carpet.

And there was the body . . . or pieces thereof. She made herself look. Charles's life might ride on their finding who had done this. She didn't have the luxury of being squeamish.

Hands, feet, head (one that looked much more like some wax sculpture for a horror film than something that had perched on shoulders and talked) sat on top of the pile. The head faced the doorway they'd come through, one hand on each side, feet on the outside of that. The rest of that pile was entrails and bones.

A square of cloth—no telling what it had originally looked like, but she was pretty sure it had been a tablecloth from the shape—was spread out on the floor next to the pile of body parts. On the square of cloth were stacks of meat cut into steaks and two racks of ribs, as if someone were planning a barbecue.

Why was the blood bothering her?

"I don't know vampires," she said, talking fast so her jaw didn't vibrate. "But I read *Dracula* when I was in high school. Would they waste all the blood like this? Or is this meant to horrify? Who do they want to frighten, and why?"

"No," said Charles suddenly. "They wouldn't waste the blood. Not without a good reason. You're right, this was deliberate. Meant to look like serial-killer stuff. That's all wrong for vampires. A vampire who left victims like this would have been killed before he—or she—did it a second time. They can afford human attention a lot less than we can."

"This is planned for effect. A lot of effort." He stared at the body parts—and smiled with satisfaction. "Too much effort, apparently."

He waved his arm at what was left of Chastel. "They cheated. We have one dead body—and there is just too much mass there, by about twenty pounds. I bet we find some commercially prepared cow in amidst the meat and that there is more of the Frenchman under the offal. Meat on bones. They didn't really have time to make a thorough job of it. It just had to look good for the audience."

"Who is the audience?" Angus asked.

"Not us," said Anna. "Me aside . . . this is bad—but to wolves who go out every full moon and hunt? There's just not a lot of horror left in blood and meat." She wouldn't point out that Angus was having a hard time pulling his eyes from the steak pile. "Especially when the victim is someone like Jean Chastel. I bet the French wolves felt bad about Michel, but said, 'good riddance' when they saw Chastel. Do you think this is for the public? To force the Marrok to *not* come out? Or is it for the fae, who have no idea what a butcher Chastel was? To add to the horror of the death so that the hunt for Charles has that righteous feel?"

"You sound like a psychologist," said Angus.

Anna shook her head. "No. Wrong Omega—Ric's the psychologist. I just watch TV and read a lot of forensic mysteries. *I* would feel a lot worse about this scene if it were Sunny. If this is the vampires—and I don't smell anyone except Charles, Michel, and Chastel, so it sounds like it has to be them—then there's a reason they did this to Chastel . . . and the other to Sunny."

"Sunny was personal," Charles said. "You didn't get close to see her body, smell it. They scared her and bled her out slowly. She hurt and suffered. Any werewolf who got near her body would know that. They wanted us to know that she suffered. This is . . . just gruesome. But it is not heartfelt. It is staged." He looked at Anna and gave her a solemn nod. "And for someone who isn't us—who, we hope, hasn't seen it yet."

"Then we need to get this cleaned up, now," said Angus and he pulled out a phone and hit speed dial. "You tell your father he's bankrolling this one: our witch is expensive. Tom?"

"Yes?" His second's voice was hushed, as if he was being quiet so as not to disturb whoever he was with.

"Get a cleanup crew—thorough and fast—and your witch. Yes, we pay her for this one, or the Marrok does, and you tell her to charge him up the nose. Get them to Chastel's place, and I'll tell you more when you get here. Yes, someone finally killed the bastard." He hung up the phone and Anna realized, with a touch of amusement, that Tom hadn't said a single word after that first acknowledgment. Angus was an Alpha who knew his word would be obeyed.

"Butcher," said Charles, thoughtfully. "Maybe this wasn't all for show. The vampires didn't mean it—but they are under orders." He looked at Anna. "I think you're right, mind you. But I also think this was symbolic. A butcher's end for the Beast. Not rage—because then the person behind this would have done it himself. But there is some connection between Chastel and the man who arranged to have this done."

Anna remembered something that the Marrok had said. "Maybe the killer doesn't want to take Chastel's place in the European hierarchy. They'd expect that, wouldn't they? That a werewolf who killed Chastel would have to step in and take over—become the Marrok of Europe? Even if it wasn't a proper challenge."

Charles smiled a little—which was not right, not in that room—but he'd been a werewolf for a very long time and likely didn't have her still-human responses to the gore. "You saved me from a worse fate than you knew when you stopped me from killing him earlier. I have no desire to do my father's job."

"I have one more question," Anna said, taking a last look

around the room. She needed to get out of there. Maybe if she were wolf at that moment, it wouldn't bother her so much, but her eyes kept looking at Chastel's head—and his dead eyes looked right back at her.

"Yes?"

"Why did they leave Michel alive?"

"I don't think they meant to," said Angus. "I think they thought he was dead. He's in very bad shape—but he's smart and used to pretending he's hurt more than he is."

Anna knew all about that one. If they thought they'd broken bones the first time, sometimes they didn't hit you a second time.

"That's it," she said, moving blindly out of the room. "That's all I can do." And she sprinted for the bathroom they'd passed on the way in. The coffee hadn't been in her stomach long enough to taste too bad. At least she hadn't had breakfast.

She grabbed a clean towel and got it wet with cold water. When she was finished, she cleaned the bottoms of her shoes. They were leather and only a couple of weeks old, and the blood hadn't been on them long. Mostly they wiped clean.

ELEVEN

MICHEL was bad. Almost-dead bad. And he wasn't going to be telling anyone anything anytime soon. Alan had him on a hospital bed—in a cage in the basement of his house twenty minutes away. The cage was necessary because seriously injured werewolves, when not attended by more dominant wolves, tended to be violent.

It was probably not useful to go talk to him until he'd had a day or so to heal, Charles decided. Tomorrow then, he'd take one of the other French wolves with him to talk to Michel.

Anna looked sick and tired—sickened, he corrected himself. She had been right. The horror of the scene was lost on him, and probably Angus as well. If the carving had been done while Chastel was still alive . . . maybe it would have bothered him more. If it had been someone he cared about, or someone he was supposed to protect—it would have been different.

But Anna was young, and despite her rough first years as a werewolf, there was a lot she hadn't seen—or maybe it was just that she could look at the murder site and not think about breakfast.

"Angus, we're going back to the hotel to get a few more hours of sleep. Would you call me when the cleanup is done?"

Angus—on the phone again—waved his agreement, and Charles touched Anna on the shoulder to get her moving.

"I thought we were going to talk to Michel?" Anna said.

"Not tonight. Let's give him some time to recover. I'm satisfied that this was done by the vampires. It wasn't me. I don't see that Michel could have done it. Even if he could have taken a wounded Chastel, which I don't really think is a possibility, there is no way a badly wounded man could take the time and effort necessary to paint such a picture. This was done coldly, professionally: vampires."

She stopped. "Why did the room smell like you?"

He pushed her forward again. "I have no idea. Angus, check it out please?"

Angus nodded without pausing in his conversation.

She took a step and stopped again. "And who won the hunt?"

"Is it important?"

"Maybe. If Chastel had the ruby ring—and Dana had access to it. The fae can put spells on objects, right?"

Charles looked over and saw that Angus was still listening to them.

"Hold a minute," Angus told whoever he was speaking to. "Valentin won it. The German wolf."

Anna said, "Shoot."

He'd never heard anyone use that word with such feeling before.

She gave him a tired grin. "Valentin snatched that bag from us. We almost got it."

"He took it from you and the Italians?" Charles asked appreciatively. "That will please Valentin—a bit of getting his own back after the Omega decided to stay with Isaac's pack."

"So no fae-magicked gem involved," Anna said.

"Seems not." Charles guided Anna through the front door and out into the cool night . . . or early morning anyway.

Ian gave them a salute with his beer can as they came out and Charles stuffed Anna into the passenger seat.

She was tired enough that it took her a few blocks before she said, "Hey. How come you are driving?"

"Because you're so tired you're slurring," he told her. "Close your eyes, and I'll get us back."

"How long can we sleep?" asked Anna, shedding her clothes before he got the hotel door fully closed behind them.

"Until we have to get up," Charles told her. He was tired, too—but he picked up her clothes and tossed them on top of a suitcase before dealing with his own in a similar fashion. He left his underwear on, as he usually did now: it seemed to make things a little easier on Anna.

He joined her on the bed, lying flat on his face and all but groaning with the pleasure of relaxation. Four in the morning, but with the curtains drawn they might see four or five hours of sleep—as long as Angus didn't have anything new to report.

She was on the far side, leaving two cold feet of mattress between them. He knew that she'd fall asleep like that . . . and then gradually move over until she was plastered against him. Then he could go to sleep, too.

"Charles?" she said.

"Hmm?"

She moved, but with his head down he couldn't tell if she'd turned away or toward him. There was a tentativeness in her voice, and Brother Wolf, the canny old hunter, told him to keep his head down and his body relaxed while their prey came to them.

"Does it bother you?" she was whispering.

He considered all the things that might be bothering him, but couldn't come up with one appropriate to this situation. "Does what bother me?"

"Tonight." Pause. "Me. My wolf." And then she didn't say anything more.

It was enough. She was talking about their earlier lovemaking. How to answer? *I'll take you any way you come to me—how about now*—didn't seem quite the right response.

"Does it bother you?" Charles asked.

A soft thump, thump, thump, and subtle vibration told him that she was tapping her fingers on the bed. Then the bed bounced as she sat up. He turned his head so he could open one eye and look at her.

She was naked. Some of the movement had been her pulling off the last of her clothes. As he watched, she reached out with her hand, leaned forward, and touched his bare back. She just held her hand there. As she sat there, her pulse rate picked up until he could see it beat in her neck—and it wasn't passion.

"Bad thoughts?" he asked.

She nodded. "It's over. Done. Has been for a long time. Why does it still have such power?" The hand on his skin fisted, pulled away, then landed back where it had been, fingers widespread.

Words. He wasn't good with them. But he'd try. "It's not over in your head. And that's all right, Anna. Don't expect it to be over and done so fast. It's like . . . like the silver left in my wound. It needs to fester out—and sometimes it'll feel worse than the original wound did."

"If I let the wolf in," she said a little bitterly, "it's not a struggle at all."

"Wolf is emotion: needs and now," he agreed. "She doesn't care about the past as long as it doesn't affect now."

"She knows you won't hurt us," Anna said, sounding frustrated. "I know, too, but it doesn't help. She can reach out and take what she wants."

He rolled over, taking his time in the doing of it so he wouldn't startle her. When he finished he was a foot closer to her and could look at her without getting a crick in his neck.

"And do you want me?"

She'd pulled her hand away when he'd moved, and now sat straight-backed and stiff. Something started to change . . .

"Not your wolf," he said. "Do *you* want me? Or is it only the wolf."

Was she only doing her best to live with the creature inside her? Giving it what it wanted? That was what his father did with his mate. Wolf to wolf they were tight as any mated pair he'd ever seen—man to woman . . . they did not match. He didn't want that for Anna.

He didn't think Anna disliked him, didn't think everything between them was her wolf. But even the possibility of it was searingly painful.

"I want you," she told him with a thumb at her chest. "I do." Then she gave him a little rueful smile. "So does she."

He went back to his original question, then. It was very important that he know the answer to this one. "Does it bother you when your wolf initiates our lovemaking?"

She dropped her eyes, not from any desire to submit, but as a human impulse to hide what she felt. "Not the way you mean," she said finally.

"And how do I mean it?"

She gave him an exasperated look.

"I'm not playing games, Anna," he told her, holding her gaze when she would have dropped it. "I need to know how to handle this. I need to know more."

"You are asking if I'm entirely willing to have sex when she starts things." Her voice was brittle with the embarrassment that colored her cheekbones.

"That's what I'm asking."

She swallowed. "Yes." And then said, in a rapid pace, like a balloon deflating, "I think I give her the idea in the first place."

Relief washed through him. Anything else he could work with. Anything. "So. Does it bother you when she initiates lovemaking in the way you mean it?"

She gave a snort of laughter. "Sorry. But it sounds stupid when you put it that way." She dropped her head, then lifted it, tossing her hair back and showing him her face, bright with embarrassment and heat. "It bothers me that she can do it without me. But I can't touch you—naked skin to naked skin—without a little help from her."

"Ah," he said. "So let's try a little play time and see if, with my cooperation, instead of hers, you can get results."

She blinked at him. "What? It's four in the morning. You're going to have to speak in shorter sentences that make more sense."

He lay flat on his back, lifting his chin in a submissive pose he'd only ever offered to his father before. "Here I am," he said. "Stuck tight." He flopped his hands as if his wrists were tied to the mattress. Wiggled his feet. "What are you going to do with me?"

*   *   *

SHE stared at him. Submissive? *Charles?* But that bared throat was still there. No threat. He couldn't have made her believe with words that he wouldn't hurt her, because she already believed the words. But his body was telling her the same thing—and that she trusted right down to her bones.

Because she trusted, she was able to move closer, until her knees bumped into his body. She put her nose against his throat and he moved to make more room, even when she opened her mouth and let her teeth rest against his skin.

Under her tongue, his pulse began to speed up. Not fear—she smelled his arousal, and the sheer, unadulterated call of that scent loosened something inside her, making her moan in pleasure. She licked the side of his neck, appreciating the taste of salt and man, appreciating the freedom he'd given her to touch and taste at her leisure.

She took her time, her touches tentative at first. It felt . . . like she was violating his privacy. Intruding.

She remembered something abruptly. "Someone told me you don't like to be touched," she told him. She couldn't remember who it had been. Asil, maybe.

His chest lifted off the bed, following her fingers when she started to lift them. Uncertain, she left her hands where they were, so he had to make an effort to keep them on him.

"Not usually," he admitted, sounding a little breathless. "But I love your touch. Touch me anytime. Any place. Anywhere." It was heartfelt and honest: and she had a sudden vision of him talking to his father and her with her hands on inappropriate places.

She was going to share the picture with him, but then she got a good look at his face and realized he meant what he'd said—and the impulse to laugh left as quickly as it had come. Deliberately, he pushed up higher, pressing her hands into him, using the muscles of his back because he kept his hands and feet where they had been.

"Pet me," he told her. "I like it."

Her heart beat so hard she could hear it—fear, a little, yes. But also there was something momentous and empowering in having Charles at her mercy. He was as good as his word: no matter what she did, his hands and his feet stayed where they were.

SOMETHING vibrated under her head.

It was such an odd sensation that—still only half-conscious—Anna tried to figure out what it was. Her ears told her there was a car motor somewhere very nearby, and she tried to figure out how she'd made it from the bed to a car without noticing.

And then she smelled the vampires.

"She's awake, Ivan," said a woman's voice.

Anna opened her eyes and saw the vampire who'd attacked Moira. The woman smiled at her.

"Now me," she said, "I didn't like Krissy. She was a pushy little bimbo. But Ivan had a thing for her—and he doesn't like you at all. So you just be a good puppy, and we'll not have any trouble, right?"

Anna didn't bother answering. She was naked, chained hand and foot and stuck in what could only be the back section of the blue minivan the vampires had been running around in. They'd removed the backseats and installed huge eyebolts to which they'd chained Anna. They were going to be paying the rental company through the nose when they returned the van. She was pretty sure that even rental insurance wouldn't cover things like drilling eye-bolts through the floor.

The woman vampire was leaning against one of the big sliding doors. Her feet were pressed against Anna's side. Next to her was a man who looked about forty-five, but he was a vampire. He'd probably been forty-five for years.

Questions bubbled to the tip of her tongue. *What do you want with me? How did you get me out of the hotel? What did you do with Charles?*

Charles wouldn't have just let them take her. She closed her eyes and felt for her end of their bond—and it was just as it usually was when Brother Wolf wasn't holding it open. Whatever had happened, Charles was all right.

The last thing she remembered was leaning down to taste the skin of his belly. Mustn't show the enemy weakness. So pick her question carefully.

"Who hired you?"

The woman smiled displaying a set of fangs. "Not my part of the show," she said. "All I know is the job. We're to box you up and ship you across the shining sea on an airplane. No harm to you if you don't give us any trouble."

Her smile got bigger. "Of course, if you do give us trouble, we get to hurt you. Fun, fun, fun."

Across the sea sounded like Europe to her, Anna thought. One of the wolves kidnapping her? Did they think that Charles couldn't find her out of the country? If so, then they were wrong. Still, it would be easier on everyone if she didn't go in the first place.

She jerked up, using the big muscles of her back and thighs for strength. The metal handcuffs cut into her skin, but she ignored the pain. Whatever her hands were chained to was tough, but the eye hook attached to her feet began to bend, the floor beneath it pulling up.

"Shit!" The man who'd been sitting by her feet looked to the front of the car. "I told you that there was no good place to attach the chains in this stinking rental."

"Shoot her," said the driver.

She couldn't get her head up and around enough to see who was driving, but she was betting on the man she'd seen at the warehouse. A shotgun flew back, thrown by someone in the front passenger seat. The male vampire she could see caught it and fired it from three feet away, hitting her in the shoulder.

CHARLES sat up and grabbed his aching head. It took him a moment to catch Brother Wolf's frantic message. *She's gone. They have her. Couldn't move. Couldn't stop them. Couldn't wake you up. Wake up!*

Anna?

She was gone—unarguably. There was no one beside him in the bed.

The room smelled of vampires and night air, both scents coming from the broken window. He grabbed his jeans and pulled them on. He grabbed shoes and socks because not ripping up his feet might let him catch up with them faster.

Seventh floor would have been impossible, but the second room he'd gotten them had been on the fifth. He jumped out the broken window, landed on his feet, and rolled to soften the fall. He got to his feet, shoulders and knees aching but functional.

He might be able to track them, even in the city—but there was a better way. He recklessly threw open the bond between him and Anna.

The first thing he discovered was that she was not far away, but she was moving fast. And she was hurt—likely her getting hurt was what had allowed him to break whatever spell it was that had put him unconscious. He felt the last trickles of it still trying to hold him—awake and aware he was able to burn away the magic. The spell was pure witchcraft. While the rest of him was focused on finding Anna, a small part noticed that the vampires seemed to have some way of accessing a lot of magic: wolf and witch.

He closed down the bond with his mate until he couldn't feel her pain, until all he had was a direction. Otherwise, distracted by worry and things he couldn't influence until he got there, he wouldn't be able to function effectively. First, find them.

He ran.

The trouble with big cities—especially Seattle with the waterways all over the place—was that he didn't just have to know where she was, but where they were taking her.

South, he thought, sprinting recklessly down the hill. What lay to the south? Beacon Hill, West Seattle, Kent, Renton, Tacoma. Most of the wolves were staying near Downtown, but he thought that the Italians might be staying somewhere in West Seattle.

Airport. Brother Wolf was quite clear and positive. Maybe he'd picked up something from Anna that Charles had missed.

Sea-Tac, he thought—about fifteen miles from the hotel. He could run faster in wolf form, but he'd lose time, and someone might see them on the highway. But if they made it that far, even Brother Wolf couldn't keep up. He'd have to steal a car—which he would do. That would leave Anna in their hands for longer. So he chose to try to catch them now.

Even in this form he ran faster than the car could go on the city streets. The vampires wouldn't want to attract the attention of the police, not with an injured woman in their vehicle. They'd obey speed limits and stop signs.

He was closing in.

It was still dark, and there was not much more traffic than there had been when he'd driven them back to their hotel. No later than five in the morning, he estimated. He hadn't been unconscious long.

They had halted directly ahead. He could see the tail-lights of a minivan no more than a block away, stopped at a red light.

He focused on the traffic light and let his will hold it red. It wasn't something he'd ever done before—and he wasn't sure it would work in a city. But the light stayed red the whole time he ran that block. Stayed red as he launched himself through the back window.

He landed on top of one of the vampires. Without forethought or planning he ripped his head off and threw it in the driver's compartment to add to the confusion. One down. Three to go. Next to his knee there was something long and hard. He grabbed it.

"Shoot him!" The driver was starting toward the back, but there wasn't a lot of room between the front seats, and it slowed him down. Gave Charles time to deal with the last vampire in the back. The front passenger opened his door and jumped out. He was running away or he planned on coming through the side door. Either way, it gave Charles a short window of opportunity where he faced only one.

The female was shouting something about the shotgun when Charles realized that the thing he'd snatched off the floor to use as a weapon was indeed a shotgun. He shoved it through her rib cage and kept going, pushing her through the side window and out into the street. She wasn't dead, but she wasn't going anywhere either. Two down. Two to go.

Anna gasped when the driver, climbing over the front seats, stepped on her.

Inside the van, Charles had the advantage. The small

space slowed him down a little—but the vampires were generally faster and more maneuverable, and being inside the van hampered them a lot more.

But inside the van meant Anna, chained to the floor, was in danger. So he grabbed the vampire, feeling the pain of being grabbed in return, and jumped out the passenger-side door when the fourth vampire popped it open. The unexpectedness of the move meant the driver was braced all wrong and Charles could put a lot of push into his jump rather than wasting his strength wrestling against the driver.

The two of them hit the fourth vampire murderously hard, and he dropped the stick he was carrying—it was the size of a cane or fighting stick. Charles didn't take the time to decide which it was—he'd never seen a vampire who carried a weapon so easily turned upon its wielder. But far be it from him to complain about another's stupidity.

Charles released his captive and, by swinging him into the side of the van, managed to get loose in return. He grabbed the stick and stabbed the downed vampire under the rib cage and up through the heart. A werewolf doesn't need a *sharpened* stake; blunt worked just fine.

That left only one.

He spun to face the van—and saw only damaged sheet metal. He inhaled, trying to pinpoint the other—and heard someone running away. He rounded the side of the van to make sure it was the driver who was running and not some terror-stricken human who had seen the carnage, but there was no mistaking the speed of the vampire for a mere human's.

"Don't leave me."

He looked down at the female vampire with the shotgun rammed through her chest.

"Sunrise," she said, as something dark and wet bubbled

out around the barrel of the gun. "Not for a long while. Kill me. Please."

With Anna hurt, he had no desire to bother questioning her. Nor did he want to leave her as a possible threat. He acceded to her wish and took care of the other vampire while he was at it. Less than four minutes had passed after he jumped through the rear window of the van, and he had three decapitated bodies and their heads stuffed in the back of the van.

Immediate danger over, he checked on Anna. She was talking to him, but Brother Wolf was more interested in seeing what made her hurt so badly. He didn't have the tools or the patience to deal with the manacles, but the chain snapped when he used the shotgun barrel to apply some leverage.

As soon as he had her free she tried to sit up and made a pained sound. She'd been hit in the shoulder from close range; the shot had barely had a chance to expand. It was a light load, birdshot. Lead. They hadn't wanted her dead, just incapacitated. It didn't mean that she might not die from it anyhow.

"I'm all right," she told him, over and over again, trying to reassure him. It wasn't true.

"Shh," he told her. "Just lie still."

His cell phone was still in his pants pocket—and it was functional. He called Angus.

"Where is Choo?" he asked as soon as the other wolf answered. "Anna's been shot."

"Anna's been shot?"

"I have three dead vampires in a blue minivan that looks like it's been in several accidents this morning. And they shot Anna. I need Alan Choo. Is he with Michel?" He hoped that he wasn't. Angus's house was in Issaquah. He needed to get Anna help sooner than that.

"The mate of one of the French wolves is a nurse. They went home with Michel. Alan's at Arthur's in the University District."

"I know where Arthur's place is."

"I'll tell the local vampires that we have some cleanup for them, and they'll take care of the bodies and the van. I'll call Alan and tell him to expect you. Do you need anyone else?"

"No." Charles hung up.

He didn't like leaving Anna in the back of the van with the dead vampires, but moving her to the front seat would only hurt her worse—and a naked, bloody woman would draw even more attention than the broken windows and dents.

"You stay there," he told her. "I've got to drive. It won't be long."

She nodded, closed her eyes. "Knew you would come," she said. "I just didn't want you to have to come all the way overseas to find me."

"Good thing I'm quick," he said.

She smiled, still with her eyes closed. "Good thing."

He had trouble shutting the side door; it was dented and didn't want to seal. After a failed effort to bend the door back into shape, he ducked back into the van and took a belt off one of the bodies. He rolled down the front passenger window and pulled the door as closed as it was going to get and tied it to the front door frame with the belt.

The vampires had left the van running with the keys in the ignition. He got in and as he shifted into drive, the light turned green.

"Charles?" her voice was tense. "Would you talk to me? I keep thinking the vampires are moving."

"They're dead," he said. "But we can talk."

He worried that he was going to have to come up with a

topic—when all he wanted to do was kill something else. But Anna came to his rescue.

"Could our Arthur really be *the* Arthur?"

"My father says that *the* Arthur was a remarkable strategist, an awe-inspiring fighter, and an extremely practical man who would have laughed himself silly at the stories of King Arthur, chivalry, and chasing after the Holy Grail. Da says there was a white lady but she bore no resemblance to Gwenevere of *Camelot* fame. Nimue, Morgain Le Fay, and Merlin, yes, but not as they are depicted. No Lancelot at all. No Round Table. Just a bunch of desperate men trying to keep the Anglo-Saxons out of their homelands. He says the real story is better than the one everyone knows, but not nearly as glamorous." He glanced down at Anna but couldn't tell if she was better or worse. "He never tells the real stories."

"So Arthur the werewolf—"

"Likes to rant about how Lancelot ruined it all," said Charles dryly. "If he is a reincarnation, he bears little resemblance to the real thing. But then there's some unhappiness between my father and Arthur; they cordially dislike each other. You have to take that into account."

"Arthur doesn't seem to dislike you," Anna said.

"We got on all right, here."

"Reincarnation?"

He shrugged. "I've never seen any evidence that it's real. But I've never seen anything that disproves it either. I believe the afterlife is better than what we have here—and it would take something extraordinary to make someone willing to come back."

"What about the sword?"

"Old, but my father says it is not Excalibur. Or if it is, it has lost all of the magic that made it Excalibur."

"There was an Excalibur, though?"

"So Da says—the result of a bargain with the fae who were not any happier with the Anglo-Saxons than the native humans were. Arthur is right that Excalibur wasn't the only weapon. There was a spear and a dagger, too."

For a few blocks Anna was silent. Then she said in a markedly weaker voice, "Your father is old enough that he knew Arthur?"

He hadn't seen any evidence of heavy bleeding, but maybe he hadn't checked thoroughly enough. He put his foot down harder on the gas pedal. "You ask him that, maybe he'll answer you. He never did me."

ALAN and a couple of people he didn't know were waiting for him outside as he drove into the driveway of Arthur's house. As soon as Charles got out of the van, he realized that the strangers weren't from Angus's pack.

"Vampires," he said.

"To take care of the mess," Alan explained. "Where's Anna?"

Charles opened the sliding door that still worked. Alan stuck his head in.

"Hey, Alan," Anna said.

"Got yourself shot," he said after a thorough look.

"Oops."

He laughed. "You'll do." He backed away, and said, "Bring her inside, and we'll get that stuff out of her.

Charles picked her up as carefully as he could. Alan held the front door open, and Charles brushed past him and stopped.

Arthur stood between him and the rest of the house. He looked horrible—his eyes hollow and his skin tone various shades of gray.

Any other time, Charles would have played the games necessary for an outside dominant coming into another's territory, but Anna was bleeding in his arms.

"Where do you want me to put her?" he said, which was as much of a concession as he was capable of making.

"Come." Arthur's voice was tired and strained, but not unwelcoming. Maybe Charles had misread his body language.

He turned and led the way. "There's a spare bedroom back here. Upstairs might be safer, but Sunny . . . Sunny's in the one upstairs."

The guest room smelled like Alan Choo, who'd evidently been sleeping here tonight. Arthur pulled the covers back farther so Charles could set Anna down.

"Angus said it was the vampires?" Arthur said.

Remembering that Arthur had a right to know, Charles explained briefly. He pulled the blankets up over her until only the wounds on her shoulder were exposed.

"Pity that one got away," Arthur said.

"Ivan," Anna told them. He'd thought Anna was unconscious, she'd been so still. "Ivan is his name."

Charles looked away from Anna for a moment, then looked at Arthur. "He can run, but I will find him."

Arthur veiled his eyes with his lashes instead of dropping his gaze, but Charles didn't care. "Yes. Tell me when you get him."

"I will."

"You think they are hired guns," Arthur looked out the window into the darkness before dawn. "Did you find out who they were working for—or why they killed my Sunny?"

"No. I wasn't in the mood to discuss things," Charles said. "Maybe Anna—"

"No," Anna murmured. "It wasn't a local werewolf. Not Angus or his pack. Or"—she glanced at Arthur and didn't mention Dana's name—"anyone else here. Someone out of the country. They wanted to fly me overseas."

"That doesn't make any sense," said Alan, coming into the room with a tray that held various surgical implements. "Killing Sunny, trying to kidnap Anna, killing Chastel. There's no pattern."

"It makes sense to someone," said Arthur. "If there's nothing more I can do?"

"No," said Charles. Having Arthur in the room with Anna wounded was trying his patience. "Thank you."

Arthur gave him a faint smile. "Call me if you need anything."

And he left them to themselves.

"I have morphine," Alan told Anna. "But wolves have different reactions to it. Some it doesn't help at all. For some it is worse than useless, doesn't stop the pain and doesn't let them brace for it either."

"No morphine," Anna said. "Just get them out."

Alan looked up at Charles.

"I'll hold her for you," he said, sliding in behind Anna so that her upper body was braced on his. That allowed him the most control. He might be a werewolf—but so was she.

"Try and relax into it," he told her.

Alan sat on the bed, too, swiveling until he was facing Anna. He set the tray on the nightstand and a bowl by his hip. He started with a pair of sharp-nosed forceps and picked out the easy ones first.

"Did you see?" Anna said, her eyes closed.

"See what?" Charles asked.

"The one-armed vampire. Wonder what he did with

the arm?" She hissed then as Alan pulled another pellet free.

"I don't know." He kissed the top of her head.

Anna didn't struggle against his hold as Alan pulled out more surface pellets. She didn't move until he had to dig deeper.

TWELVE

ANNA was sweating and swearing—and Charles was fit to be tied and a fair bit on his way to needing restraint himself. Alan had nerves of steel, because his hands were steady even though Charles couldn't keep his growls to himself. Finally, Alan dropped the forceps into the bowl.

"All right," he said. "There is still lead in there. I can smell it, but I'll be damned if I can find it. At least it is not silver. An X-ray machine would be able to locate the rest."

"We have one of those in Aspen Creek," Charles said.

"Or you can let the remainder fester out. There isn't a lot—I don't think it's enough to make her sick."

"That's where my vote goes." Anna's luminous skin was greenish, and there were dark circles under her eyes. "No more probes, please."

Charles slid out from behind her. "You'll change your mind when they start festering," he predicted. "But you can wait if you'd like."

"I'll do that." She huffed indignantly. "Festering. What a lovely thought."

He kissed her lightly, then took a good look at the manacles they'd used on Anna. "I can pick these," he said, "if Arthur has the right tools around."

"Go look," Anna told him. "If I'm going to fester, I'd like to do it in comfort. And these things are not comfortable. Plus they're tacky."

Charles was smiling when he left the room, shutting the door behind him. While she was hurting, and he had to get her help, he hadn't even thought about her nudity. But he didn't want Arthur walking in on her, so he shut the door.

The house was dark, and he thought Arthur must have gone back to bed—morning was still a while away. He wasn't going to sleep again, not in Arthur's house—and he wasn't going to move Anna until she'd healed up a bit.

He went to the kitchen and opened drawers to see if he could find anything useful.

"Charles?" Arthur's voice. It came from the room that he kept his treasures in.

"Yes," he answered. "I'm looking for something to get the manacles off Anna. You wouldn't happen to have a lockpick kit, would you?"

"I probably have something that would work," Arthur said.

Charles stopped sorting through the kitchen implement drawer, lifting his head. There was something . . . odd about the other man's voice.

Maybe it was nothing. Maybe. He removed a fillet knife from the block and slid it into his jeans pocket.

"That would be cool." He was careful to keep his throat loose, so Arthur wouldn't have any reason to think Charles had noticed anything different. "She's tough, she'd handle it—but I want them off." He moved unhurriedly through the dark living room . . . and caught Sunny's lingering scent from the couch nearest him.

Poor thing. He hadn't known her well enough to do more than feel sorry for her. No wonder Arthur was off. Oddly, the sympathy he felt for Arthur was far more sincere than any mourning he could do for Sunny.

He tried not to think about how much worse tonight could have been. Anna, they wanted to kidnap. Not kill.

Their taking her made him angry, so angry that not even killing three of them soothed him. Or Brother Wolf, either.

If they had killed her . . . he would have joined her. He paused, not having worked that out before. But it didn't particularly bother him. If she died, he would follow. Just as he would have followed her wherever they had planned on taking her had they succeeded. She was his and he hers.

"Charles?"

His phone rang. "I'll be right there. Angus is calling."

He opened the phone, "Yes?"

"Your Anna was spot on. About an hour ago—fifteen minutes after the cleanup crew left Chastel's place—we had police all over the place. Someone had called in a report of screaming, dogs howling, gunshots, and hell-all-knows else. They brought in luminol—the stuff that glows in the presence of blood. We owe Moira big-time because they found squat. The last witch we had could never have cleaned up that well. The police are still tearing the place apart—but they're being nicer about it."

"Trap sprung too late," said Charles—aware that Arthur had come out to listen.

"Yes." Angus paused. "And your scent? Moira found clothes in one of the . . . well, in the mess of body parts. As best we can figure, someone snitched the clothes you wore to the hunt, dragged them around the room, and dumped them."

"Deliberate."

"Absolutely. And not even the fae can pin it on you now. I know you left the hunting grounds in a completely different set of clothes."

"Good."

"On another interesting news front . . . that van? The local vampires who were doing the cleanup on it recognized the stick you poked through one of the bad guys. She called it a spellcatcher."

Charles frowned. "Spellcatcher?"

"Vampire hocus pocus, apparently. Very secret—the vampires here *really* don't want trouble with your father over this to tell us this much. Only a couple of vampires can make them—and they charge a lot for them. If our team of out-of-town vamps were hired guns, they were successful and expensive to be able to purchase such a thing. Apparently this stick can absorb up to four spells, and the person it's tuned to can use it to cast them, even if that person wouldn't normally be able to do magic."

"That would explain the shadows spell and the Look-Not-At-Me the vampires used when they attacked Anna the first time. And how they kidnapped Anna while we were both in the hotel room—they must have used the spellcatcher to put us out with a witch's sleep spell."

"The thing to remember is that it can only absorb spells given to it voluntarily by the spell caster. Means a wolf gave them the shadows spell and the Look-Not-At-Me."

"Confirming Anna's theory," Charles said. He was pacing. There were many things he did not like about cell phones—but not tangling himself up in cords was a definite benefit.

"Is Anna all right?"

"She'll be fine as soon as a few more chunks of lead fester out, and I get some locks picked so she doesn't have to explain her interesting choice in jewelry."

Arthur was leaning against the door frame of his treasure room, making no effort to pretend he wasn't listening.

"Good." Angus cleared his throat. "You did good, son."

The "son" made Charles smile. He was older than Angus by a few decades. "I think so. She's—she completes me."

"Tell her that," Angus advised humorously. "Women like to hear their men get all tongue-tied."

"I'll do that."

He shut the phone.

"Cleanup crew?" asked Arthur.

And Charles realized that there was a lot Arthur didn't know. "Chastel was killed last night in a particularly bloody fashion that required some quick action."

"Was it you who killed him?"

"No. Vampires."

"Ah." Arthur looked away. "Chastel. Odd to think of him being dead at last. It couldn't have happened to a better person." He looked back and gave Charles a broken smile. "And I guess it did, didn't it? Poor Sunny." He rubbed his face, hiding it for a minute. "Sorry. Sorry. So Chastel required a cleanup crew?"

Charles considered offering sympathy—and decided it wouldn't help. "Anna suggested that the murder was so bloody—especially given it was vampires who'd done it—"

"The vampires killed Chastel? You are sure?"

Charles nodded. "Ironic, considering how many wolves I know who would have loved to kill him."

"Who called the police? The vampires?"

Charles shrugged. "The timing is off. The police were

meant to find the scene in all its glory." Maybe to keep his father from bringing the werewolves out. Maybe to keep the wolves away from the scene so whoever had tried to frame Charles for it would have an easier time. Without access to the murder site, the werewolves might never have determined how Charles's scent appeared in a place he'd never been. "But they gave us too much time. The police won't find anything now."

"I suppose not. Angus is remarkably efficient."

"And, I believe, his second's daytime job is with the police. Tom knows what they are looking for and how to keep them from finding it." Charles paused.

It occurred to him that he could see Arthur hiring someone to do his killing for him. But he dismissed his suspicion. Sunny had been killed. A wolf would never kill his own mate.

Even so, Charles gave in to his impulse to throw out some bait. "Whoever called the police did it hours too late. It might have worked if he'd called right after the job was done." He shook his head. "That's what's been bothering me, I think. The incompetence of it all. Most wolves are better hunters. The vampires made a try for Anna—right before we came over here for dinner, as a matter of fact. They failed—and lost two of their pack doing so. Michel, one of the French werewolves, was with Chastel when he was killed. And they left him for dead. He'll survive, and in a few days he'll tell us exactly what the vampires said when they attacked. Maybe they told him who hired them."

"Hired?"

"They're pros. Hired to come to Seattle to do at least three things." Charles ticked them off on his fingers. "Kidnap Anna. Kill Sunny. And kill Chastel—making his death horrible and bloody, something that screamed 'Monster' to the police."

Charles hummed thoughtfully to himself. "It wasn't the vampires who were incompetent. If they had known what they were facing when they tried to kidnap Anna the first time, they would have succeeded. Someone underestimated the escort I sent out with Anna. Thought that the only one who would be a problem was Angus's second, Tom. Chastel's death was . . . masterful. Any humans who'd walked in, who'd seen pictures of it, would remember it for the rest of their lives. But the person who was supposed to call the police was too slow."

Charles had been watching Arthur out of the corner of his eye. The wolf's face showed nothing but polite interest. His body, on the other hand, had been tightening with anger throughout Charles's whole speech.

"Incompetent," he said again. And watched Arthur's fist clench.

Arthur.

His father had been suspicious of the death of an Alpha who'd recently been killed in London. Tough man and very dominant—decapitated in a car accident. Could have been deliberately arranged.

Charles resumed pacing, ignoring Arthur as if he weren't there at all. So Arthur didn't realize he'd given himself away.

Taking out Chastel made sense. Chastel was a threat to Arthur. Kept Arthur from expanding into Europe. His death left a huge power vacuum—and Arthur would have stood no chance in a fair fight against Chastel. He couldn't have just assassinated him and left the murder open, though—if anyone knew Arthur had taken the coward's way of killing Chastel, they would never have followed him. Arthur was not Bran, he wasn't strong enough to rule a continent based on his own power—he'd need them to be willing subjects. He'd need to pin Chastel's death on someone else.

Charles didn't think Arthur cared one way or the other about the werewolves' coming out. He was precisely the charismatic kind of wolf that Bran planned on introducing the public to first. But making Chastel's murder look as though it was designed to attract human attention was a way to send suspicion elsewhere. There were a lot of wolves who were unhappy about his father's plans. Bran would not believe Charles had killed Chastel, after all—so Arthur needed a nameless villain for Bran to blame. Someone who hired the vampires, then conveniently disappeared.

That whole butcher thing . . . was Arthur making an observation. Chastel was a barbarian—Arthur clearly his superior. He wouldn't see the similarities. In his mind, a brute who killed for pleasure was uncivilized. Arthur didn't kill for pleasure.

Chastel ruled by killing all who challenged his place— and by terrifying the rest. Arthur . . . had started out killing the Alphas in Great Britain, then stopped. Or found a better way to dispose of the wolves who would challenge him. Bran could figure it out from here. As far as Charles was concerned, Arthur and Chastel were just two sides of the same coin—all the need for power and none of the need to take care of what was theirs. Arthur wouldn't see it that way, though perhaps he needed to make that more clear with the brutal method used to dispose of Chastel's body.

Sunny.

If the reason for hiring the vampires was that it would have been difficult for a werewolf to attack an Omega, hiring them to kill your own mate, who was Omega, or nearly so, would have been imperative.

And suddenly the attempted kidnapping of Anna made so much more sense. Arthur wasn't the only werewolf to have his own jet—but he did have one. And Anna was what Sunny could have been. Omega. Valued not so much because of who she was—but for who everyone else would think her to be. Prize possession. And, unlike Sunny, she would live forever. Sunny had been getting old, as humans did. Arthur's pain at that knowledge had been genuine. So he'd had her killed to spare himself the suffering. From his reactions at the warehouse, Charles rather thought Arthur had underestimated the pain of her death. He hoped so.

Casually, he pulled his phone out and set it to text. "Forgot to update Da," he said. "He'll be eating breakfast about now and doesn't like it interrupted. I'll text him about the happenings of tonight, and he can call me about it at his leisure." No lies for Arthur to hear. He kept the text message simple. IT IS ARTHUR.

He kept the phone tilted away from Arthur so he'd think he was still texting Bran and typed out a message for Angus. DON'T CALL. SEND HELP HERE. ARTHUR IS VILLAIN. He deemed it a little melodramatic, but it was short and simple and impossible for Angus to misinterpret. He hit SEND.

He could handle Arthur. Arthur had not been wolf enough to take Chastel. But Anna and Alan Choo were here, and they needed him to keep them safe as best he could—and that meant calling in help.

"You were looking for lockpicks," said Arthur.

"Yes."

"I have some in there." Arthur tipped his head to indicate his treasure room. "I've been packing things up—I won't be coming back here."

Charles followed him in. It looked as if Arthur had been doing exactly as he said. The tapestries were off the wall, set into two-by-four frames to keep them stable and slid into the kind of plywood rough-lumber shipping crate museums used to transport artwork. A smaller wooden crate had already been sealed. The only thing left out was the box that held the sword.

"I understand the rest," Charles said, running his fingers over the wood that protected the old sword. "But how did you bribe Dana into breaking her word?"

He looked up and watched Arthur go very still. The British wolf . . . altered subtly. Lost the aura of grief almost entirely.

"The same way I got the vampires to do my bidding. Offered her something she wanted." Arthur smiled. "Even that wouldn't have worked if you hadn't ticked her off."

"How did I do that?" As soon as Charles asked the question, he remembered Dana's extreme reaction to the painting his father had sent her. It was lost, that place that had once been hers, and his father meant to gift her with a remembrance—but maybe she'd thought it was a taunt, instead.

Arthur threw up his hands theatrically. "How should I know? Fae are easily offended. As for what I offered her—" He motioned to the sword case.

"That is not Excalibur," Charles said. "When she discovers you don't have it, she'll be . . . offended."

Arthur ran his fingers gently over the display case—and slid open a dark chunk of wood on the end. "There is something to be said about hiding things in plain sight."

The sword he removed from the hidden compartment wasn't the one that had been on display—though it looked very like. Both were swordsmen's weapons rather than movie props. As soon as this once-hidden sword left the case, the hair on the back of Charles's neck came to attention.

Excalibur or not, there was no denying that the sword in Arthur's hand was a fae blade: he could feel its magic on his skin, could smell it.

Arthur was a swordsman, Charles knew. He'd studied fencing and had received the same sort of martial training that Charles himself had. Arthur's balance was right and his grip—neither too tight nor too loose—showed all that training had not been wasted.

He hadn't been worried about *a* sword, but *that* sword . . . Charles was a dead man, most likely. But Angus would be coming with help. Enough help that even with the sword, Anna should be safe. All he had to do was delay as long as possible. And Arthur always had loved to perform.

"Anna won't go with you," he told Arthur. "She won't stand by your side. She'll wait until you take your attention off her for a moment, then she'll gut you."

Arthur smiled. "You really don't believe in reincarnation, do you? Or fate. I came here to kill Chastel and your father. Chastel I had an answer for. For your father, I needed more."

"Why my father?"

Arthur looked at him as though he was stupid. "Because I am he, of course. King Arthur. It is my destiny to be the high king." .

Madness indeed, thought Charles

"But my father didn't come."

"No," agreed Arthur. "Fate is an odd thing. Do you know just who Dana is?"

"Obviously you are going to tell me," said Charles dryly.

"I wonder if your father does. This is what I mean by fate—that I who was Arthur would find Nimue, the Lady of the Lake, here. I knew a couple of decades ago that she was here in Seattle—the first time I saw her, in fact. I knew that there would come a time that it was important—so I bought Sunny this house."

Obviously, Charles thought, it wasn't going to be hard to keep Arthur monologuing.

Arthur's smile turned sly. "I didn't find Excalibur in an archaeological dig—though that's what I was doing at the time. At Cambridge I made friends with a boy whose family was old Cornish gentry. He invited me home for Christmas. I discovered that they'd been guarding a treasure for so many generations that they'd forgotten all about it. It took me to find it again. It was hidden under the flagstone in the carriage house. A sword in the stone—so to speak." He laughed at his own cleverness.

"The boy's older sister looked enough like Dana to be her twin." With his free hand, he rubbed his thumb over his first two fingers. "A little research, and insight becomes knowledge. So I knew when I saw Dana I had the perfect thing to bribe her with." He swung the sword gently. "She had no idea it wasn't resting beneath the stone where she'd placed it until I showed it to her—a photograph. I am not stupid."

"I could disagree with you on that," Charles said. "You've done a number of stupid things that I can pick out. But trying to get the best of a Gray Lord is the stupidest by far. You never had any intention of giving her the sword."

Arthur bobbed his head—a polite agreement. "The first deal would have been honest. Excalibur isn't the only thing I discovered there. I had other weapons, you know. I offered her the dagger. She refused—and made it clear she would hunt me 'to the ends of the earth,' I believe. I know her, you see, but she doesn't know me. Doesn't believe I am Arthur."

Charles knew which Arthur he was talking about.

"But my father didn't come."

"No, you did. And you brought her with you."

"Her?"

"Gwenevere. My white lady."

And then Arthur proved that he wasn't as stupid as Charles had started to believe. Because without telegraphing his move by so much as a breath, while Charles was still absorbing the idea that Arthur wanted Anna because he thought she was *his*, Arthur struck.

The sword in his stomach didn't hurt, just robbed Charles of his strength. Of his ability to move.

He heard Anna cry out, but his attention was on the icy cold that was sucking him down.

As his legs collapsed, Arthur followed him down. "A swift fight," Arthur said, "is the best kind of fight. I know you. When your father didn't come, I was so disappointed. But when I saw her . . . saw my Gwenevere, I knew." He grimaced. "She was mine, and you had her, just like before. I could have killed you cleanly, you know. But I want you to suffer. Lancelot."

"There was no Lancelot, fool."

For a moment Charles thought that he'd said those words, he'd thought them so hard. But the voice was a woman's.

Dana.

Arthur jerked the sword free and stumbled back until he regained his feet. As soon as the steel left his body, the coldness dissipated. Charles put a hand to his belly to staunch the bleeding. It hadn't gone all the way through— Arthur had wanted him to suffer—so if he could keep from bleeding to death, Brother Wolf could heal them. The wound was small enough to heal fast.

Sharp steel, Brother Wolf told him, *cuts swiftest, hurts least, heals soonest.*

Charles gave the pack magic a little tug and received a bounty in return. He wasn't the Alpha, but his father could grant him help if he chose. And Bran was a generous leader. Pain faded. No need to advertise that he was not dying, though. Not yet. He stayed collapsed, out of the way. *Don't pay attention to me, I'm not a threat.* Charles could become less noticeable if he had to, though not as well as Bran—his da had the technique perfected. It is easier to go unnoticed, Bran liked to say, when everyone is focused on something else.

"Give me the sword," she said.

"She is my sword," Arthur said, taking a tighter grip and pulling the point up into a guard position. "Mine from the first. She came to my hand from yours—and when I died, it was not I who gave her back."

Dana moved into Charles's view. She'd dropped the glamour—or adopted a new one. It wasn't so much that she changed anything, but she had become *more*. And Anna was right, she was riveting. *Good. Keep Arthur's attention.*

Charles moved his hand, and when blood didn't pour out, moved his shirt and looked at the scab. Too fresh to move yet, but soon.

"You stole it," Dana said, her voice low and fierce. "It is not yours. Was never yours. The King may indeed come again—it was foretold so. But that is not you. Has never been you. You are not Arthur."

"You are not meant to know me," Arthur told her. "And we are quit of our bargain. Chastel didn't kill Charles, as you promised. And when Charles defeated the Frenchman— you were unable to find another way to kill him, to kill Charles. You failed. I owe you nothing."

She lifted her hand. "*Caladbog. Caledfwych.* Excalibur. I have delivered it to the hands of great men, fighters, heroes all. Your hands profane it. A coward who hires his deaths and kills those better, smarter, stronger than he."

"You can't take it from me," Arthur said. "Not unless you kill Charles. And you cannot harm me as long as Charles still lives. I know how fae bargains work."

I wouldn't be so confident if I were you, Arthur, thought Charles. *I thought my father had worked out a bargain with her—and look what happened to us. Excalibur meant more to her than her word, and it still does.*

"Fine," she said, and flung out a hand.

And Charles had the very odd experience of seeing himself fall all the way to the floor while he sat and watched. Which was better than the vision he had briefly had of himself falling dead.

"You can't kill like that," said Arthur, his voice breaking with sudden fear. He raised the sword between them, as if the blade could hold off fae magic—which, if it were Excalibur, and that appeared to be nearly certain—it might possibly do.

Arthur was right, thought Charles, as he got to his feet. Dana couldn't kill like that—but she could fling illusions of death all day long. His wound was still sore, but unlikely to open up and let him bleed to death when he moved.

"Can I not?" Dana asked. "What do you know of the fae? Not as much as you believe, I think. If the bargain is complete, give me the sword."

While she kept Arthur occupied, Charles pad-footed over to the display case. The sword left there was not Excalibur, but it was a fine sword. A replica, he thought, created a long time ago to protect the original. He tore the box open and took the sword to use it for the purpose for which it had been forged.

Arthur spun to see what the noise was and, from his face, he could now see Charles—either the noise had broken the illusions, or Dana had let them drop.

"Arthur Madden," Charles said formally. "For murder of innocents on the Marrok's territory, you have been found guilty and condemned to death."

He didn't have to say anything more because Arthur raised the sword and came for him.

Arthur might have had years of martial arts behind him—but Charles had been trained by his father, a man who had actually used a sword like this to stay alive.

Charles was stronger and faster, and Arthur was afraid of him.

All that said, Charles had never actually used a sword in real combat before.

Remember, the memory of his da's voice echoed in his ears, *wolves are not human. If you engage another wolf and hit his blade full strength, you're going to destroy your sword. If you need to preserve your weapon, turn blows away and strike body, not metal.*

His brother's voice chimed in helpfully, *Avoidance is better than a block—less risky.*

So Charles slipped away from the first strike Arthur aimed at him. He kept both feet on the floor—ghosting over the hardwood. Rat-stepping allowed him to strike with better balance and to shift direction faster.

The room was small. The swords were short. It meant there was little chance to disengage, and fighting was done close range.

"You're dead," Arthur said. "I killed you."

"You stabbed me with steel and gloated overly much," Charles murmured, keeping his mind on saving his sword. Sliding blocks, moving aside, turning, letting Arthur do the work for the moment. It visibly unnerved the British wolf when he didn't hit anything, so Charles concentrated on not being there when Arthur's sword snaked out.

"I heal pretty damn fast from small wounds like that." No need to mention pack magic—let Arthur eat fear.

Charles was aware of Dana, who had moved back from the actual fight until she stood just outside the room. He'd made the command decision to ignore her. She was not an ally, not anymore—but it was to her advantage if he won this fight. He didn't care if she took Excalibur. She might have broken her word, but he, and more important, his mate, had taken no direct harm from it. Brother Wolf was inclined to hold her somewhat responsible for Anna's wound, but all Dana might have done to avert that was tell him about Arthur.

Arthur was losing it. The smooth, practiced attacks became random and unfocused. Charles stepped up his pace. No longer just dodging interleaved with intermittent blocks, he also began to weave in attacks: two strikes from the left, and a turn and block; right, left, right, down and again—patterns practiced and refined for years—never forgetting that Arthur's sword was probably less damage-prone. Arthur failed to completely block a strike and a long red line appeared across his chest.

The pain of it, or perhaps the fear, lent sudden impulsion to Arthur's return strike, and he hit the other blade squarely. Charles's sword shattered. He let the energy from Arthur's blow spin him around. He ducked around Arthur's unarmed left side and rolled behind, drawing the fillet knife from the back of his pants. With all the force he could muster he stabbed Arthur in the spine, just where it connected with the skull. And the knife, being an expensive, well-crafted tool, slid between bone, through the softer disk, and severed the spinal cord.

Arthur fell forward, his sword rolling away from his hands.

"I—" Arthur said before he lost the ability to speak.

Charles picked up the fae blade and severed the British wolf's neck entirely. Then, blade in his hand, he looked at Dana.

"Did you know he was going to kill his mate?" he asked.

She smiled apologetically. "He held the sword hostage."

"Not an answer," he told her. "But I suppose the life of a human does not matter, not to you. They are so short-lived anyway. What was her life worth? Or Chastel's—he was a monster, right? What were their lives worth when measured against a sword such as this?"

"Sarcasm does not suit you," Dana said with dignity.

"No," Charles said. "I suppose not. He hired you to kill my father?"

She nodded. "I refused until he offered me Excalibur. She was entrusted to me, she is the reason for my existence—and this fool had found her."

"And my father didn't come." While he had the sword, she would talk to him—and Charles wanted to know exactly what she'd done so he could inform his father.

"No. I knew Bran wouldn't—the elements told me so. But I had to find a reason for that fool to bring Excalibur to me. His fortress in Cornwall is guarded against fae; I needed him to bring her here. I intended to make no bargains with Arthur—just get the sword back."

"You would not have killed my father?"

"Not if he stayed in Montana. And he did stay in Montana, didn't he? But then you chose to come in his stead—and you brought something with you that Arthur wanted more than he wanted your father's death. I was to engineer matters so Chastel killed you. It would have accomplished two things: ensured that Chastel was not at his lethal best when Arthur's assassins came to call—and your death would leave your mate free for Arthur's claiming."

Charles took a deep breath. He had no grounds to convict her of wrongdoing. She had killed no one, spilled no blood—not even Arthur's. Intent was not enough for him to act against her nor was his dislike of her moral compass.

Suddenly, urgently, he wanted nothing so much as a shower to rinse off the blood, sweat, and dirty deeds of this night. He opened his hand until he held the sword's hilt by two fingers and held it out to her. "This is yours—he admitted to the theft. Take better care of it this time."

She took it with her left hand and her knuckles whitened as she sighed like a lover satisfied at last. She held out her right hand. "No hard feelings?"

He looked at the hand and felt no urge to take it. He had hard feelings aplenty.

"Please," she said.

He took her hand. "My father will talk to you about this. You broke your word to him."

Her hand tightened on his, and she looked down. "I know. I know. And I can't have that. No one must know. If no one knows, it will be all right. You understand."

For the second time that night Charles found himself on his knees with very little idea of how it had happened. He looked at his hand, still in Dana's grip—blue patterns ghosted down his arm from her hand.

As he collapsed fully on his side, the pain began, but he couldn't open his mouth.

"If you had been human, you would already be dead," Dana said. She brushed a strand of hair that had escaped his braid away from his face. "This will take longer, but it will leave no traces that can be followed. Your father will suspect, doubtless, but as long as no one knows my part, it will be fine."

She bent down and kissed him on the cheek. "I do like you, Charles. I would never have made a bargain with Arthur to slay you but that I owe your death to your father. He gave me a reminder of that which I can never regain—I only return the same to him, as I promised you I would."

Brother Wolf growled, but the pain kept them motionless on the hard floor.

"TELL her we're about *fourteen* minutes out," Angus said as soon as he answered the phone. "And, as tempting as it is, I won't be driving randomly around the block, so I suspect the next time she makes you call, we'll be *thirteen* minutes out."

Alan had been holding his phone out to make sure Anna heard it. "Yes, sir," he said, and ended the call.

Anna knew she should apologize, but it was beyond her. Once they realized that the noise they'd heard a few minutes after Charles had closed the door was a locking mechanism—and that the room they were in was as secure a place to hold werewolves as she'd ever seen, they'd discovered Alan's phone didn't work. It had taken them a while to find the stupid black box that had kept Alan's cell phone from calling out—a cell phone disrupter.

When they called Angus, he'd already been on his way, alerted by a text message from Charles. The Marrok was about thirty minutes out of Seattle. He'd had a bad feeling earlier, and when Charles hadn't answered his phone, Bran had climbed aboard the jet and headed to Seattle.

At this rate, Anna thought, he'd beat Angus here. It had been ten minutes since the noise—identified as a sword fight by Alan—had stopped. Eight minutes since Charles had shut down their bond so tightly that all she could tell was that he was nearby and not moving.

Her wounds had closed, though there were a few itchy spots and a couple of sore places. She'd grabbed a sheet and wrapped it around her like an impromptu dress. As she paced, the short lengths of chains that dangled from her wrists and ankles made cheerful sounds that annoyed her. They probably annoyed Alan worse, but he didn't say so.

Sixteen minutes after their last call, the door unlocked.

"Sorry," Tom said. "We had a little trouble finding the electronic lock—it was in the room with Arthur's body."

"Charles?"

"Moira's looking after him," Tom said.

Anna found Charles lying on his side in Arthur's trophy

room amidst a scattering of steel shards, blood, and gore. Moira was kneeling beside him with both of her hands on his bare shoulder. "I have him stabilized right now, but it's not going to stay that way. Someone put a death curse on him. He's fighting it, and I'm helping."

Anna looked at his face. He wasn't unconscious, and every muscle of his body was tight, the veins standing out as if he were lifting weights.

"How do we stop it?" Anna asked, not recognizing her own voice. She knew enough about magic to keep her hands off.

"Find out who put it on him and make them take it off," Moira said. "Or kill them."

"Can you tell who did it?"

Moira shook her head. "This is a new one to me. I can't even tell if it is witchcraft, fae, or some sort of werewolf trick—it's too entwined with his magic. And his magic is something I've never encountered."

"His mother was an Indian shaman's daughter," said Angus.

"And his father is witchborn," said Anna without considering if it was something Bran would want bandied about. Witchborn meant Charles had a lot more magic than the average werewolf—maybe that would help Moira keep him alive.

She looked around the room, trying to put together what might have happened so she could figure out how to fix it: a broken sword, a kitchen knife, Arthur dead. Magic . . . the vampires had been able to use magic, and there was one vampire left. Or it might have been the fae woman.

"How long?" she asked Moira.

"Until I can't hold it anymore," the witch told her. "An hour. Maybe two."

"The Marrok's coming." Angus sounded grim. "If anyone can fix this, he can."

There had been only one fight in this room. Charles and Arthur's. Whoever had taken Charles down was someone who'd taken him by surprise. Something the vampire would never have managed.

She needed to think. Needed to find whoever was hurting Charles and kill them.

"If Charles was right when he sent you that text, and Arthur was the villain—then Arthur had her killed," Anna said. "His own mate."

"Or the person who bespelled Charles," Angus said.

She looked at the neat cut that had sliced through Arthur's neck. Execution style, Charles style. She didn't argue with Angus, but her wolf was certain: Arthur had killed his wife. "I'm going to see if I can find some clothes."

"You and Sunny are about the same size," said Angus. "I don't think she'd mind you borrowing her clothes."

She followed the scent of death into Sunny's room. Ignoring the body laid out on the bed, she went to the chest of drawers and grabbed a pair of bright pink sweats and a T-shirt. After dressing, she slipped on socks and Sunny's tennis shoes, which, wonder of wonders, fit like a glove.

Anna started out the door, paused, and looked at the dead woman. "My husband took care of your killer."

Sunny's mouth opened and sucked in air. Anna froze.

The dead woman said, "Anna Latham Cornick, mate of Charles Cornick, Omega of the Aspen Creek Pack. Wolf. Sister. Daughter. Lover. Beloved."

Sunny's eyes opened, filmed-over and dead, and her head turned until they looked straight at Anna. "She who was Nimue, Lady of the Lake, and is now Dana Shea has broken faith, broken her word. She must be punished, and you we have chosen as the instrument of our justice. We gift you with Finding and with this." Sunny's hand lifted, and in it was a dagger with a blade a few inches longer than her forearm. The handle was bone or ivory, it was difficult to tell. "Take Carnwennen as the means. Your mate's life as the reason. Our geas as the cost. True love your reward. Remind her of the Wild Hunt."

Anna made no move to touch the dagger. "Who are you?"

"We are the Gray Lords. The one who makes the dead talk is she who takes the dead of the battlefield." Sunny's body jerked, the dagger fell from her hand to the bed. "Hurry, or he will die, and you will be left with justice and vengeance your only reward."

Sunny's eyes closed, and her body was once more just a body. Anna reached over her and took the dagger, part of her waiting for Sunny to grab her wrist. But nothing happened until she touched the dagger.

Then, magic curled up her hand, first warming her skin where it touched the dagger, then cooling it. A gift of Finding, the Gray Lords had said, and a reward of true love.

"Where is Dana Shea?" she said. And she knew.

Thirteen

SHE took the stairs in two jumps and ran out the door, brushing past Tom and ignoring Angus's shout. She ran past the parked cars and out into the street, turning down toward the water. Of course Dana would be headed toward the water.

"Where are you going?" Tom asked, running beside her.

"Carnwennen the means," Anna told him, showing him the dagger.

He stumbled once, but caught up to her. "Fae shit," he said.

"The Gray Lords," Anna agreed. "Carnwennen the means. Justice the cause. True love the reward. Their geas the cost."

"Zapped," he said, pulling out his cell phone. "Yeah, Angus. The fae got to her. Best I can figure it, they're sending Anna out after Dana—can't think they'd be concerned with the vampire who escaped, and he's the only other player in this. She's speaking goobledygook, but it sounds to me like maybe they've promised her it'll save Charles."

"Stay with her. Help her if you can." Angus sounded frustrated. "He's going to kill me if something happens to her."

"Charles?" Anna asked through the haze that kept her running away from him.

"Yes, him too—though I was talking about Bran."

She made an impatient sound.

"Charles is still with us," Angus said. "Moira says *if* Dana did this, that probably it'll stop with her death. But fae are hard to kill."

"Oh, I think that the dagger they gave Anna will kill a fae all right," Tom said. "Stinks to high heaven of magic. And it has a name. Fae things that have a name will usually kill just about anything. Do you know of a dagger called— Carnwellen?"

Angus repeated the question for the only one at Arthur's house who couldn't just listen in to the whole conversation. "Moira, do you know of a dagger called Carnwellen?"

"Carn*wennen*?" Moira squeaked.

"Probably. Tom said the other."

"Carnwennen was King Arthur's dagger. Little White Hilt, it means. Arthur used it to hunt the Very Black Witch."

"It has a white hilt," observed Tom. "Doesn't look all that little to me. 'Bout as long as her forearm, almost enough to be a short sword instead of a dagger."

"It couldn't have been too little," said Moira, when Tom's reply had been repeated for her. "He supposedly cut the witch in half with it."

Anna saw Tom look at the dagger again.

"Yes," he said. "I think it might be good for something like that."

"Keep safe," Angus told him.

"Remember," Moira said, urgently. "Never trust the fae."

Anna frowned, "The troll told us that."

"Told you what?" Tom asked.

But Anna was more concerned with finding Dana than in repeating herself. A paved trail broke off from the road, and Tom caught her arm, pulling her to a stop. "Anna, are we going to Dana's boat?"

"I don't know," she told him—and pointed her finger. "That way."

"We could have taken a car, you know?" he said, folding his cell phone closed with one hand and stuffing it into a pocket.

He was wrong. "No, no car."

His eyebrows lowered. "Of course not. Fairy magic, eh? Cold iron." He took a good look at her wrist manacles. "I would have thought those would keep you safe."

"I have to go," she told him intensely. "Now."

"This is the Burke-Gilman Trail," he told her. "If you are headed to Dana's boat, this trail goes right by her dock. It's a more direct route than running down the road—and we're much less likely to attract interest with that thing. Not many people out on a jogging path in the middle of winter at this hour of the morning."

Then he let her go. Let her decide.

She ran down the trail, stretching her legs and letting the hunt take her. Wild Hunt. It was early morning, but the darkness still kept watch over them, darkness and the faintest sliver of the moon. It was almost the time of the dark of the moon, she thought, but there was still light to hunt by tonight.

THEY were nearly to the docks when the geas faded. She could see Dana's houseboat—but was able to force her legs to walk. Once she had slowed, it wasn't such a hard thing to stop altogether. The manacles were doing the trick, she thought, because it seemed like her hands and feet returned to her control before any other part of her body.

"Tom?" Anna asked, panting.

"All praise to the Virgin Mother," he said. "You're back with me."

"Magic," she said.

"Right. What happened to you?"

She told him, speaking faster as her tongue started working right again.

"Dead bodies talking, eh?" he said. "Nasty." Then he called Moira and Anna told the story to the witch—and presumably all the werewolves gathered around the phone.

"She who takes the dead . . ." Moira sounded exhausted. "That would probably be one of the Morrigan. Babd or maybe Nemain, probably not Macha. Sorry, you don't need that. My concentration's shot. They want you to kill Dana. Why?"

"She broke her word," Angus said. "Now she's got to be an example. I don't like them using Anna to do it."

"Wild Hunt," Anna said. "They called the Wild Hunt, I think that's what they said. Some of it was a little difficult to interpret. It sounded like the hunt was just to be me."

"They sent a wolf stuck in human form with a dagger—however enchanted—after a woman who is a Gray Lord," Angus said heavily, to whoever else was listening—or maybe just to himself. "I don't think she was meant to succeed."

She is Nimue, the Lady of the Lake. Brother Wolf spoke to her in clear words for the first time. His voice sounded like Charles, but not quite and it thundered through their bond.

After the words, he added a flood of information that had no words. Pain that he tried to keep veiled from her—not hiding it, but protecting her from it. The dagger was part of a treasure stolen by Arthur—including Excalibur, which Dana now had. Worry and command—she was to return to Arthur's apartment and wait for the Marrok. She was to stay away from Dana. He thought she was being used to return the dagger to Dana, for safekeeping.

He thought she was only a warning, meant to be destroyed after she delivered her message.

And then Brother Wolf was gone again—and the bond felt . . . weaker.

"Never trust the fae," Anna said. She believed Brother Wolf. But she was the only one who had heard him, thank goodness, or they would not let her do what she needed to.

"Moira. How is Charles?"

"Not good."

She knew that, felt it while Brother Wolf communicated with her. "How long does he have?"

"I can help for maybe fifteen minutes more—and then it's just a matter of time. He's in a lot of pain, I think, and that doesn't help."

"If he—" She had to suck in her breath and try again. "If he had died before you got there, would you have been able to tell what had killed him? That it was a death curse? That a fae had laid it upon him?"

"No," Moira told her. "I can't tell who laid it upon him now. If he were dead, probably no one could even tell for certain that it was magic that killed him. If Charles hadn't still been fighting it—"

"And Dana had no way to know that Angus and I both know that she's broken her word to Bran. She would have thought Charles was the only one." She was talking to herself. "How far out is the Marrok?"

She wasn't even sure Bran could help. She'd learned he wasn't infallible, just scary.

"He'll be landing at Sea-Tac in ten minutes."

"Not soon enough," Anna said. She ended the call.

"What are you planning?" Tom asked.

"I think that's too cerebral a name for it," she told him. "I'm playing it by ear. But I think this is Charles's only chance." It was meant to be her death. Charles was dying.

The phone rang.

Tom looked down at it. "Angus. He might tell us to go ahead."

"And if he doesn't?"

Tom turned his phone off. "Do we go in together, or do you want me as backup?"

She thought about it. "She likes men. I think that this might go better if you come with me." She looked again. "But let me borrow your jacket." People underestimated her all the time. Maybe the Gray Lords had, too.

THE water was black under the floating dock, and Anna had no desire whatsoever to play. She knocked at the door, glad for Tom at her back.

"Who is it?" Dana's voice sounded as if she were standing beside them.

"You know who it is," said Anna, not bothering to raise her voice—Dana could hear her. "I have something for you. A gift, a warning—it depends upon you."

"I'm in the studio." The door opened.

Anna led the way through the boat and up the stairs to the studio.

The lights were on, and otherwise the scene was very much like the one the fae had set the first time Anna had been here. She was working on a painting that Anna could not see. The painting the Marrok had sent was hung on the left-hand wall, all by itself. A sword leaned casually against the same wall, but closer to the far side of the room than to the middle. It looked very much like the one Arthur had shown her, had claimed to be Excalibur. From what Brother Wolf told her, this one was likely to be the real thing. Its duplicate was shattered all over Arthur's treasure room, having spent itself defending her mate.

"The Gray Lords sent me here to attempt to kill you," Anna told the fae woman, who had not looked up from her painting.

"Brother Wolf thinks I'm a messenger," Anna continued, "sent here to warn you that if you do this again, the Wild Hunt itself will be sent to you. He believes I've been sent to bring you their gift. And for you to kill." She took a deep breath. "And I think he is right."

The fae looked up from her painting. She was beautiful. Not a cold, flawless beauty, but striking. This was a woman who would be terrible in her anger and fierce in battle. Anna felt the same fascination for Dana that had hit her the very first time she'd seen her.

Anna took a deep breath and closed her right hand over the steel manacle on her left wrist. When she looked again, Dana was still beautiful—but Anna didn't feel as though she was being sucked into her beauty anymore.

Dana smiled, as if Anna's struggles amused her. "Who is Brother Wolf?"

"A friend." Anna didn't want to give Dana anything she might use. "I was meant to come here and attack you—but they didn't count on the little present Arthur's vampires left me with." She showed Dana one of her wrist manacles and shook one foot to make the chains jingle.

"Their failure left me with a few options—and you as well. If I had attacked you, and you killed me . . . you would be in their power, wouldn't you."

"I am a Gray Lord—I answer to no one."

"When Charles dies. When you kill me—the Marrok would hunt you down. You'd be forced to die or leave this continent. To go back to Europe. To be under their thumbs."

Dana's lips thinned with anger and—Anna's nose told her—a wisp of fear.

"You said you brought me a gift?"

Dana was just trying to change the subject, Anna judged. But Anna was in control of the conversation.

"You didn't know," she said, sounding, with some effort, relatively sympathetic, "when you cursed Charles, that we all knew you broke your word to protect the wolves attending this conference, did you? I saw, Angus saw—and we told Bran and Charles. Not enough for an accusation. But more than enough that if Charles died of unnatural causes, Bran would look right at you."

The fae put down her paintbrush and used it as an excuse to look away. But Anna could tell a lot more from scent than she could from her expression, anyway. The scent of panic was an old friend. She wasn't afraid of Anna. She was afraid of the Marrok. Good. Hopefully it would be enough.

Anna strolled around the painting, until she stood only a couple of feet from Dana.

"Nimue, Lady of the Lake," Anna said, calling upon the part of her that soothed and calmed. "Take the curse off my husband. My word on it that no word of your deceit makes its way out into the world." *And my word is good,* she thought, but she didn't say it. "The Marrok will not hunt you, nor harry you out of his lands."

The fae stared at the painting on the easel. Picasso was a wiser choice than Vermeer, Anna thought inconsequentially. Not even experts could agree on what Picasso was trying to say with his paintings. No one could tell Dana she'd gotten it wrong.

"No," said Dana, her voice thick with rage. She raised her hand and pointed it at the painting, not hers, but the one on the wall—the Marrok's gift. "I have not hurt so in a thousand years. Look what he did to me. Every time I look at that, it feels . . . it feels as it did the day I had to leave it. I vowed before the both of you that I would repay him in kind. That he would pay, and pay in the same way I do—with the same sorrow. I lost my home, he loses his son. I will go back to Europe, and he will—"

Anna stabbed her with the dagger she'd concealed in Tom's jacket. Under the ribs and through the heart—just like her favorite forensic TV show had taught her.

The fae's eyes flashed surprise, just for an instant, before there was nothing in them at all.

" 'No' was the wrong answer," Anna informed her.

"Don't move," said Tom, and he used the sword that had been sitting against the wall.

Anna pulled the dagger out of the body and cleaned it with a rag Dana had on the small table with her paints. Trying to avoid thinking about what had just happened. And failing miserably.

"That's six headless bodies this trip," she said, hating that her voice shook. "And I'm not counting the first two vampires we killed—because their bodies are dust. Six is just a bit much, don't you think?"

"Maybe she'd have stayed dead," Tom told her. "I don't know much about killing fae. Cold iron is supposed to do the trick—and that dagger's got plenty of that, nice sharp cold iron. But I for damned sure didn't want to run into her ever again after this, so there's no harm in making sure."

"Would you . . . would you call?" Had she been in time? Did it even work? Was Charles dying while she stood here?

Tom took the bloody rag from her and wiped the sword

clean with a few efficient swipes. Then he handed it to her and pulled out his cell.

"Hey, Moira," he said. "How's Charles?"

"Better." Moira sounded half-dead. "Not good. Not good by a long shot. But the curse dissipated a few minutes ago. He'll make it."

"That's what happens when an Omega goes negotiating," Angus commented. "Even the fae can't stand against one."

Tom looked down at Dana's body. "Just so," he said. "Though I don't know that anyone expected exactly this result."

THE troll, in his guise as a street person, was waiting for them just outside the door. He was leaning against the boat, smoking a cigarette and watching his feet.

Tom stepped in front of Anna.

"Well," said the troll, soft-voiced. "I guess that showed 'em. Wasn't no one thought ye had it in ye, Lady. Most especially that one." He tilted his head at the boat.

"She was going to kill my mate."

The troll nodded. "And yourself, too, sounded like. She should have knowed that some people take things like the killing of mates right to heart, all right." He stubbed the cigarette out on his thumb and tossed it into the water. "I'm supposed to take possession of the—"

Anna stepped around Tom and held out the dagger in one hand and the sword in the other.

"They aren't mine," she said. "I don't want them."

The troll stepped back, then had to do some fancy footwork to keep from falling in the water. "Don't you be wishing those on me. *Don't* you. I'm supposed to take possession of the body. We'll see to it Ms. Dana Shea doesn't get discovered." He seemed calmer once Anna let her hands drop and quit holding out the weaponry. "That's better, there see. Now I'm supposed to ask you to watch over those a little bit longer. Someone will be along to collect them later. Someone *else*." And just in case she hadn't gotten it, he said. "Someone not me."

"All right," Anna said. "Agreed."

He pulled off the old trench coat he was wearing. "Happen you might want to bundle things up in here. It'll keep 'em out of sight—a little magic . . . and a lot of material."

She bit back a thank-you. Tom, who took the coat, didn't seem to have the same trouble.

"I'll see that the coat goes to whoever gets the weapons," Tom said instead. "Maybe they can return it."

The troll nodded once and went into the boat.

"Troll," said Tom thoughtfully, and knocked twice on the side of the boat with his knuckles. "I don't suppose I needed to cut the head off, after all. *Bon appetit.*"

THEY were maybe halfway back, although Anna was stumbling tired, so her estimate of distance could have been way off, when she noticed an expensive but anonymous car purring at a junction between the path they were on and a cross street.

"I see it," said Tom, moving between her and the car.

Very conscious of what she was carrying, Anna didn't protest. She didn't want the sword—but there were a lot of people she didn't want to have the sword either. Like the vampire who'd gotten away.

She dropped back a dozen feet and let Tom take the lead. If only the sword had been a gun. She knew how to use a gun.

The back door of the car opened and Bran got out.

Tom didn't look relieved. So Anna broke into what was supposed to be a run but came out as a faster shuffle. "It's good, it's good. Tom, meet Bran Cornick, the Marrok. Bran, this is Tom. I don't remember his last name, but he saved my life."

"Tom Franklin," Bran said. "Thank you. Anna . . ." He shook his head. "Words fail me."

"Here." She shoved the coat with sword and dagger at Bran. "*You* take these. I don't want them. Someone is supposed to come pick them up later."

"Ah," he said, and looked down at the battered material. "Seattle is not the place I would have expected to encounter these." He seemed to know what he held even though they were both still wrapped up.

Tom grinned. "Seattle is a city with a certain . . . *panache*. Never know what you are going to find when you come for a visit. Good food, friendly people, ancient legendary weapons. Always something different."

"Get in the car," Bran told them. "They're all on the way to Angus's house."

"Charles?" Anna couldn't help but sound anxious.

"He wanted to come with me," Bran said. "But I told him he'd have to wait until he could walk under his own power. He's on his way to Angus's if he's not already there." He got in the car, and Anna slid in next to him, leaving the window seat for Tom.

Bran gave her a laughing glance. "He wasn't happy with me. Or you either. Expect him to yell at you because you scared him badly this time."

"Sounds unfair, to me," Anna said, though it didn't bother her. "I risk my neck to save him, and he yells at me." Charles was alive, he could yell at her all he wanted to.

"If it gets to you, just shed a few tears," muttered Tom. "He'll shut up. Works for Moira."

"Arthur's dead, Dana is dead. Five of the six vampires are dead," Anna said. "There's only one villain left."

"We don't have to worry about the vampire who escaped," Bran told her. "The local vampires found him and took care of it. They are apparently sending Angus proof."

"Good," said Tom.

"Good" was the wrong word, Anna thought. *"Good"* shouldn't apply to headless bodies and dead people. But she didn't have a better word.

Anna had to ask. "Bran? Could you have done anything to stop the fae from killing Charles? Should I have waited for you?" *Did I just kill unnecessarily?*

He must have heard her unspoken worry. "In human courts, the least of the charges facing Dana would have been conspiracy to commit murder. Charles confirms that she knew Arthur planned on killing Sunny. Jean Chastel. Charles. She was in the process of killing Charles. That's attempted murder." He shook his head. "Do not regret her death."

"She was the Lady of the Lake," Anna said in a small voice.

"And being famous should have made her immune to the consequences of her actions?"

He pulled her head toward him and kissed her forehead. *"Ego te absolvo.* There is some Latin for you, my dear. I absolve you of your guilt. You did well. The only way I could have stopped her was the same way you did. And I would have been too late."

"De duobus malis, minus est semper eligendum," she murmured. "Her death was the lesser evil."

CHARLES sat in lone splendor on a huge couch in the middle of Angus's spacious living room—while the other ten or twelve people present made themselves at home on the other side of the room.

Anna surveyed the scene. "Okay," she said. "Who's been being a grouch."

He looked at her. For such a look, she thought, she'd have done a lot more than kill. He patted the couch beside him, but she crawled into his lap instead.

"I've had a really bad night," she said. "Any chance we can get some sleep?"

Charles kissed her, a long, involved kiss that took no prisoners. When he was finished, she licked her lips, and said, in a voice that was a little breathless, "Does that mean no?"

"I would slay dragons for you," he told her. "I suspect that finding an unoccupied bedroom will be easier."

She pulled away a little, just far enough that she could see his face. "Dragons, huh. Well, I killed the Lady of the Lake for you, sir."

He cupped her face in his hands, "I'm sorry, Anna."

Te absolve, indeed, she thought. Faced with Charles's warm and undeniably living flesh, she would have killed the fae over again. "I'm not," she said. "I love you."

Angus sighed. "Lovebirds," he said.

Turn the page for an exciting excerpt from
the next Alpha and Omega novel

FAIR GAME

by Patricia Briggs

Available now from Ace Books!

PROLOGUE

A FAIRY TALE

Oɴᴄᴇ upon a time, there was a little girl named Leslie.

The year she turned eight, two things happened: her mother left Leslie and her father to move to California with a stockbroker; and, in the middle of a sensational murder trial, the fae of story and song admitted to their existence. Leslie never heard from her mother again, but the fairies were another matter.

When she was nine, her father took a job in a strange city, moving them from the house she'd grown up in to an apartment in Boston where they were the only black people in an all-white neighborhood. Their apartment encompassed the upper floor of a narrow house owned by their downstairs neighbor, Mrs. Cullinan. Mrs. Cullinan kept an eye on Leslie while her dad was at work, and by her silent championship eased Leslie's way into the society of the neighborhood kids who casually dropped by for cookies or lemonade. In Mrs. Cullinan's capable hands, Leslie learned to crochet, knit, sew, and cook while her dad kept the old woman's house and lawn in top shape.

Even as an adult, Leslie wasn't sure if her dad had paid

the old woman or if she'd just taken over without consulting him. It was the kind of thing Mrs. Cullinan would have done.

When Leslie was in third grade, one of the kindergarten boys went missing. In fourth grade, one of her classmates, a girl by the name of Mandy, disappeared. There were also, throughout the same time period, a lot of missing pets—mostly kittens and young dogs. Nothing that would have attracted her attention if it weren't for Mrs. Cullinan. On their daily walks (Mrs. Cullinan called them "busybody strolls," to see what people in their neighborhood were up to), the old woman began stopping at missing-pet notices taped in store windows and taking out a little notebook and writing all the information in it.

"Are we looking for lost animals?" Leslie asked finally. She mostly learned from observation rather than by asking questions because, in her experience, people lied better with their lips than they did with their actions. But she hadn't come up with a good explanation for the missing-pet list and she was forced, at last, to resort to words.

"It's always good to keep an eye out." It was a not-quite answer, but Mrs. Cullinan sounded troubled, so Leslie didn't ask her again.

When Leslie's new birthday puppy—a mutt with brown eyes and big feet—went missing, Mrs. Cullinan had gotten tight-lipped and said, "It is time to put a stop to this." Leslie was pretty sure her landlady hadn't known anyone was listening to her.

Leslie, her father, and Mrs. Cullinan were eating dinner a few days after her puppy's disappearance when a fancy limousine pulled up in front of Miss Nellie Michaelson's house. Out of the dark depths of the shiny vehicle emerged two men in suits and a woman in a white flowery dress that looked too summery and airy to be a good match for the men's attire. They were dressed for a funeral and she for a picnic in the nearby park.

Unabashedly spying, Leslie's father and Mrs. Cullinan left the table to stare out the window as the three people entered Miss Nellie's house without knocking.

"What are they . . . ?" The expression on Leslie's father's face changed from curious (no one ever visited Miss Nellie) to grim in a heartbeat, and he grabbed his service revolver and his badge. Mrs. Cullinan caught him on the front porch.

"No, Wes," she said in a strange, fierce voice. "No. They are fae and it's a fae mess they've come to clean up. You let them do what they need to."

Leslie, peering around the adults, finally saw what had gotten everyone in a tizzy. The two men were carrying Nellie out of her house. Nellie was struggling, her mouth wide open as if she were screaming, but not a sound came out.

Leslie had always thought that Nellie looked as though she should be a model or a movie star, with her sad blue eyes and downturned soft mouth. But she didn't appear so pretty right then. She didn't look frightened—she looked enraged. Her beautiful face was twisted, ugly, and, at the same time, breath-stealingly scary in a way that would haunt Leslie's dreams.

The woman, the one in the airy-fairy dress who'd come with the men, exited the house about the same time the men finished stuffing Nellie in the backseat of the car. She locked the door of Nellie's house behind her, and when she was finished she looked up and saw the three of them watching. After a pause, she strolled across the street and down the sidewalk to them. The woman didn't appear to be walking fast, but she was opening the front gate almost before Leslie realized that she was heading for them.

"And what do you think you're looking at?" she said mildly, in a voice that had Leslie's father thumbing the snap that held his gun in the holster.

Mrs. Cullinan stepped forward, her jaw set like it had

been the day that she'd faced down a couple of young toughs who'd decided an old woman was fair game. "Justice," she said with the same soft menace that had sent the boys after easier prey. "And don't get uppity with me. I know what you are and I'm not afraid of you."

The strange woman's head lowered aggressively and her shoulders got tight. Leslie took a step behind her father. But Mrs. Cullinan's retort had drawn the attention of the men by the limousine.

"Eve," said one of the men mildly, his hand on the open car door. His voice was mellow and rich, as thick with Ireland as Mrs. Cullinan's own, and it carried across the street and down the block as if there were no city sounds to muffle it. "Come to the car and keep Gordie company, would you?" Even Leslie knew it wasn't a request.

The woman stiffened and narrowed her eyes, but she turned and walked away from them. When she had taken his place at the car, the man approached them.

"You'd be Mrs. Cullinan," he said, as soon as he was on their side of the street and close enough for quiet conversation. He had one of those mildly good-looking faces that didn't stand out in a crowd—except for his eyes. No matter how she tried, Leslie could never remember what color his eyes were, only that they were odd and strange and beautiful.

"You know I am," Mrs. Cullinan said stiffly.

"We appreciate you calling us on this and I would like to leave you with a reward." He held a business card out to her. "A favor when you need it most."

"If the children are safe to play in their yards, that is reward enough." She dried her hands on her hips and made no move to take the card from him.

He smiled and did not put down his hand. "I will not leave indebted to you, Mrs. Cullinan."

"And I know better than to accept a gift from the fairies," she snapped.

"Onetime reward," he said. "A little thing. I promise that

no intentional harm will come to you or yours from this as long as I am alive." Then, in a coaxing voice, he said, "Come, now. I cannot lie. This is a different age, when your kind and ours needs must learn to live together. You could have called the police with your suspicions—which were correct. Had you done so, she would not have gone without killing a great many more than the children she has already taken." He sighed and glanced back at the car's darkened windows. "It is difficult to change when you are so old, and she was always in the habit of eating small things, was our Nellie."

"Which is why I called you," Mrs. Cullinan said stoutly. "I didn't know who it was taking the little ones until I saw Nellie over by our backyard two nights ago and this child's puppy was missing in the morning."

The fae looked at Leslie for the first time, but Leslie was too upset to read his face. "Eating small things," the man had said. Puppies were small things.

"Ah," he said after a long moment. "Child, you may take what comfort you can that your puppy's death meant that no more would die from that one's misdeeds. Hardly fair recompense, I know, but it is something."

"Give it to her," Mrs. Cullinan said suddenly. "Her puppy's dead. Give her your reward. I'm an old woman with cancer; I won't live out the year. Give it to her."

The fae man looked at Mrs. Cullinan, then knelt on one knee before Leslie, who was holding very tightly to her father's hand. She didn't know if she was crying for her puppy, the old woman who was more her mother than her mother had ever been—or for herself.

"A gift for a loss," he said. "Take this and use it when you most need it."

Leslie put her free hand behind her back. He was trying to make up for her puppy's death with a present, just like people had tried to do after her mom had left. Presents didn't make things better. Quite the opposite, in her experience. The giant teddy bear her mama had given her the night she left was buried in the back of the closet. Although Leslie couldn't stand to get rid of it, she also couldn't look at it without feeling sick.

"With this you could get a car or a house," the man said. "Money for an education." He smiled, quite kindly—and it made him look totally different, more real, somehow, as he said, "Or save some other puppy from monsters. All you have to do is wish hard and tear up the card."

"Any wish?" Leslie asked warily, taking the card, more because she didn't want to be the focus of this man's attention any longer than because she wanted the card. "I want my puppy back."

"I can't bring anyone or anything back to life," he told her sadly. "I would that I could. But outside of that, almost anything."

She stared at the card in her hand. It had one word written across it: GIFT.

He stood up. Then he smiled—an expression as merry and light as anything she'd ever seen. "And, Miss Leslie," he said, when he shouldn't have known her name at all, "no wishing for more wishes. It doesn't work like that."

She'd just been wondering . . .

The strange man turned to Mrs. Cullinan and took her hand in his and kissed it. "You are a lady of rare beauty, quick wits, and generous spirit."

"I'm a nosy, interfering old woman," she responded, but Leslie could see that she was pleased.

As an adult, Leslie kept the card the fairy man had given her tucked behind her driver's license. It looked as clean and fresh as it had the day she'd agreed to take it. To the shock of her doctors, Mrs. Cullinan's cancer mysteriously disappeared and she'd died in her bed twenty years later at the age of ninety-four. Leslie still missed her.

Leslie learned two valuable things about the fae that day. They were powerful and charming—and they ate children and puppies.

ONE

Aspen Creek, Montana

"Go home," Bran Cornick growled at Anna.

No one who saw him like this would ever forget what lurked behind the Marrok's mild-mannered facade. But only people who were stupid—or desperate—would risk raising his ire to reveal the monster behind the nice-guy mask. Anna was desperate.

"When you tell me you will quit calling on my husband to kill people," Anna told him doggedly. She didn't yell, she didn't shout, but she wasn't going to give up easily.

Clearly, she'd finally pushed him out to the very narrow edges of his last shred of civilized behavior. He closed his eyes, turned his head away from her, and said, in a very gentle voice, "Anna. Go home and cool off." Go home until *he* cooled off was what he meant. Bran was Anna's father-in-law, her Alpha, and also the Marrok who ruled all the werewolf packs in his part of the world by the sheer force of his will.

"Bran—"

His power unleashed with his temper, and the five other wolves, not counting Anna, who were in the living room of his house dropped to the floor, even his mate, Leah. They bowed their heads and tipped them slightly to the side to expose their throats.

Though he made no outward move, the speed of their surrender testified to Bran's anger and his dominance—and only Anna, somewhat to her surprise at her own temerity, stayed on her feet. When Anna had first come to Aspen Creek, beaten and abused as she'd been, if anyone had yelled at her, she'd have hidden in a corner and not come out for a week.

She met Bran's eyes and bared her teeth at him as the wave of his power brushed past her like a spring breeze. Not that she wasn't properly terrified, but not of Bran. Bran, she knew, would not really hurt her if he could help it, no matter what her hindbrain tried to tell her.

She was terrified for her mate. "You are wrong," Anna told him. "Wrong. Wrong. Wrong. And you are determined not to see it until he is broken beyond repair."

"Grow up, little girl," Bran snarled, and now his eyes—bright gold leaching out his usual hazel—were focused on her instead of the fireplace in the wall. "Life isn't a bed of roses and people have to do hard jobs. You knew what Charles was when you married him and when you took him as your mate."

He was trying to make this about her, because then he wouldn't have to listen to her. He couldn't be that blind, just too stubborn. So his attempt to alter the argument—when there should be no argument at all—enraged her.

"Someone in here is acting like a child, and it isn't me," she growled right back at him.

Bran's return snarl was wordless.

"Anna, *shut up*," Tag whispered urgently, his big body limp on the floor where his orange dreadlocks clashed with the maroon of the Persian rug. He was her friend and she trusted the berserker's judgment on most things. Under other circumstances she'd have listened to him, but right now she had Bran so angry he couldn't speak—so she could get a few words in past his stubborn, inflexible mind.

"I know my mate," she told her father by marriage. "Better than you do. He will *break* before he disappoints you or fails to do his duty. *You* have to stop this because he can't."

When Bran spoke, his voice was a toneless whisper. "My son will not bend or break. He has done his job for a century before you were even born, and he'll be doing it a century from now."

"His job was to dispense *justice*," she said. "Even if it meant killing people, he could do it. Now he is merely an assassin. His prey cling to his feet repentant and redeemable. They weep and beg for mercy that he can't give. It is destroying him," she said starkly. "And I'm the only one who sees it."

Bran flinched. And for the first time, she realized that Charles wasn't the only one suffering under the new, harsher rules the werewolves had to live by.

"Desperate times," he said grimly, and Anna hoped that she'd broken through. But he shook off the momentary softness and said, "Charles is stronger than you give him credit for. You are a stupid little girl who doesn't know as much as she thinks she does. Go home before I do something I'll regret later. Please."

It was that brief break that told her this was useless. He did know. He did understand, and he was hoping against hope that Charles could hold out. Her anger fled and left . . . despair.

She met her Alpha's eyes for a long moment before acknowledging her failure.

Anna knew exactly when Charles drove up, newly returned from Minnesota where he'd gone to take care of a problem the Minnesota pack leader would not. If she'd been deaf to the sound of the truck or the front door, she'd have known Charles was home by the magic that tied wolf to mate. That was all the bond told her outright, though— his side of their bond was as opaque as he could manage, and that told her a whole lot more about his state of mind than he probably intended.

From the way he let nothing leak through to her, she knew it had been another bad trip, one that had left too many people dead, probably people he hadn't wanted to kill.

Lately, they had all been bad trips.

At first she'd been able to help, but when the rules changed, when the werewolves had admitted their existence to the rest of the world, the new public scrutiny meant that second chances for the wolves who broke Bran's laws were offered only in extraordinary circumstances. She'd kept going with him on these trips because she refused to let Charles suffer alone. But when Anna started having nightmares about the man who'd fallen to his knees in front of her in mute entreaty before his execution, Charles had quit letting her go.

She was strong-willed and she liked to think of herself as tough. She could have made him change his mind or followed him anyway. But Anna hadn't fought his edict because she realized she was only making his job harder to bear. He saw himself as a monster and couldn't believe she didn't also when she witnessed the death he brought.

So Charles went out hunting alone—as he had for a hundred years or more, just as his father had said. His hunt was always successful—and, at the same time, a failure. He was dominant; he had a compulsory need to protect the weak, including, paradoxically, the wolves he was there to kill. When the wolves he executed died, so did a part of Charles.

Before Bran had brought them out to the public, the new wolves, those who had been Changed for less than ten years, would have been given several chances if their transgression came from loss of control. Conditions could have been taken into account that would lessen the punishment of others. But the public knew about them now, and they couldn't allow everyone to know just how dangerous werewolves really were.

It was up to the pack Alpha to take care of dispensing commonplace justice. Previously, Charles had only had to go out a few times a year to take care of bigger or more unusual problems. But many of the Alphas were unhappy with the new harshness of the laws, and somehow more and more of the enforcement fell to Bran and thus to Charles. He was going out two or three times a month and it was wearing on him.

She could feel him standing just inside the house, so she put a little more passion into her music, calling him to her with the sweet-voiced cello that had been his first Christmas gift to her.

If she went upstairs, he'd greet her gravely, tell her he had to go talk to his father, and leave. He'd come back in a day or so after running as a wolf in the mountains. But Charles never quite came back all the way anymore.

It had been a month since he'd last touched her. Six weeks and four days since he'd made love to her, not since they'd come back from the last trip she'd accompanied him on. She'd have said that to Bran if he hadn't made that "Grow up, little girl" comment. Probably she should have told Bran anyway, but she'd given up making him see reason.

She'd decided to try something else.

She stayed in the music room Charles had built in the basement while he stood upstairs. Instead of using words, she let her cello speak for her. Rich and true, the notes slid from her bow and up the stairway. After a moment she heard the stairs squeak under the weight of his feet and let out a breath of relief. Music was something they shared.

Her fingers sang to him, coaxing him to her, but he

stopped in the doorway. She could feel his eyes on her, but he didn't say anything.

Anna knew that when she played on her cello, her face was peaceful and distant—a product of much coaching from an early teacher who told her that biting her lip and grimacing was a dead giveaway to any judge that she was having trouble. Her features weren't regular enough for true beauty, but she wasn't ugly, either, and today she'd used some makeup tricks that softened her freckles and emphasized her eyes.

She glanced at him briefly. His Salish heritage gave him lovely dark skin and exotic (to her) features, his father's Welsh blood apparent only in subtle ways: the shape of his mouth, the angle of his chin. It was his job, not his lineage, that froze his features into an unemotional mask and left his eyes cold and hard. His duties had eaten away at him until he was nothing but muscle, bone, and tension.

Anna's fingers touched the strings and rocked, softening the cello's song with a vibrato on the longer notes. She'd begun with a bit of *Pachelbel's Canon in D*, which she generally used as a warm-up or when she wasn't sure what she wanted to play. She considered moving to something more challenging, but she was too distracted by Charles. Besides, she wasn't trying to impress him, but to seduce him into letting her help. So, Anna needed a song that she could play while thinking of Charles.

If she couldn't get Bran to quit sending her mate out to kill, maybe she could get Charles to let her help with the aftermath. It might buy him a little time until she could find the right baseball bat—or rolling pin—to beat some clarity into his father's head.

She deserted Pachelbel for an improvised bridge that shifted the key from D to G and then let her music flow into the prelude of Bach's *Cello Suite No. 1*. Not that that music was easy, but it had been her high school concert piece so she could practically play it in her sleep.

Her fingers moving, she didn't allow herself to look at him again, no matter how hungry she was for the sight of him. She stared at an oil painting of a sleeping bobcat while Charles stood at the door and watched her. If she could get him to approach her, to quit trying to protect her from his job . . .

And then she screwed up.

She was an Omega wolf. That meant that not only was she the only person on the continent whose wolf would allow her to face down the Marrok when he was in a rage, but also that she had a magical talent for soothing wolfish tempers regardless of whether or not they wanted to be soothed. It felt wrong to impose her will on others, and she tried not to do it unless the need was dire. Over the past couple of years, Anna had learned when and how to best use her ability. But her need to see Charles happy slipped over the barrier of her hard-won control as if it wasn't there at all.

One moment she was playing to him with her whole self, focused solely on him—and the next her wolf reached out and calmed Charles's wolf, sent him to sleep, leaving only his human half behind . . . Charles turned and walked purposefully away from her without a word. He, who ran from nothing and no one, exited their house by the back door.

Anna set down her bow and returned her cello to its stand. He wouldn't come back for hours now, maybe not even for a couple of days. Music hadn't worked if the only thing holding Charles in its spell was his wolf.

She left the house, too. The need to do something was so strong it had her moving without a real destination. It was that or cry, and she refused to cry. Maybe she could go to Bran one more time. But when the turnoff for his house appeared, she drove past it.

Like as not Charles was headed to Bran's to tell his father what he'd done for the wolves of the world—and it would be . . . awkward to follow him, as if she were chasing him. Besides, she'd already talked to Bran. He knew what was happening to his son; she knew he did. But, like Charles, he weighed the lives of all of their kind against the possibility that Charles would break under the strain of what was necessary, and thought the risk acceptable.

So Anna drove through town, arriving at a large greenhouse in the woods on the other side. She pulled over and parked next to a battered Willys Jeep and went in search of help.

A lot of wolves called him the Moor—which he disliked, saying that it was a vampire kind of thing to do, take a part of who a person was and reduce him to it with a capital letter or two. His features and skin showed traces of Arabia by way of North Africa, but Anna agreed that certainly wasn't the sum total of who he was. He was very beautiful, very old, extremely deadly—and right now he was transplanting geraniums.

"Asil," she began.

"Hush," he said. "Don't disturb my plants with your troubles until they are safe in their new houses. Make yourself useful and deadhead the roses along the wall."

She snagged a basket and started picking dead flowers off Asil's rosebushes. There would be no talking to him until he'd accomplished what he intended, whether that was to calm her down before they talked, get some free labor, or merely keep the silence while he tended his plants. Knowing Asil, it could be all three.

She worked for about ten minutes before she got impatient and reached for a rosebud, knowing that he always kept an eye on anyone working with his precious flowers.

"Remember the story of Beauty and the Beast?" remarked Asil gently. "Go ahead. Take that little bloom. See what happens."

"'Beauty and the Beast' is a French fairy tale and you are a mere Spaniard," Anna told him, but she took her fingers off the bud. Beauty's father had stolen a flower at great cost. "And in no way are you an enchanted prince."

He dusted off his hands and turned to her, smiling a little. "Actually, I am. For some definitions of 'prince.'"

"Hah," said Anna. "Poor Belle would find herself kissing your handsome face and then, poof, there would be the frog."

"I think you are mixing your fairy tales," Asil told her. "But even as a frog I would not disappoint. You came to talk fairy tales, *querida*?"

"No." She sighed, hopping up to sit on a convenient flat table next to a bunch of small pots that held a single pea-sized leaf each. "I'm here to get advice about beasts. Specifically, information about the beast who rules us all. Naturally I sought you out. Bran has to quit sending Charles out to kill. It is destroying him."

He sat on the table opposite hers and looked at her with the space of the narrow aisle between them. "You do know that Charles lived nearly two hundred years without you to take care of him, yes? He is not a fragile rosebud who needs your tender touch to survive."

"He's not a killer, either," Anna snapped.

"I beg to differ." Asil spread his hands peaceably when she snarled at him. "The results speak for themselves. I doubt that there are any other wolves with so many werewolf kills under their belt outside of present company." He indicated himself with a modest air that was a tribute to his acting skills, since he didn't have a modest bone in his body.

Anna shook her head at him, her hands curling into fists of frustration. "He isn't. Killing *hurts* him. But he sees it as necessary—"

"Which it is," murmured Asil, clearly patronizing her.

"Fine," she agreed sharply, hearing the growl in her voice but unable to keep it down. Failing so spectacularly with Bran had taught her she needed to keep her own temper in check if she wanted to convince old dominant wolves of anything. "I know that it is necessary. Of course it is necessary. Charles wouldn't kill anyone if he didn't see that it was *necessary*. And Charles is the only one dominant enough to do the job who is also not an Alpha, since that would cause trouble with the Alpha of the territories he must enter. Fine. It doesn't mean that he can continue like this. Necessary does not mean possible."

Asil sighed. "Women." He sighed again, theatrically. "Peace, child. I *do* understand. You are Omega and Omegas are worse than Alphas about protecting their mates. But your mate is very strong." He grimaced as he said it, as if tasting something bitter. Anna knew that he didn't always get along with Charles, but dominant wolves often had that problem with one another. "You just have to have a little faith in him."

Anna met his gaze and held it. "He doesn't bring me with him anymore when he goes. When he came home this afternoon, I used my magic to send his wolf to sleep, and as soon as the wolf was quiet he left without a word."

"You expected living with a werewolf to be easy?" Asil frowned at her. "You can't fix everyone. I told you that. Being Omega doesn't make you Allah." Asil's long-dead mate had been an Omega. Asil had taught Anna all that she knew about it, which he seemed to believe gave him some sort of in loco parentis status. Or maybe he just patronized everyone. "Omega doesn't mean power without end. Charles is a stone-cold killer—ask him yourself. And you knew it when you married him. You should quit worrying about him and start worrying about how *you* are going to deal with accepting the situation you got yourself into."

Anna stared at him. She knew that he and Charles weren't bosom buddies or anything. She hadn't realized that he didn't know Charles at all, that Asil saw only the front he put on for everyone else.

Asil had been her last, forlorn hope. Anna levered herself off the table. She turned her back on Asil and strode to the door, feeling the heavy weight of despair. She didn't know how to make him, to make *Bran*, see how bad things were. Bran was the one who counted. Only he could keep Charles home. She had failed to persuade her father-in-law. She'd been hoping that Asil might help.

It was still light out and would be for a few more hours, but the air was already stirring with the weight of the waxing moon. She held the door open and turned back to Asil. "You are all wrong about him. You and Bran and everyone else. He *is* strong, but no one is that strong. He hasn't picked up an instrument, hasn't even sung a note for months."

Asil's head came up and he stared at her a moment, proving that he knew something about her husband after all.

"Perhaps," he said slowly with a frown, rising to his feet. "Perhaps you are right. His father and I should speak."